Slim Pickins' in
Fat Chance, Texas

Books by Celia Bonaduce

Fat Chance, Texas Series

Welcome to Fat Chance, Texas

Slim Pickins' in Fat Chance, Texas

Venice Beach Romances

The Merchant of Venice Beach

A Comedy of Erinn

Much Ado About Mother

Slim Pickins' in Fat Chance, Texas

Celia Bonaduce

LYRICAL PRESS
Kensington Publishing Corp.
www.kensingtonbooks.com

LYRICAL PRESS BOOKS are published by

Kensington Publishing Corp.
119 West 40th Street
New York, NY 10018

All Kensington titles, imprints, and distributed lines are available at special quantity discounts for bulk purchases for sales promotion, premiums, fund-raising, educational, or institutional use.

Special book excerpts or customized printings can also be created to fit specific needs. For details, write or phone the office of the Kensington Sales Manager: Kensington Publishing Corp., 119 West 40th Street, New York, NY 10018. Attn. Sales Department. Phone: 1-800-221-2647.

Lyrical Press logo Reg. U.S. Pat. & TM Off.

First Electronic Edition: January 2016
eISBN-13: 978-1-60183-431-7
eISBN-10: 1-60183-431-4

First Print Edition: January 2016
ISBN-13: 978-1-60183-432-4
ISBN-10: 1-60183-432-2

Printed in the United States of America

To my friend
Pete Voggenthaler

Aloha oe

ACKNOWLEDGMENTS

First of all, I'd like to thank that great time-suck, Google. When writing a novel, there are probably worse ways to spend your time than researching what you don't know. Of course, there are better ways—like writing the book. But as soon as you give yourself permission to investigate ravines, or mules, or fan belts, hours can pass before a word is written. Where would Fat Chance, Texas, be without research?

But sometimes, even Google doesn't have the answer. At that point, I reach out to the experts. Miraculously, they get back to me! Thanks to Sally Hill for her knowledge of planes and women pilots and to Dr. Ed Hellman, professor of viticulture at Texas Tech for sharing his expertise on the history of grape-growing in Texas.

With every book comes book launches. Before a reading I feel like a thirteen-year-old, afraid nobody is going to show up at her party. Then the friendly faces start arriving. I am so grateful to new readers who are taking this amazing journey with me of their own free will—and to my friends and family, who still arrive at my events as if they just can't wait to hear it all again. Thank you for cheering me on. You amaze me.

Thanks to Myrna Everett and Kimberly Rouleau for your inspiration and to Laura Chambers, Mary Asanovich, Gene Asanovich, Dori Berman, Patricia Rogerson, Cheryl DiVitale, my nephew Dominic Bonaduce, and my mother Elizabeth Bonaduce for your help rolling this one up the hill.

Gratitude should be flooding the streets of New York City as I thank my agent Sharon Bowers, my editor Martin Biro, and everyone at Kensington Publishing. You guys continue to rock my world.

To my husband, Billy, who spends hours editing my work: Your red pen is a valentine. I love you.

PART ONE

CHAPTER 1

H e was here.

From the boardwalk Dymphna Pearl looked up past the end of Main Street. She knew what that small cloud of dust rising over the town meant. Another chunk of road was giving way on the trail that wound its way up and out of Fat Chance. Her stomach knotted. Dymphna could only catch a foreign syllable or two coming from the trail. She might not know much Spanish but it was clear by the tone of the man's voice that *he* didn't know the ropes.

The dust settled and the tirade finally stopped. Dymphna heard Pappy say, "What the hell made you think wearing a pair of new four-hundred-dollar boots to a place called Fat Chance, Texas, was a good idea in the first place, Pilgrim?"

She didn't hear much else because suddenly the two men spilled off the trail and onto Main Street. Dymphna ducked back into the café, but watched from the window. The visitor was in his mid-thirties, with the solid build of a soccer player. His black hair sparkled blue in the hot Texas sun. It was good hair.

He'll never be able to get a haircut like that in Fat Chance.

The man was smaller than Pappy, but Pappy was a mountain. Dymphna thought Pappy must be at least eighty, but he carried the younger man's large suitcase as if it were filled with cotton balls. As they advanced, Dymphna saw that Pappy looked as grim as his companion. When the two men reached the café, Dymphna caught Pappy's eye through the screen door. From behind wire spectacles, annoyance radiated from his green eyes. His massive white beard twitched. In Spanish or English, these two guys were not happy campers. Dymphna yanked the café's screen door open and greeted them with as big a smile as she could manage. It was indirectly because of Dymphna that the man was here. He was Fernando Cruz, the possible gift from the gods who might save the town from slow death.

"You must be Dymphna," Fernando said accusingly.

"Yes," Dymphna said. "And you must be Fernando."

"And this is Fat Chance, Texas . . ." he said, his voice trailing off as he looked up and down the street.

"After you," Pappy said, ushering Fernando into the café.

Pappy and Dymphna hurried after him, Pappy dropping the suitcase at the door. Fernando's deep scowl morphed into one of complete disbelief.

"Wow, this place is a hot mess," Fernando said as he surveyed the café.

Dymphna looked around the room. She tried to think back to the first time she saw the café, the first time she saw *any* building in Fat Chance, Texas, almost a year ago. She had come to love the town. But looking at the place through a newcomer's eyes, she could see how he might be a little stunned. The café, like every other building in town, listed to the left. The town had more animals than people. The trail, which came down a steep ravine from the highway, was impossible for any car, no matter how stalwart, to navigate.

"Yes, I guess it *is* a mess," she said. "But what did you expect from a café in the middle of a ghost town?"

"I guess my romantic nature got the better of me." Fernando shrugged. "I was hoping for the ghost of Wyatt Earp, cowboys panning for gold, tumbleweeds . . ."

"We have tumbleweeds!" Dymphna burst out. She and Pappy followed Fernando to the kitchen. Fernando opened cabinets, cranked the burners on the stove, and studied the oven door. When he reached for the oven knob, Dymphna swiftly threw herself between Fernando and the stove.

"Stop!" she said, putting her hand on his chest. "Don't. Touch. That. Dial."

"Because . . . ," Fernando said slowly, as if speaking to a child—or a lunatic.

Dymphna hurried to explain that a mother mouse had chosen the oven as a safe place to have her babies. Once that was discovered, the townsfolk always slammed the oven door once or twice to let her know she should get the kids out for a while.

"You're kidding, right?" Fernando said, and smiled as if to let them know he was in on the joke. But Pappy had joined Dymphna at the oven, intent on saving the threatened mice, should Dymphna's diminutive stature and, at 29, her relative youth not prove enough of a threat. Fernando sighed and stepped back. Obviously, he found not only the entire idea of doing business in Fat Chance insane but also its inhabitants.

Fernando took off his conspicuously new cowboy hat and laid it on the scarred counter. He wiped the sweat from his face with a blindingly white handkerchief and folded it carefully back into his pocket. He took another long, silent look around him and, judging from his expression, saw no reason to change his first impression.

Dymphna made no move to speak. She was looking around the room with a growing sense of despair. He was right—this place was a hot mess!

"The whole damn place looks like it was left over from another century," Fernando said.

"The whole damn place IS left over from another century," Pappy said. "The town dates back to the eighteen hundreds, and you're standing right now in a bona fide 1958 café. And it's a damn good one too."

"If I promise not to disturb Mrs. Mouse, may I take a look at that stove, please?" Fernando asked.

Dymphna and Pappy exchanged a look. Dymphna wasn't sure if Fernando was humoring them or they were humoring him, but she and Pappy backed away from the stove. Pappy watched the newcomer carefully, waiting for one false move.

"When was the last time this oven was calibrated?" Fernando asked.

"In 1960?" Dymphna guessed. "You'd have to ask Cleo."

"Cleo?" Fernando asked, still poking around the tiny kitchen. "The woman who used to run this café? Isn't she a gazillionaire? What was she doing here? What are *you* doing here?"

"That's a long story."

"Honey, a cab dropped me off at the top of the hill two hours ago, and there's apparently no phone reception unless you're standing in the middle of what you euphemistically call a street—and then only if you're lucky. I've got plenty of time for a long story," he said, examining a dented kettle. "Shall I make us some tea?"

"I'm in," Pappy said. "Meet you in the dining room."

Pappy and Dymphna went into the next room and hurriedly selected three reliable chairs. The room hadn't been used in ages—not since Cleo left five months ago. But from the time the small group arrived in Fat Chance a year ago until Cleo gave up and hightailed it back to Beverly Hills, the tiny uneven space with five tables had been the heart and soul of the community. Dymphna shot a peek at Fernando. He didn't flinch at the reference to the "dining room."

"Do you think the fact that he's making tea for us is a good sign?" Dymphna whispered to Pappy as they sat and waited for Fernando to appear.

"A sign of what?" Pappy asked.

"A sign that he might stay and run the café."

"I have no idea." Pappy shrugged. "Why do you care?"

"I . . ." Dymphna did care, but she couldn't think of a reason why. "Don't *you* care?"

"Of course I do," Pappy said. "I want a decent cook around here again."

Fernando, gingerly tucking his cowboy hat under his arm, came in with three chipped mugs and set them on the table. He laid his hat carefully on the table, took a seat, and stared first at Dymphna, then at Pappy. "OK," he said. "Tell me about this town."

"Now hold on," Pappy said. "We're the ones looking for a cook. We should be asking *you* questions, not the other way around."

"Nice try, old timer," he said. He looked at Dymphna. "So, about Fat Chance . . ."

Dymphna had practiced telling the story to herself in front of a mirror. She wanted the events to sound casual and plausible instead of baroque and insane. No need to frighten the poor man at the onset. She launched into the proceedings that had brought her here: how the late billionaire "Cutthroat Clarence" Johnson had left Fat Chance, a ruined town in the Texas Hill Country, in his will to a group of six total strangers and two of his relatives, his daughter Cleo and his grandson Professor Johnson. Cutthroat felt he had robbed all of them or their relatives of their chance at the American Dream, and left them each a building in the town—with the proviso that they had to stay and see what they could do with the place in six months. At the end of the six months, there would be compensation, three years' salary, which made it an equal gamble for all.

"And then what?" Fernando asked. "I mean, that was over a year ago."

"Well, we failed miserably," Dymphna said cheerfully. "I mean, I guess there was a reason he was a billionaire and the rest of us are barely scraping by. Whatever his vision was when he looked at this place, we sure didn't see it. But most of us realized we were happier here than we'd ever been anywhere else, and decided to stay."

"Most of you?" Fernando asked.

"Yes," Dymphna said. "By the time the six months were up, we had the original eight beneficiaries, plus Pappy, who had been watching over the place, and before long, two guys from the next town over moved in. Twin brothers, who are champion-quality bowlers. Those were really great days! We really thought we'd be able to make something of the place! But within months, we'd lost not only Cleo and her nephew, but all the young guys."

Dymphna registered the slight disappointment in Fernando's eyes.

"No young bowlers?" Fernando asked.

"No. Rodney and Rock got an offer to be the faces of a new bowling alley in Austin called Rock 'n' Rodney's," Dymphna said. "It was a dream come true!"

"This place is full of dreamers!" Pappy snorted. "One more, two less, doesn't make any difference."

"So, you're not a dreamer?" Fernando asked.

"No, I'm not," Pappy said. "I'm also not one of the beneficiaries."

"He was here when we arrived," Dymphna said.

"I'm the mayor and the banker," Pappy added. "And the sheriff."

Dymphna cringed. She had hoped not to go down this road so soon. She knew Fernando probably thought Pappy was crazy. She remembered when they'd first arrived in Fat Chance—they all thought Pappy was crazy. They were all still pretty sure he was, but, well, now they loved the town—and Pappy was part of it.

"This has certainly been interesting," Fernando said, standing up. "But I'm not sure this is the right . . . opportunity . . . for me."

Dymphna felt her cheeks burning. She had never met Fernando before, but he was here because of her. When she first got to Fat Chance and discovered her farm was rampant with wild berries, she'd called her good friend Suzanna, who owned a tea shop called *The Rollicking Bun . . . home of the epic scone* in Venice, California. Dymphna had remembered Suzanna always bragging about one of her childhood buddies, Fernando. Not only was he a lifelong friend, he was also the pastry chef at the Bun until he opened his own B and B on Vashon Island. Fernando apparently had the world's best jam recipes, and Suzanna was sure he would part with them for "family" or, in Dymphna's case, sort-of-adopted family. He had, and the recipes were as good as Suzanna said they were. Dymphna was now making jars of jam that added to her larder and her income.

Dymphna didn't want Suzanna—or Suzanna's sister Erinn, or their mother, Virginia—worrying about her, so she tended to embellish how well things were going in town when she spoke to them. No harm done, until Suzanna sent an e-mail to Dymphna, letting her know that the fabulous Fernando had sold his share of the B and B to his partner and was looking for a new place. Suzanna thought Fat Chance sounded like a ground floor opportunity, and Fernando was very excited about checking it out. Without admitting to her pack of white lies, Dymphna convinced herself that he might actually like the place.

Fernando, Dymphna, and Pappy turned toward the door as Thud, the enormous bloodhound that shared Dymphna's farm, bounded into the room. Thud sensed the new blood and raced to welcome Fernando to town. The dog reared back, then jumped. He put his front paws on Fernando's shoulders, knocking his chair over. Fernando and Thud landed on the floor, the dog looming over the man. Drool ensued. Dymphna hoped Fernando found this charming, but suspected by Fernando's involuntary yowling that he was not a dog person.

Dymphna pulled the dog off him and Pappy righted his chair. Fernando wiped the dog slobber from his face, this time stuffing his no-longer-white handkerchief into his jeans.

"Tell him how great this place is, Pappy," Dymphna said as she lugged Thud back outside.

"I won't lie to you," Pappy said, looking Fernando right in the eye. "Fat Chance is an acquired taste."

They all thought of the place as a ghost town, but it was actually a study in "arrested decay." The structures had been maintained, but only to the extent that they would not be allowed to fall over or otherwise deteriorate in a major way. That explained why the town was a mishmash of buildings from the turn of the twentieth century, with electricity, running water, a few 1950s appliances—and a faint Internet signal.

"I have to get up to the farm," Dymphna said to Fernando as they all stood in front of the café. "I've got to shear my goats. Do you want to come up?"

"Less than anything on earth," Fernando said.

"You go on," Pappy said to Dymphna. "He'll be fine here."

Dymphna hesitated, but realized there was nothing she could say or do to make Fernando decide to stay. She and Thud headed up to the farm, the two men watching them until they were two small specks on the horizon. The speck that was Thud bounced all the way up the hill.

"Who's maintained the buildings all these years?" Fernando asked.

"I have," Pappy said proudly. "Been here for more years than I can remember."

"Why?" Fernando asked. "Why have you been here so long?"

"Can't say. Probably same sort of reason you're here."

"Oh, I doubt that," Fernando said.

"You might not stay." Pappy shrugged. "But you could have gone anywhere. Back to Napa or Los Angeles. You could have gone to Chicago or New York. But you decided to check out Fat Chance. Not business as usual, you got to admit that. You were looking for something different. And you found it."

Pappy's words seemed to hit home.

"OK," Fernando said. "You may be right. I'm willing to try to find out what you see here that I don't."

"I'll be happy to show you the—"

"No, Pappy," Fernando said, looking a little uncomfortable calling a complete stranger "Pappy." "I don't want you to *show* me. I want to go find it. You know, the unvarnished truth."

"Unvarnished is pretty much business as usual around here," Pappy said. "As a matter of fact, you'll be hard-pressed to find anything varnished."

Fernando put his new hat back on his head, adjusting the angle just slightly until he felt it was doing its best for him. "I guess I'll mosey around," he said.

"Just watch out for the snakes and—" Pappy stopped abruptly. "Right. Get on with you."

CHAPTER 2

Fernando looked up and down Main Street, hands on hips, as if daring the place.

OK, Fat Chance, show me something.

He took a few steps and dust kicked up all around him. He lifted one foot and rubbed his boot on his jeans—hadn't anyone around here in the last hundred years heard of asphalt? This dirt was killing his new boots. He rubbed his other boot clean and was relieved to see the dust didn't seem to have caused any permanent damage. He took a few more steps, then looked down at his boots once again—they were as dusty as before he'd tried to clean them.

Whatever!

He stumbled, but righted himself quickly, glowering at the ground where a large rock had deliberately found its way into his path. He kicked the offending rock with all the pent-up frustration he'd been feeling.

"Damn," he said, as pain shot up his ankle.

The rock was unmoved by the activity. Even the ground in this backwater town was against him. He looked around again. Fernando wanted to figure out his best approach to this scouting expedition and, more importantly, to make sure that his futile fight with a boulder hadn't been witnessed by any of the other inhabitants.

From the look of things, it appeared the café was pretty much in the center of the town. Any way he walked he would see—what? More dirt surrounded by a bunch of falling-down buildings?

He jumped up on the weathered boardwalk, which was smooth from years of sunshine and footsteps. Most of the buildings were on the boardwalk, but as he looked back toward the trail he and Pappy had managed to climb down, he remembered seeing an intriguing building on the other side of Main Street. He looked at the other end of town, where another building stood apart from the others. He flipped a coin—the far end of town won.

At least this way I'll be closer to the trailhead after I've looked around.

Eyeing the loose dust of Main Street, he headed back down the boardwalk toward the far end of town. Dymphna and Pappy said a handful of people lived and worked here, but there wasn't a soul moving in the whole town as far as he could see. He reached the end of the boardwalk and realized he'd have to walk through the deep dust to reach the building that sat defiantly apart from the other buildings. He saw a creek peeking out from behind the buildings on the boardwalk, meandering gracefully in front of a two-story building and babbling brightly in the sun. Fernando tiptoed through the dust and stood, studying the front porch. He was a sucker for front porches. This one looked directly down Main Street. If the porch wasn't so battered, if the building wasn't so precariously leaning to one side, and if there was anything to see down Main Street, this would be a great spot.

He started across the little bridge that spanned the creek. He shielded his eyes and looked up at the sign hung over the eves.

The Creakside Inn.

He let out a laugh.

"What's so damn funny?" came a dry voice from a corner of the porch.

Fernando jumped. An old woman with the most unruly white hair he'd seen since—well, since Pappy took off his hat—walked out of the shadows.

Startled that he was actually face-to-face with another human being, Fernando continued up the path.

"Hold up there, city boy," the old woman said. "This is my place and you weren't invited in. Now, unless you are looking to rent a room, I suggest you get on about whatever business brought you here, and get off my property. And rumor has it you are not interested in renting a room."

"Rumor has it?" Fernando said. "There are enough people in this place to start a rumor? I've only been here a few minutes."

"We're a well-oiled machine."

"Sorry, ma'am," he said in what he felt was a calm, reassuring tone. "I'm just lookin' around your li'l place here, makin' m'self familiar . . . y'know."

"Just because this is a ghost town in Texas, there's no reason to be dropping your Gs," the old woman said.

He stayed where he was on the bridge, but put his hands on his hips. "So, tell me more about this rumor."

"I heard you came to look over the café, but you didn't like it."

"I never said I didn't like it."

"Did you?"

"Did I what?"

"Like the café?"

"No, it's a train wreck!"

"OK, well, at least you're not crazy," the old woman said. "You can come up on the porch now."

As Fernando made his way up the rickety steps, the old woman approached him. He noticed she was wearing a faded gingham dress with a double ruffle at the hem. Her hands were shoved into the pockets. He tried to sneak a peek at her hands—what if she had a pistol in there? The old woman noticed.

"And what are you looking at?" she asked.

"Your apron," he said quickly.

"What about it?" she asked, her eyes narrowing.

"You didn't strike me as the ruffle type."

She stared at him through a mass of wrinkles, which suddenly broke into a grin.

"You got that right," she said, putting out her hand. "I'm Bertha. They call me Old Bertha behind my back, but never to my face."

Fernando suspected that was a wise move on the part of the townspeople. Old Bertha offered him a seat, indicating the porch swing. Now that both of her hands were out of her pockets and he could see there was no gun, Fernando relaxed. He took the seat offered him. Bertha perched her ample bottom on the porch railing. Fernando held his breath, but the wood didn't splinter under her.

"I guess this is your place?" he asked.

"Yep."

"Anybody ever rent a room?"

"I bet you'd be surprised if I said yes," she said.

"I won't lie," he said, looking around. "I'd be very surprised."

"I don't like your tone, city boy. You're making some pretty rash judgments about what's happening in Fat Chance, based on not much of anything but a sore foot!"

"I was hoping no one was looking."

She glanced up at him and giggled like a little girl. "Oh yeah, I saw it. You sure did put that rock in its place."

"Not my finest hour," Fernando admitted, then softened his tone. "So, tell me about you."

Old Bertha stared hard at him. "I'll bet you say that to all the old ladies, don't you? I'll make a deal with you, city boy. You play straight with me, I'll play straight with you."

"I never play straight," Fernando said in his most flamboyant voice.

"Oh, you are good," she said, putting her hand up for a high five.

Fernando smacked her hand. They were going to get along just fine.

Old Bertha told him she had two lodgers. One was Powderkeg, who was a carpenter and leather worker. His shop was at the other end of town. He was also the ex-husband of Cleo, the billionaire's daughter who left town so quickly. Old Bertha suspected that Powderkeg was still in love with his ex-wife, but even though the old woman was pretty sure there was "some hanky-panky going on" while Cleo had been in town, he hadn't been enough to hold her.

The second lodger was Polly, who, at twenty-three, was the youngest person in Fat Chance. Fernando noticed that Old Bertha lit up when talking about the young woman—almost like a mother bragging about her daughter—or in this case, a grandmother bragging about her granddaughter. Polly ran a millinery shop on the boardwalk called Polly's Tops, Hats and Tails, and made dazzling hat confections that she sold online and in a gift shop in the nearest "big town"—Dripping Springs, with its population of nearly 1,800. Powderkeg also sold his leather crafts there, as did Titan.

"I thought you only had two lodgers," Fernando said.

"Did I say anything about Titan living here?" Bertha asked testily. "He lives over at the forge."

"The forge? You mean that glorified lean-to over by the trailhead? What does he sell, horseshoes?"

"He does sell horseshoes, but mostly to the local cowboys," Old Bertha said.

"Local cowboys?" Fernando brightened, looking around as if waiting for them to materialize.

"Not local-local," Old Bertha said. "We've got a few ranches nearby. Apparently he's a real artist when it comes to horseshoes. But he also makes jewelry and bowls out of metal. He sells them over in Dripping Springs. They get a tourist trade over there that we can't seem to get going here."

"The fact that you don't have a real road has got to be a stumbling block," Fernando said dryly.

Old Bertha nodded and sighed.

"Let me get this straight," Fernando said. "You, Pappy, and Dymphna live in this town, plus Powderkeg, Polly, and Titan. Is that right?"

"That's about it, yeah."

"Why haven't I seen them then—Powderkeg, Titan, and Polly, I mean."

"Why should they put themselves out to meet you?"

"Are they hiding?" Fernando looked around, slightly alarmed.

"I wouldn't say they were hiding, exactly. But, you know, rumor has it . . ."

"OK, OK," Fernando said, not wanting to inflame the rumor mill. "So you guys each have a business here in Fat Chance?"

"Mostly," Old Bertha said. "But I've got two. I run the grocery store. It was originally left to a kid named Wally Wasabi, but I took it over when he left. Doesn't really take a whole lot of time running this boardinghouse, as you can imagine."

"Why did Wally . . ."

"Wasabi."

"Why did he leave?" Fernando looked down Main Street as the town baked in the sun. "Besides the obvious."

"He got a deal with a publisher in New York City," Old Bertha said. "What do you think the odds are of becoming a successful writer in New York City?"

Probably better than becoming a successful grocer in Fat Chance, thought Fernando.

CHAPTER 3

As she and Thud walked up the hill, Dymphna wondered if there was anything she could have said to make Fernando stay. She thought about her conversation with Pappy. Why did it matter to her what Fernando thought of Fat Chance? No matter how much Pappy groused, the town had managed without their café for months now. If Fernando decided to walk back up the hill and never look back, nothing would really change. So that couldn't be it. Was she worried that Fernando would tell Suzanna and her family about Dymphna's little white lies? No, she didn't think that was it either. As a matter of fact, that might be a relief!

Dymphna could see Main Street from her farm. She tried not to think about Fernando or worry about his decision, but she kept sneaking peeks to the spot in the road where there was the only cell phone reception. Fernando still wasn't standing on it. The last she saw of him, he was, improbably, sitting on the porch of the Creakside Inn with Old Bertha. Dymphna admonished herself—she had work to do, she couldn't stand here all day worrying about something over which she had no control. She suddenly realized what was bothering her. Fat Chance was like beauty—it all depended on the eye of the beholder. And while Fernando would either see the beauty of the place or he wouldn't, she loved this little town and she wanted him, as an impartial outsider, to love it too.

Fat chance.

Dymphna and Thud went into the house. Dymphna filled the bloodhound's bowl with water and left him happily lapping, as she headed to the barnyard. She approached the goats as quietly as possible, her hands—which were hiding a large pair of scissors—behind her back. Contrary to popular belief, goats were incredibly intelligent and had memories like an Italian plotting a vendetta. Twice a year, her four Angora goats—Udderlee, Catterly, Sarilee, and Down Diego—had to be shorn. Sarilee had borne two kids, but they were still babies and wouldn't be shorn for another season. Having been through three shearings already, if the adult goats saw the scissors, they'd hightail it into the pasture. Dymphna's farm was fenced, but the goats only stayed inside the fence if they felt like it.

When she first arrived at the farm, she'd kept the goats in the barn while she spent hours securing the old fence. Confident the goats would be safely corralled, she'd let them into the yard, where they played picturesquely. Pappy was visiting the first time Dymphna saw the goats leap the fence. Thud had gotten into the yard and was bounding around joyously. But the goats wanted none of him. They gracefully hopped almost vertically into the air and over the enclosure. While she stood there in shock, Pappy didn't miss a beat of his story, a well-worn tale of how he had managed to get his Volkswagen bus up the trail before the road gave way entirely during a torrential rain. She had interrupted him.

"My goats just took off!"

"I see that," Pappy said. "So, like I was saying, I felt the tire slipping and—"

"But . . ." Dymphna watched her goats scampering toward the creek. "My goats just . . . took off."

"What's your point?" Pappy said, clearly annoyed that his story about his VW bus had been derailed.

"I didn't know they could do that," she said.

"Well," Pappy said. "Now you do."

"Then, why . . . Why build a fence in the first place?"

Pappy looked at her with a mixture of pity and annoyance. "You're the one who built the fence. You tell me."

Dymphna watched the goats playing down by the creek.

"Can you picture the horse pastures of Kentucky?" Pappy asked, pity finally winning out.

"Of course," Dymphna said. "Green rolling fields with white fences for miles."

"That's right. Lots of times the fence is only four feet high. So, when you think about it, any horse worth his salt could jump over it. But he doesn't. And do you know why?"

"No," Dymphna answered.

"'Cause he doesn't want to," Pappy said. "Same with the goats. They'll hang out most of the time, but if you give them a reason to scoot, they'll scoot."

Dymphna smiled at the memory. She'd used a lot of energy trying to outsmart her goats. Now she quietly approached them. She scratched Udderlee's head, feeling a little guilty trying to trick the beautiful animal into a forced separation from her hair. It suddenly occurred to Dymphna that she should put all the goats in the barn and bring them out one at a time for their shearing. One small woman against four goats just wasn't fair. She knew she could ask any of the men who remained in town for help—Pappy, Powderkeg, and Titan were always happy to lend a hand—but she felt that this was her land and she should solve her own problems.

If Professor Johnson were still here, a lot of things would be different, she thought. For one thing, perhaps their relationship might even have progressed to a point where she no longer called him "Professor Johnson."

Professor Johnson was their benefactor's grandson. Another of the original heirs, Professor Johnson had been included in the will because Cutthroat Clarence thought his grandson's life could use a little shaking up. Cutthroat confessed, via a DVD played for his beneficiaries after his death, that he'd ignored his grandson during his life and wanted to make it up to him. Dymphna thought back to the somber man, on sabbatical from his university, who first boarded the RV to Fat Chance: his serious expression, his determined posture as he led Thud onto the bus that would take them all to Texas. Dymphna remembered thinking that he did not look like a man excited by the prospect of adventure. But he'd proven Dymphna wrong. Professor Johnson, solemn expression and all, embraced the possibilities of Fat Chance. He had worked day and night, determined to turn the ramshackle saloon into a museum about Fat Chance. By the time the six months imposed on the beneficiaries was up, so was his sabbatical. As much as he wanted to stay, Professor Johnson had responsibilities in the world outside their little ghost town, and he wasn't the type to turn his back on them. Dymphna tried not to let her mind wander. She didn't want to think about how little time the two of them actually had spent together.

They corresponded by e-mail regularly and had a hit-or-miss phone conversation once a week. They were both shy by nature, and the fact that Dymphna had to make the call from the middle of Main Street didn't give them much opportunity to warm up, let alone heat up, a conversation. The greatest indication that Professor Johnson harbored strong feels for her was the fact that he'd left his beloved bloodhound, Thud, to watch over her. Sometimes, when she worried that Professor Johnson might lose interest in her and never make it back to Fat Chance, she'd hug Thud—her living, breathing security blanket. The bloodhound was better than any promise or piece of jewelry. Thud was a pledge of Professor Johnson's allegiance.

The other goats tried to get in on the scratching action. Dymphna attempted to lean the shears against the barn without alerting the animals, but Down Diego was not fooled. He bellowed furiously and all the goats followed him over the fence. Dymphna stared after them, hands on hips.

"Should we go get them?" she asked the chickens. "Or wait till they come back and try again tomorrow?"

"That's up to you," said a deep voice.

Startled, she looked up. Leaning against the fence stood a tall, lean man with a shock of movie-star-quality hair. His blue-white teeth glinted in the sun. He was wearing sunglasses, but she was pretty sure there had to be emerald-green eyes under them. This man was too gorgeous for plain old brown eyes.

"I hope I didn't scare you, Dymphna," the man rumbled.

She was immediately on guard. How did this stranger know her name?

"Do I know you?" she asked, backing up toward her shears. She could see Thud at the window, inside the house. He was jumping up and down, trying to get out. She really wished he had opposable thumbs right about now.

"No," the man said, pulling off his sunglasses. "But I know you. Well, I know Thud."

He continued to smile. His eyes *were* emerald green. He made no attempt to come in through the gate.

"How do you know my dog?" she asked, stalling for time. If she couldn't get to the shears, She'd consider throwing a chicken at him if things got weird.

"I'm sorry! I really should introduce myself. My name is Constantino Valentine."

OK, nobody is really named Constantino Valentine, thought Dymphna.

"I'm a veterinarian," he continued. "Thud was my patient . . . after his snake bite."

Dymphna's breath caught. She still couldn't think about that terrible day months ago without a chill running up her spine. Thud had saved the life of Dodge Durham, a man from a neighboring ranch. Dodge was no friend of anyone in Fat Chance, but he had found the dog after Thud saved him from a rattler. Dodge nursed the dog back to health with the help of a vet so this man's story held together, but still . . .

"That was a while ago," Dymphna said, not ready to let her guard down.

"I know," said Constantino. "I would have come sooner, but I've been out of the country. But once you've met him, Thud sort of stays with you, you know what I mean?"

Dymphna did know. She looked over at the house, where Thud continued to bay at the window. He seemed frantic to get out, but now Dymphna could see that he just wanted to see their guest. Constantino followed her gaze and caught sight of the dog. His entire face lit up.

"There's the big guy," he said, heading over to the house.

Constantino walked over to the window and tapped on the glass. Thud put his paws up and licked the inside of the window. It was obvious Thud knew him and was happy to see the man. Dymphna relaxed.

"May I let him out?" Constantino asked.

"Sure," Dymphna said. "I think he's going to break the window if you don't."

Constantino opened the front door and Thud came hurtling out, jowls and ears flapping. He jumped on the man on the porch, but Constantino was ready for him. With his paws on Constantino's shoulders, the dog was almost as tall as the vet.

Dymphna walked over to the house. Constantino tried to push the dog to the ground, but Thud sprang back up. The vet just laughed and continued to wrestle with him.

"Thud!" Dymphna commanded. "Get down."

Thud ignored her.

"I'm so sorry," Dymphna said. "He has terrible manners."

Dymphna suddenly remembered her own manners.

"Would you like some iced tea?" She picked up a large screw-topped jar of sun tea on the porch railing. "I just brewed some this morning."

"Sure!" said Constantino, finally getting Thud to stay on the ground. "That sounds perfect."

Dymphna ran into the house and returned with two glasses of ice. She opened the jar and poured the fragrant tea.

"It's mint tea, Doctor Valentine," Dymphna offered.

"Love it." He took a glass from her. "But call me Tino. Everyone does."

"That's pretty informal for a doctor," Dymphna said, thinking fleetingly of her maybe boyfriend, Professor Johnson.

"Well, when you're up to your elbow in somebody's mare, you tend to get to the informal stage pretty fast."

Dymphna felt the color rising in her cheeks, which surprised her. She had been around animals her entire life and she certainly knew her way around a farm. But there was something about Dr. Valentine's wicked grin that made his barnyard banter feel almost like . . . flirting.

Every morning, he woke up in confusion. With his eyes still closed, Professor Johnson uncurled his wiry frame and patted the nightstand for his glasses. He sat up as he put them on. The enormous room, filled with the finest décor, was not in his apartment in Los Feliz nor in Fat Chance. Sunlight filtered through the room, as if demanding he rise and shine, damn it. But Professor Johnson, with his PhD in natural sciences, knew the sun was not pointing rays at him personally. He had to face the facts: He'd awakened, as he had for the last six months, in one of the four guest rooms at his aunt Cleo's mansion in Beverly Hills.

Spring was in the air—even in Los Angeles, where spring was always in the air. He'd wanted to visit Fat Chance over the university's spring break, but he had to work on another grant proposal, his only real hope at getting back to Texas full time, and wireless access being what it was in Fat Chance, he had opted to stay in California. He had told himself that summer was just around the corner, and, even if he didn't get one of the myriad grants he'd applied for, he would at least be able to spend the summer there. Now there were whisperings that he was going to be given a new summer course to teach. He could "just say no," but he knew academic politics. In the long run, turning it down would hurt him.

Now there was no Dymphna, no Thud, no progress on his proposal to the university. He took his glasses off, put the pillow over his eyes, and refused to meet the morning until the last possible instant.

When Professor Johnson finally came down for breakfast, Cleo was already in the solarium. She was absently running French manicured nails through her highlighted hair. No amount of upkeep was too large or too trivial to be overlooked by Cleo Johnson-Primb. Cleo's Lafont reading glasses were perched on the end of her nose. She took them off as soon as she heard her nephew enter the room.

"You don't need to take your glasses off," he said, heading to the sideboard for coffee. "It is only I."

"Force of habit, darling," she said.

Professor Johnson added sugar to his coffee. His aunt took hers black, but as soon as he'd moved in, she'd added the sugar bowl to the sideboard.

"Did you know there's a new trend in housing? Living in less than six hundred square feet? It's a whole *lifestyle* apparently," Cleo said, putting her glasses back on and returning to the *Wall Street Journal*. "Even the Republicans have heard about it."

"A whole six hundred feet? That doesn't seem unreasonable," he said, sitting opposite his aunt. "Dymphna's cabin is probably only five hundred square feet—if that."

He and his aunt had a psychological game of chess going. She didn't like discussing anyone or anything that had to do with Fat Chance, Texas. He was at her house only because he was trying to save enough money to get back there as soon as possible. Once Cutthroat's estate had made good on the Fat Chance challenge and distributed generous amounts of money to his charities, Cleo was Cutthroat's primary beneficiary. Professor Johnson's aunt now had discretionary income coming out her chemically peeled pores—but he didn't want any of it. At thirty-two years of age, Professor Johnson had been making his own way for many years now and he saw no reason to change.

"Any word from the university?" his aunt asked.

"Nothing concrete." He shook his head.

He wasn't sure if his aunt wanted the university to come through with the funding or not. They never discussed it. What was clear was that his aunt didn't want him to return to Fat Chance anytime soon. He knew it didn't really have anything to do with *him*. She just looked a little less awful if she wasn't the only one who had turned her back on Fat Chance as soon as she could.

Professor Johnson was uneasy about having left Fat Chance at all. Of course, he had his responsibility to the university. But was that enough reason to give up a shot at real happiness with the only woman with whom he'd ever really connected? Was that enough reason to leave his dog? He knew leaving Thud to watch over Dymphna was the right thing to do. It was even selfish in a way. He rested easier knowing that Thud was there to protect her. He couldn't stand the thought of her all alone on that ramshackle little farm.

Dymphna and Tino collapsed against the hay bales, exhausted and out of breath.

"Wow!" Dymphna panted. "Thank you."

"Are you kidding? I should be thanking *you*," he said, straightening his shirt.

"You're just saying that." Dymphna could feel her cheeks heating up.

"No, it's true. It's been a while. But I guess it's like riding a bicycle. You never forget."

"That doesn't seem like the kind of thing you'd learn at school," Dymphna said.

"Nah." He shook his head, then rested it against the hay bale. "I was raised on a small spread in Montana. These things pretty much come naturally to a farmer, I guess."

Dymphna leaned back into the hay as well. "Well, you showed me a thing or two."

Tino reached over and carefully pulled a piece of straw from her hair. As if snapping out of a daze, Dymphna sat up and stared at the goats they had just finished shearing. She suddenly found it easier to look at them than at him.

The four shorn goats raced around the pen, their mohair piled high near the house. Thud sniffed at the mohair suspiciously. Now that Dymphna and Tino weren't in the act of actually shearing the goats, she found herself unexpectedly self-conscious.

"Well," she said, trying to wrangle her hair into submission. "It was extremely nice of you to help."

We were only shearing goats! she thought. *So then why do I feel so guilty?*

CHAPTER 4

Fernando left the Creakside Inn armed with a mix of facts and innuendo about Fat Chance. Old Bertha certainly had her opinions about everybody and everything. He'd learned never to dismiss the observations of old women, and Old Bertha did seem to have her finger on the pulse of this dead town.

He headed back the way he'd come, listening to the sound of his boots echoing on the boardwalk. He had to admit—it was a romantic, very Western sound.

He stood still for a moment, flashing back to the movie he'd seen on the plane. The Longest Something or Other. The Longest . . . what? Yard? Nope. The Longest . . . Ride! It starred Clint Eastwood's kid, Scott. Fernando never put in his earbuds, so he wasn't exactly sure if the kid could act or not, but he was sure good-looking. He had to admit, the thought of riding rough with Scott Eastwood as his wingman had its appeal. Sleeping on the ground, a saddle for his pillow.

Fernando shook his head. Nope, not in his wildest dreams could he picture himself doing that. He couldn't even imagine doing it on purpose. His idea of roughing it was a night in a hotel that served powdered eggs for breakfast.

He turned his attention back to the boardwalk, just in time to skirt another bunch of tumbling tumbleweeds. He wondered briefly why anyone bothered to write songs about the damned things. He looked around again, trying to get a better sense of just where everything was in this less than dynamic hub.

Back on the boardwalk, Fernando stood in front of the first store. The beautifully carved sign above it read: The Boozehound Saloon.

Might as well start here. Maybe I can get a stiff drink.

Fernando wondered if he should knock. Deciding it was a place of business, and therefore knocking was probably not the right protocol, he turned the knob and the door squeaked open. The place was deserted.

This must have belonged to the billionaire's nephew—Professor Somebody or Other—the one who left town at his first opportunity.

Fernando smiled as he realized he was judging the man for leaving after six months, when he himself was planning on leaving at the first opportunity.

He took a deep breath. He could smell the years of whiskey soaked into the floorboards. Even under a thick layer of dust, it was impossible to disguise the workmanship of the bar, with its marble top and heavily carved base. He went behind the bar but there was no booze.

Of course there was no booze. *No man smart enough to leave this place is dumb enough to leave his booze behind.*

But there was a player piano! Intrigued, he walked over and studied it. He saw a sliding panel above the keyboard and moved it gently to the left. Inside was a scroll of music. He leaned in and could just make out the faded printing that read "A Bird in a Gilded Cage." Fernando was tempted to try to make the thing play, but he had no idea how to operate it. Reluctantly, he slid the panel back in place. He'd have to leave town without ever knowing if the poor bird got out.

In the center of the saloon were a few beautifully crafted display cases. It was as if the place was a museum, not a saloon.

Well, I guess when you're a saloon owned by a professor, things happen.

Fernando saw that Cleo's Café was attached to the saloon, something he hadn't really noticed when he was having his powwow with Dymphna and Pappy. He walked through the archway into the café.

These tables should be turned the other way . . .

He mentally shook the image out of his head. *You do not redecorate when you are leaving.* He resolutely walked out the door of the café.

As he made his way back uptown, he saw city hall, the jail, and the bank, all clearly marked with signs. He knew these buildings all belonged to Pappy, so he pressed on. The next shop was Polly's Tops, Hats and Tails. He looked at the display window. There were decorated cowboy hats, steampunk hats, Victorian hats, Mad Hatter tea party hats. Ribbons, bows, feathers, and sequins in every conceivable and inconceivable combination. The display took his breath away. He could see the shadow of a figure inside, but he hesitated at the door. Old Bertha had said Polly could be a little prickly. That observation, coming from somebody as snappish as Old Bertha herself, made him a little leery. But, he reasoned, he had nothing to lose—and he really wanted to meet the woman behind the creations in the window, so he went in.

"Hey," said the woman who must be Polly. "You must be the guy everyone is talking about."

"News travels fast," Fernando said.

"Let's face it," Polly said. "It doesn't have all that far to go."

Polly was tall, with dyed red hair pulled up in two pigtails. The pigtail holders were a complicated affair of ribbons and bits of hardware. She had a row of silver stud earrings in graduated sizes marching down her earlobes and sported a tiny diamond nose stud as well. The hair needed work, he thought, and the nose stud looked uncomfortable to him, but he admitted that was a personal prejudice.

"I'm not staying," he said.

"That's not exactly a surprise," she replied. "None of the young guys stay. It's slim pickins' around here as far as that goes."

"I'm thirty-five," Fernando said. "I'm not that young."

"I think Titan's about that age. Young enough to go, old enough to stay."

"I'm not staying," Fernando repeated.

"I know. You said that. Here, come hold this."

Polly was standing at a large butcher-block table in the center of the store, working on a felt top hat. The hatband was made of leather and was styled to look like a miniature corset. Polly was lacing up the corset with black lace and needed Fernando to hold the knot while she made a bow. Once the bow was puffed to her satisfaction, she started digging around in a box of what looked like gears from old watches.

"You do amazing work," Fernando said.

"That's the thing about Fat Chance," Polly said distractedly. "There's nothing else to do. We're all doing stuff we never dreamed of."

"Maybe that's what your benefactor had in mind."

"That's probably wishful thinking." She attached two small watch hands to the hat. "I'm pretty sure Cutthroat wasn't into the arts. I think he was hoping we'd figure out how to be . . . you know . . . financially successful. It still might happen, but all of us who stayed are spending more than we're making."

"Try this," Fernando said, picking up a coil. He handed it to Polly, who beamed and added it to the hat.

"Of course, the rent's cheap." Polly smiled.

"Old Bertha told me about you guys. The ones who stayed. And I know about Chloe . . ."

"Cleo," Polly corrected. "Yeah, and Professor Johnson, her nephew. Yeah, they left—Cleo couldn't get out of here fast enough. Professor Johnson had a commitment to a university. He didn't want to go. You can't blame him for leaving."

I wouldn't blame anybody for leaving, thought Fernando.

He had put his own brown cowboy hat on the table. Polly picked it up and studied it.

"This seems sort of plain for you," she said.

"I wasn't sure what sort of impression I needed to make."

"Since you're leaving, I guess you don't have to make any impression. Want a red feather?"

Fernando accepted his hat, now sporting an embroidered headband and a jaunty red feather.

He studied himself in the mirror.

"I love it," he said, admiring himself from all angles.

"Let me get a picture." Polly grabbed her iPhone. She surprised Fernando by coming around to get in the picture with him.

"Since we barely use our phones for anything that requires cell phone reception," Polly explained, "I've become a cell phone photographer."

Polly held up the phone in classic selfie mode—opening her mouth in the required young female "I'm having the *best* time"—and snapped a picture of them both.

"Eat your heart out, Instagram," Fernando said.

"Really." Polly nodded. "Actually, when we go to Dripping Springs, I jump online at the Internet café, but whatever pictures I've taken are old news by then."

"Don't worry about that," Fernando said. "I never become old news."

He left Polly to her wizardry and selfies. Next door to Polly's shop was the town grocery store. He peeked in. Old Bertha was sitting behind the counter, reading a paper. He opened the door and leaned in.

"I didn't see you go past Polly's," he said. "How'd you get over here?"

"Ever heard of a back door?" Bertha pointed a thumb toward the rear of the store. "We're swankier than we look, I guess."

Fernando saluted her and closed the door. There was only one store left on the boardwalk. The sign simply said Carpenter. He grabbed the door handle firmly—he'd gotten used to almost forcing the warped doors open. But this door gave immediately.

This guy is a carpenter, after all.

The front of the store was no bigger than the others. Certainly not big enough to do large or even medium-size wood projects. There must be a workroom out back. There was no one in sight. He looked around at the displays of leather belts with their intricate, delicate, ornate buckles, and at the wooden carved bowls, walking sticks, and chess sets. There was even a wooden square-shaped man's ring. Fernando couldn't resist. He tried it on and went to the window to look at it in the light.

"I can give you a deal on that," came a gravelly voice.

Fernando spun around, yanking at the ring. "Oh, I was just trying it on," he stammered.

"That's what it's there for," the leathery man said.

"You must be Powderkeg," Fernando said, still trying to get the ring off his ringer.

"You must be Fernando," Powderkeg said, nodding at the ring. "Want a hand with that?"

Fernando held out his hand and Powderkeg pulled. Fernando heard his knuckle pop, but he tried not to wince.

"That's the trouble with these square rings." Powderkeg scooped out some sort of grease from a jar onto a dirty rag. "They get stuck. I haven't perfected this yet."

Fernando closed his eyes as Powderkeg wrapped the filthy rag around his finger. The ring glided off.

"Thanks," Fernando said. "It really is a beautiful piece of work."

"Don't mention it." Powderkeg stared at Fernando with his piercing eyes set in deep, leathery wrinkles. "How long are you here for?"

"Not long," Fernando said. "I came from—"

"Washington," Powderkeg said. "We know."

It occurred to Fernando that the people of Fat Chance actually didn't need cell phone reception. News just seemed to get around.

"Yeah, Washington," Fernando said. "It took a while to get here, so I'm just looking around before I head back."

"Can I answer any questions for you?" Powderkeg asked, polishing the ring and putting it back on the stand.

If you mean can you get me to stay, the answer is no. "You're very talented. You have three years' salary in your pocket. Or under your mattress. Or in the bank. Why are you here?"

"I get to do what I want, when I want, and really concentrate on leather and wood in a way that wouldn't be possible in the outside world. And nobody bothers me," Powderkeg said. "Where else would I be?"

As Fernando left the shop, he thought over Powderkeg's answer. After years in the bed and breakfast trade, the thought of pursuing his baking without someone ringing for more soap or different towels seemed incredibly appealing. He was surprised by the wave of sorrow that swooshed through his mind. Hadn't he done what he wanted? He'd built up a great business—okay, maybe not great but definitely a solid business—in a place he loved, doing things he wanted to do. No other B and B on the island had prettier views—inside and out. And that kitchen! It was everything he'd always wanted in a kitchen. *Enough,* he told himself. *I did it . . . it is done! Now I'm looking for something new.* He looked around rather regretfully. *And so far this isn't it!*

But as he looked down the boardwalk, he realized that keeping this band of eccentrics happy would probably be impossible. *It's a nice, quiet place,* he thought. The only sound was a plane that crisscrossed the sky from time to time.

It had been a nice dream while it lasted.

Fernando had come to the end of the boardwalk. He faced the trailhead and realized it was probably time to try his luck at getting cell phone reception in the center of town. As he stepped back onto the dust of Main Street, he noticed the forge. He started across the street, contending with the dirt devils and their evil plot to wreak havoc with his boots. He was just about to give up on his plan when he saw a man come from inside. Fernando sucked in his breath. Was this gorgeous creature a mirage? Surely no mere mortal could look like this: a shirtless mountain of a man, his ebony skin gleaming in the sun, taut muscles flexing. This must be Titan. Fernando wondered if the intense sun was affecting his brain.

Titan met Fernando's eyes. He smiled, showing even, white teeth. Fernando smiled back.

Why didn't anyone tell me about this fabulous man? Maybe I should stay at least a little longer . . .

Fernando took a step toward Titan, but was stopped in his tracks by a sunbaked, one-eyed bird, who rushed him like a dog after a postman. Fernando squeaked.

"Fancy!" Titan said in a melodious, silky voice. "Come back here! Bad bird!"

Fernando backpedaled as Titan scooped up the flapping bird.

"I'm so sorry," Titan said. "She's just very protective."

"That's all right," Fernando said, trying to recover his dignity. He pulled out his cell phone and waved it at Titan. "I'm just going to make a call . . ."

CHAPTER 5

"A little to the left," Polly said from the boardwalk. She was watching Fernando, who stood in the middle of Main Street, trying to find some cell phone reception. With the phone to his ear, he took a step sideways.

"Oh, sorry," Polly said. "I meant my left—your right. Take a step the other way."

Fernando took a step in the opposite direction. He noticed that Titan was watching him from the front door of the forge. He took this as a compliment and stood a little straighter. Then he noticed that Powderkeg and Pappy were watching him from a bench on the boardwalk and Old Bertha was peeking at him from behind the curtain of the grocery store.

What a bunch of whackjobs!

He gave Polly a thumbs-up as he heard a voice on the other end of the call.

"Your Taxi Service," the faint voice crackled. "This is Amanda."

"Thank God!" Fernando said, cupping his hands around the phone as he noticed his audience leaning in. "Can you send a cab to Fat Chance?"

"Just a moment, sir," Amanda replied. "I'll look that up."

"Don't put me on hold," Fernando replied, slightly hysterically. "The phone reception here is really wonky. Just . . . do what you have to do and stay on the line, please."

"All right, sir," Amanda said. "Just a minute."

Fernando stood riveted to his spot, heart lurching every time the phone made a snap or crackle. Pappy's words earlier had some truth in them—Fernando was looking for something new or interesting to do. The day he signed over his share of the B and B to his partner, Andy, he certainly felt a touch of regret, but mostly he felt exhilarated. Ready to start a new adventure. He was very disappointed that Fat Chance had turned out to be, at best, a run-down ghost town and at worst, a lunatic asylum. He vaguely thought of how he would break the news to Suzanna and her family that the place was a dump. His eyes drifted up the hill to Dymphna's farm.

Maybe I shouldn't say anything. She seems safe and happy enough, he thought.

Fernando watched a small plane circling overhead. If worse came to worst, maybe he could flag it down.

"Sir, I see no city called Fat Chance in our service area," Amanda said.

"It might not be on the map," Fernando said, panic rising.

"Sir," Amanda said in her robotic tone, "we use satellites. If Fat Chance, Texas, existed, we'd know."

"No, no you wouldn't. It's off a highway . . ."

"Which highway?"

"I don't know!" Fernando usually paced when he was upset, but he willed himself to stay on his mark. "I didn't pay attention. But it's at the bottom of a hill, down a dirt road that cars can't navigate."

"Then we couldn't pick you up, even if there was a town called Fat Chance." Amanda's robotic tone was tinged with just a hint of annoyance.

"Amanda, listen to me," Fernando said, fishing a business card out of his pocket. "I have your business card right here! You guys delivered me to the godforsaken town earlier today."

The silence from the other end of the line made Fernando's stomach drop. "Hello?"

"Is there a name on the business card?" Amanda finally asked.

"Yes! The card says 'My Taxi Service Is Your Taxi Service—Jerry.'"

"Oh." Amanda's voice had returned to the neutral position. "Jerry."

"Yes, Jerry," Fernando panted. "Please send Jerry. He picked me up in Dripping Springs and he knows where Fat Chance is."

Fernando couldn't believe he'd apparently stumbled upon the only taxi driver in the world who knew where Fat Chance was, but one was all he needed.

"Jerry no longer works for Your Taxi Service," Amanda said.

"Of course he does," Fernando said. "He just dropped me off a few hours ago."

"Yes, sir," Amanda said. "That was his last fare. Is there anything else I can help you with?"

"You haven't helped me with anything yet! I need a ride! I can meet your driver at the top of the hill."

"Address at the top of the hill, please."

"There *is* no address at the top of the hill, Amanda!" Fernando said, pacing up the street. "I'm in the middle of nowhere."

He could sense the dead air before he realized he'd left the cell phone sweet spot. He took the phone from his ear and glared at it.

"You should have told her that you'd meet the cab in Spoonerville," Powderkeg called from the porch.

"Where is that?" Fernando asked, not moving from the center of the street.

Powderkeg pointed vaguely toward the north. The biplane buzzed low again.

"It's a little supply town for a big ranch called the Rolling Fork," Titan added, yelling over the noise of the plane. "We get stuff there, too."

"It's on the map," Polly added with a smirk, squinting into the sun to watch the plane disappear.

"Is it walking distance?" Fernando asked no one in particular.

"Not in those new boots, it ain't," Pappy said. "It's about four miles."

"I guess I'll have to chance it," Fernando said. "I'd like to be back on the road by nightfall."

"We've got ourselves a boardinghouse here," Pappy said.

Fernando noticed Pappy said this in a very loud voice as he stared at the grocery store. Fernando looked up—the plane was nowhere in sight, so there was no need for the rise in volume. It must be for the benefit of Old Bertha, who was still peering out the grocery store window. The curtain fluttered shut and Pappy's face fell. It occurred to Fernando that perhaps there was something going on between the two old-timers, but he had enough to think about.

"I think I'll try my luck in Spoonerville," Fernando said. "How do I get there?"

"Easiest way is to follow the creek," Powderkeg said.

"Easiest way is if I drive you," Pappy said, getting off the bench.

"You have a car?" Fernando asked, looking around.

"Not down here," Polly said. "Up at the turnout."

"That VW bus," Titan said, walking out of the forge with Fancy the buzzard on his arm. Fernando tried not to take a step back. "You must have seen it."

"I did." Fernando thought about the old bus with its roof replaced by canvas. *I just couldn't imagine that it ran.*

"Pappy calls it the Covered Volkswagen," Titan said, inching closer with the buzzard.

"Cute," Fernando said.

Titan beamed and looked at Fancy. "Did you hear that, Fancy? Our visitor thinks you're cute."

Fernando didn't correct him. At least Titan got one thing right— Fernando was a *visitor*.

"If you want a ride, I'll meet you in the grocery store in ten minutes," Pappy said. "That suit you?"

"Sure." Fernando tried not to sound as relieved as he felt. "Thank you."

"If you're going to Spoonerville, Pappy," Polly said, "can I go too? I have some new hats to drop off."

"I'll come too," Powderkeg said, getting off the bench and stretching. "Somebody needs to harass Dodge Durham, just to let him know we're still here."

Polly, Powderkeg, and Pappy disappeared from the street, leaving Titan and Fancy in the middle of Main Street with Fernando. Fernando didn't want to move as long as that one-eyed bird was staring at him.

"Dodge Durham is a rascal," Titan said. "You need to be careful around him."

I'm beak-to-beak with a hungry-looking buzzard and this guy wants me to be careful around some dude named Dodge?

"Thanks for the tip." Fernando took a careful step away from Fancy.

"It was nice to meet you," Titan said. "We don't get many visitors down here."

I'll bet.

"I better get into the grocery store." Fernando jerked his thumb in the direction of the store. "I wouldn't want to miss my ride."

He watched as Titan and Fancy went back to the forge. Titan seemed like a nice guy. In other circumstances, Fernando could see the two of them working out at a gym somewhere that wasn't here.

But that bird!

Fernando saw his suitcase leaning against the front of the grocery store. He'd forgotten all about it. Who'd put it there? The last time he saw it, it was leaning against the café door. This was such a strange group. He stooped to pick up his suitcase and then thought better of it. These people might be a little odd, but if someone was making sure his suitcase moved with him, he didn't really want to insult any-one by insinuating that he was worried someone was going to run off with his belongings.

Why am I worrying about any of this? What do I care what they think?

He could see Old Bertha rushing behind the counter as he let him-self into the store called Wally's Groceries. A tinny bell tinkled as he entered.

"Hey, Miss Bertha," Fernando said. "I hope I'm not interrupting you."

"Depends," Old Bertha said. "If you've come to buy some gro-ceries, then you aren't interrupting me."

Fernando usually had a way with cantankerous old women, but that was because they typically loved his cooking. Since he wasn't planning on cooking for this old bat, it might be an uphill battle.

But I'm on my way out, so what does it matter?

He looked around the store—slim pickins', to be sure. There were no real aisles, just a few shelves lining the walls and a very noisy glass-front refrigeration unit in one corner. He could feel Old Bertha's eyes on him every second. Miss Hospitality she was not.

He pulled a garish red soft drink from the refrigerator case. A teardrop of condensation dripped down the words Big Red. He held it up to Old Bertha. "What is this?" he asked.

"If the label is anything to go by, I'd say it's a soda called Big Red," Old Bertha said. "It's very popular in Texas. It's like a cream soda."

"But it's red," Fernando said. "Cream soda isn't red."

"It is in Texas."

"Do you have any sparkling water?" He put Big Red back in the case.

"There might be a bottle left over from when Cleo was around." Old Bertha heaved her heavy behind off the stool. "She was the only one who drank the stuff."

She lumbered over to the refrigerator case and then stood with her hands on her hips, looking at the paltry offerings.

"Nope," she said.

"I can see that," Fernando said. "Maybe you have some in the back?"

Old Bertha just snorted. "Maybe they have sparkling water in Spoonerville." She plodded back behind the counter. "They're a little more uptown than we are here in Fat Chance."

Fernando settled for a club soda. He put the bottle on the counter. "How much do I owe you?"

"Depends."

"On what?"

"What do you pay for a club soda where you're from?"

"I don't know. Maybe two dollars?"

"OK," Old Bertha said. "That'll be four dollars."

"I just said it's about two dollars where I come from," Fernando protested.

"I heard you," Old Bertha said. "But you know how things cost way more at an airport? It's like that."

Evidently, Old Bertha wasn't going to be any more charming selling groceries than she was being the proprietor of the boardinghouse.

Fernando had had about enough. "Cut the crap, Bertha," he said. "While I was walking around town, I got a little intel on you. I know, for example, you were a bookkeeper for some pretty sophisticated companies. So enough with the crusty-old-woman routine."

"You got me there." Old Bertha glared at him.

"So let's try this again. How much do I owe you?"

"Four dollars."

Fernando put a five on the table.

"I don't have any change," Old Bertha said. "Go pick out something else."

Fernando sighed and started looking at the random merchandise. There was dried salami, cans of tuna fish, packages of rice and ramen, two apples, and four pairs of socks. An entire shelf full of jam and jelly caught his eye. He picked up one of the jars. On the handwritten label, it said Strawberry Jelly—Made with Love by Dymphna. All the jars had the same handmade labels. Blackberry, plum, peach—Fernando couldn't believe the variety.

"Find something you like?" Old Bertha asked.

"All these jams," Fernando said, holding up a jar in her direction. "Is all this fruit growing around here?"

"If Dymphna's making fruit jelly," Old Bertha said, "it stands to reason she's got some fruit."

Pappy stuck his head in the door.

"You ready to go?" Fernando asked.

Pappy shook his head. "Bus is acting up."

"What else is new?" Old Bertha asked no one in particular.

"So now what?" Fernando asked. "I go back to standing in the middle of Main Street and hope for a signal?"

"You could," Pappy said. "Or you could walk to Spoonerville. But you won't get there till after dark." Pappy looked down at Fernando's boots. "If you could get there at all."

"So I'm *marooned*?"

"Just for the night," Pappy said. "I'm sure I'll have the bus working by tomorrow."

Fernando gasped. "I can't believe this is happening to me."

"Exactly what is happening to you, young fella?" Pappy asked. "It's my bus that's broken down, not yours."

"Fine," Fernando said. "I'll stay the night and then leave in the morning."

"OK then," Pappy said. "I'll go tell the troops that the trip to Spoonerville is postponed."

"Just till tomorrow, right?"

"Just till tomorrow." Pappy turned to Old Bertha. "Jumpy little guy, isn't he?"

Fernando watched Pappy walk onto the boardwalk. He took a few deep breaths. "Well, Miss Bertha, what do you charge for a room over at the boardinghouse?"

"How much do you pay for a room at a boardinghouse where you're from?" she asked.

CHAPTER 6

"Poor thing," Titan said. "He must have just freaked out when you told him the bus was down."

"Yep," Pappy said. "You'd think it was the end of the world—like he was a hostage or something."

"Well, isn't he?" Titan said. "Can you imagine being stuck in Fat Chance against your will?"

"Culture shock is good for the system," Powderkeg said, shoulder deep in the engine of the Volkswagen. "He'll be fine."

Powderkeg, Titan, and Pappy huddled around the battered VW bus on the turnout about Fat Chance. The bus hadn't been down the trail in years. Pappy couldn't remember if that was due to the trail finally washing out, the age and condition of the bus, or a combination of both. While Powderkeg clanked around in the rear engine compartment, Pappy started tightening the straps of the canvas he'd stretched over the VW's roofline. The roof had rusted away years before. Pappy improvised, making the thing look like a combination Conestoga wagon and avant-garde art instillation. The Fat Chancers all called it the Covered Volkswagen.

"Stop rocking the boat," Powderkeg's muffled voice said from deep in the engine.

Pappy reluctantly stopped fidgeting.

"How's everything lookin' in there?" Pappy peered over Powderkeg's shoulder into the rear compartment that housed the ancient engine.

"Should be OK now," Powderkeg said. "Not sure this fan belt will hold though. It looks as old as the one I replaced."

"You know parts are hard to come by," Pappy said. "I bought a box of spare fan belts so I wouldn't run short."

"When?" Powderkeg studied the broken belt in his hands.

Pappy shrugged. "I don't know. Twenty years ago?"

"Yeah," Powderkeg said. "Knock yourself out and buy some new ones. Rubber dries up over time."

"Don't we all?" Titan said.

"Anyway," Pappy said, "tomorrow, while we're in Spoonerville, I'll order some new belts."

"Just enough for two years," Powderkeg said. "Let's not go crazy."

Pappy looked up at the sky, a worried expression on his face.

"What's up, Pappy?" Powderkeg asked.

"I was just wondering about that biplane," Pappy said. "I haven't seen it around these parts in quite awhile."

"We've *never* seen it," Powderkeg said, squinting upwards. "And we've been here a year."

"That's Mikie's plane from the Rolling Fork Ranch," Pappy said. "It's usually only up there if some livestock are missing."

"I can't believe a ranch the size of the Rolling Fork hasn't lost any livestock in a year," Titan said.

"I'm sure this is a last-ditch effort," Powderkeg said. "It's not cheap to fly a plane like that."

"You got that right," Pappy said. "This must be something big."

The men returned their attention to the VW. As the shadows started to lengthen, Powderkeg started packing his toolkit.

"Crap," Powderkeg muttered. "I don't see my 3/8 inch spark plug socket. Titan, can you . . . Titan?"

Powderkeg looked up to see Titan staring at the sky. Powderkeg and Pappy exchanged a confused look—the sky was clear.

"What are you looking at, son?" Pappy asked.

"It's been quiet for at least an hour," Titan said.

"What do you mean?" Powderkeg asked.

"There's been no sign of the plane for over an hour," Titan said. "That must mean they found whatever they were looking for, right?"

"It's getting on to dusk," Pappy said. "It might just mean they're giving up for the night."

Powderkeg stood up from the VW engine as a pickup truck pulled into the turnout.

"Speak of the devil," Pappy said. "That's Mikie's truck."

"Who's Mikie?" asked Powderkeg just as the pickup's door swung open.

"You know," Pappy said impatiently, shooting a glance at a worried-looking Titan while pointing to the sky. "The pilot."

The door blocked Titan, Powderkeg, and Pappy's view of Mikie, except for weather-beaten leather boots, topped with boot-cut jeans, landing in the dust. Then Mikie stepped out from behind the door.

She had wheat-colored hair, which she'd tied up in a ponytail and thrust through the back of her black baseball cap. She wore an untucked white cotton T-shirt that fluttered in the breeze. Powderkeg tried to close the long-gone engine compartment door as Mikie approached, and caught his finger in the process. Titan started to coo over Powderkeg's cracked fingernail, but Powderkeg gave him a warning look that said he wasn't about to look like a sissy in front of this woman.

"Hey, Mikie," Pappy said. "Long time no see."

"Hi, Pap," Mikie said, coming over and giving Pappy a hug. "Well, Dodge isn't exactly ready to throw out the welcome mat for you guys."

Powderkeg noted the suntanned crinkles around the woman's eyes, guessing her to be in her forties. A little young perhaps for his sixty-three years, but stranger things have happened. After all, he was in pretty good shape, if he did say so himself.

"Dodge doesn't own the Rolling Fork," Pappy said. "He just runs the store at Spoonerville. What do I care what he thinks?"

"What do you care what anybody thinks, Pappy?" Mikie said, giving Pappy another hug.

"How about an introduction, Pappy?" Powderkeg said, doing his best casual cowboy-lean on the gate.

"Oh sure, sure," Pappy said. "Powderkeg, Titan, this is Lacey Carmichael. We call her Mikie. She's a pilot for the Rolling Fork. Mikie, meet Powderkeg. He does some carpentry and leather work. And Titan, who works our forge . . . and makes earrings."

"And bowls and platters," Titan added, offering his hand, which Mikie took in a firm handshake.

"I've seen your work in a store down in Dripping Springs, haven't I?" Mikie said. Then she turned to Powderkeg. "And I've seen your stuff down there too. You make belts, right?"

"That's right," Powderkeg said, impressed.

"I bought one." Mikie gathered the hem of her T-shirt to expose the waistline of her jeans. She revealed a hand-tooled leather belt with a filigree buckle. Powderkeg also caught a glimpse of a pierced belly button—and Titan caught a glimpse of him catching a glimpse.

"We were just talking about you," Pappy said as Mikie smoothed the hem of her T-shirt. "Seems like you were pretty busy this afternoon."

"Yeah," Mikie said, her eyebrows furrowing. "It's Rocket."

"He got out again?" Pappy asked disapprovingly.

"Rocket is Dodge's prized longhorn," Mikie explained to Powderkeg and Titan. "A real escape artist."

"He's like Houdini," Pappy said. "With horns."

"Rocket is a prized stud," Mikie said. "The Rolling Fork is happy to keep him around. The problem is, he keeps jumping the fence."

"Did you find him?" Titan asked.

"Nope." Mikie shook her head. "Looked for hours. I'll start again in the morning."

"Will he be all right?" Titan asked, his voice rising.

"Probably," Mikie said. "He's big and mean, so he's got that going for him. But if his horns are stuck in some brush or in a tree, he won't be able to fight off any predators."

"Dodge isn't going to like that news," Pappy said.

"I know," Mikie said with a slow smile. "Why do you think I'm driving around instead of telling him?"

Pappy chortled—a sound that startled both Titan and Powderkeg.

Mikie dug into the rear pocket of her jeans and pulled out a well-creased map. She leaned over the back of the bus next to Pappy. Powderkeg tried to study the map instead of the jeans.

"We followed his regular path. It's always led us to him before, but this time there was no sign of him. There's lots of places we won't see him from the sky . . . especially down here near the rock spurs." Mikie traced a path going east from her starting point. "It's mucky down there and difficult to navigate. If that's where he is, he either can't get out or doesn't want to. Either way, we're going to have to do some hardcore hiking in the morning."

"He'll be all alone tonight?" Titan asked.

"Afraid so," Mikie said. "Look. I gotta get some sleep if I'm going to start this hunt all over again tomorrow."

"We'll keep our eyes open," Pappy said.

"Nice meeting you, gentlemen," Mikie said.

"Likewise." Powderkeg lifted his sweat-stained hat to reveal a full head of russet hair plastered to his head.

"Hat hair, hat hair," Titan whispered, putting his huge hand over the crown of Powderkeg's hat and smoothing it back on his friend's head.

Powderkeg and Pappy watched Mikie's long legs and tight butt as she headed back to the truck. Suddenly, she bent over, giving the men an even better view. She stood up, turned back, and faced them. She threw something to Powderkeg. He caught it.

"Somebody lose a 3/8 inch spark plug socket?" she asked.

They watched her drive away.

"I'll say this for her," Powderkeg said. "That woman can pack a pair of jeans."

Titan looked at her jeans, head cocked in artistic contemplation. Mikie turned back to them suddenly and the men's eyes darted to their feet.

"Oh, Pappy, I almost forgot," she said. "That special delivery you had sent over to the store? It's there."

"That's great news," Pappy said. "I'll be over in the morning to pick it up."

"I would," Mikie said. "Dodge wasn't all too happy when it arrived."

"Understood." Pappy tried not to smile. He didn't really care if Dodge was happy or not.

"You should say something to her before she gets away," Titan whispered to Powderkeg.

"What should I say?" Powderkeg asked, watching as Mikie headed to the truck again.

"I don't know. But she's leaving again, so you better think of something."

"Hey, Mikie," Powderkeg called.

Mikie had already opened the truck door and had one booted heel on the running board of the battered truck. She looked at Powderkeg expectantly. So did Titan and Pappy.

"I know your name is Lacey Car*michael*," Powderkeg said. "But why would a pretty girl like you want to be called Mikie?"

Mikie's expectant half-smile disappeared and then so did she. In an instant, she was in the truck, driving away.

"Did I say something wrong?" Powderkeg asked.

"Women these days—especially accomplished pilots—don't exactly want to be referred to as "pretty girls," Pappy said. "I'm an old man who's lived in a ghost town for thirty years. How come I know that and you don't?"

Powderkeg stared after the cloud of dust, which was all that remained of Lacey Carmichael's visit.

He turned back to see Titan starting down the trail into Fat Chance. "Whoa, Titan. What's the rush?"

Titan turned around, his face stricken. "I can't just let that poor cow stay out all night. I'm going to go look for him."

Powderkeg and Pappy watched as Titan rounded the bend in the trail.

"Let's hope Rocket takes more kindly to being called a cow than Mikie did to being called a pretty girl," Powderkeg said sourly.

Night was moments away. Titan was worried he'd never find Rocket before the entire landscape was pitched into darkness. He stood stock-still, hoping to hear any sound that might indicate a six-hundred-pound bull was in distress. But he only heard the rushing of the creek. He looked toward a small grove of cedar trees upstream, then up at the sky. It was certainly possible that if Rocket got himself tangled in the branches of a cedar, Mikie would have missed him when she flew overhead. As the sun continued its plummet, Titan took a deep breath and headed toward the trees. It was his only hope.

Titan entered the grove. The branches of the trees seemed knitted together, forming a canopy of shadows. In the darkness, he thought he heard a faint rustle. He tried to keep his heart still. As his eyes adjusted to the low light, he saw the bull.

And the bull saw him.

"You doing OK, fella?" Titan asked.

Rocket snorted and shook his horns, which rattled in the branches. Titan was ashamed of himself for being relieved the bull was caught fast. Trying to slow his heart, he took a step toward the bull. Without breaking eye contact, Rocket bellowed.

"Okay, okay," Titan said, taking a step back. "We'll take this slowly."

Titan wasn't sure what to do. Obviously, Rocket didn't want him to come any closer. But Titan couldn't imagine that the bull wanted Titan to leave, either. One thing was clear: Rocket was distressed.

"So, you're Rocket," Titan said, hoping the bull would calm down when he got used to Titan's voice. "I'm Titan."

Rocket lowed, but this time didn't shake his horns. Titan took this as a good sign.

"Your people are worried about you, you know. I guess if I belonged to Dodge, I'd run away too. Did you know that he tried to trick us into losing our town? He thinks because it used to belong to his family a hundred years ago, he should own it now. But life just doesn't work that way."

He tried to take another step forward, but Rocket snorted again.

"I mean, I lost something more important than a town. I lost my mom when I was just a kid. My mom was a singer—she was super famous. Mama was a great dancer, but not a great singer. Cutthroat Clarence, the guy who left this town to us, worked with my mom. I was too young to know any of this, but Cutthroat and his people tried to make it seem like my mom was singing in concerts when she wasn't. My mom wanted to tell the truth when she got nominated for a Grammy, but Cutthroat said no, there was too much at stake. He felt guilty because my mom got hit by a car after she got caught lip-synching. She died. That's why he left me a building here in Fat Chance."

Titan could hear Rocket's hooves scratching at the ground, but it didn't sound threatening. He hoped he was reading this right. He wasn't really up on bull behavior.

"Just shows you the different ways you can handle things," he continued. "Dodge just figures since his family owned the town, he's *owed* the town. Cutthroat could have never given me another thought, but he tried to make things right. And I'm going to make something of myself here, I know it. Not for Cutthroat, you know, but for my mom."

It had gotten so dark in the cedar grove that Titan could only catch sight of Rocket's majestic horns flashing now and then in the moonlight. He could still hear the bull breathing, but the head shaking and snorting had stopped entirely. It was getting cold standing so near the creek. Titan felt it was time to make his move. He inched closer.

"I make horseshoes," he said. "I know you don't need any, but I come around the Rolling Fork and Spoonerville from time to time. I could come visit you."

Titan carefully stretched out his hand and laid it on the longhorn's shoulder, which Titan knew was called the "crop." The bull didn't move.

"That's a good boy." He gingerly released some of the tangled branches. "Wow, these trees have got you good."

Rocket remained still.

"Too bad we're here alone in the dark." Titan quickly but gently liberated a little more of Rocket's left horn. "This would make a great YouTube video. You know, like the guy who rescued the whale from a jumble of fishing gear. The great part was, the whale didn't kill the man who was saving him. He just let the human help him. When the whale was free, he jumped around in the ocean, thanking the human with a big thump of his tail before he went on his way."

Titan wasn't sure if Rocket was getting the subtext, but it was worth a shot. The longhorn was almost free. There was one more stubborn branch. Titan didn't see any way around it. He would have to break the branch, which might startle the bull. But there didn't seem to be any other option. He grabbed the branch with both hands and snapped it in two. In an instant, Rocket was free.

The bull was startled, but didn't move forward. He shook his head violently, and then snorted at Titan. Titan swallowed as Rocket leaned his head from side to side, making sure he was completely unencumbered. Titan stood, frozen, with the offending tree branch in his hands. He knew that he was at the mercy of the bull. He remembered hearing something about bulls not being as docile as the castrated steers. Titan thought this seemed backwards; he thought losing your testicles would piss any animal off big-time. But this was not the case and Titan was now standing head to head with a testosterone-laden longhorn.

"Remember the whale I was talking about?"

Rocket suddenly seemed to snap out of his contemplation. He snorted, shook his head violently, and ran out of the grove. Titan knew the bull would find his way home.

He leaned back against a tree and looked up at the sky.

"What do you think of that, Mama?"

CHAPTER 7

Cleo put on another coat of mascara and sighed. As the daughter of one of the richest men on earth, she'd traveled the entire world—Paris, London, Hong Kong, Moscow, Monte Carlo—but always managed to return to the world of the Ladies Who Lunch, unscathed. It had been a year since she'd been the café owner and cook in Fat Chance, Texas, but she felt the town had left its mark. Weekly trips to the dermatologist and med-spa had certainly returned her baby-smooth complexion, but there was a gleam in her eye now—a knowledge of the world beyond that of the rich and famous—that she just couldn't shake.

Last month, Cleo hosted the Beverly Hills Garden Society in her home, as she always did. The group had started work on the garden tour they called the Beverly Hills Annual Spring Fling. After everyone had been served coffee, which they drank, and petit fours, which they ignored, Cleo casually mentioned that—just perhaps—they might consider touring some of the gardens south of Wilshire.

"You want to tour the Flats?" Her friend Annette gasped, trying not to sneer at the part of town where there were homes that sold for under five million dollars and—if one could believe it—apartments.

"Yes," Cleo said. "Just the other day, I noticed some beautiful lawns on La Peer Drive with amazing roses. It occurred to me it might give the Fling some new life."

"I don't understand," Janet said. "What's wrong with the life we already have?"

"Everything," Cleo said before she could stop herself.

"What I don't understand," Marsha said, "is what were you doing on La Peer?"

* * *

Cleo's attorney, Wesley Tensaw, was in the library waiting for her. After her stint in Fat Chance making meals that had to be served on time, her customary habit while in Beverly Hills of making everyone wait twenty minutes now seemed silly. But she knew what was expected of her as the primary recipient of Cutthroat Clarence's fortune. So she sat in her dressing room while her two-thousand-dollar-an-hour attorney cooled his heels downstairs. She knew they didn't have anything important to discuss. Just the monthly visit to check in—and put in the time to make his Tesla payment.

She studied her face in the vanity mirror. She knew she looked older since giving up Botox. Without the miracle drug keeping her face smooth, at age fifty-three, tiny lines were reappearing at the corners of her eyes. She reminded herself to be careful not to betray any emotions now that they'd show on her face again. She thought about being in Fat Chance, where there was always something real to think about, real problems to be solved. Living in Beverly Hills was like living in Lotus Land. Problems were solved *for* her. Like so much about her life in Southern California, Botox now seemed ridiculous.

She looked at her watch. She'd only been keeping Wesley waiting ten minutes, but she couldn't stand it any longer. She stood up, gave herself one last look in the mirror, and headed down to the library.

Wesley had helped himself to the scotch, as he always did. He saluted her with her own Waterford tumbler as she entered the room.

"Your timing is off," Wesley said, looking at his watch. "I wasn't expecting you for eight more minutes."

"Very funny," Cleo said, although she reddened. She had no idea her ruse was so transparent. "You've been well, I hope?"

"Can't complain," Wesley said. "Golf game is improving. They have a great new pro over at the club. Have you heard?"

"No." Cleo sat in an armchair by the fireplace. "I haven't been over to the club in a while." The club seemed as boring as everything else.

As Wesley prattled on about his golf game, Cleo looked around the room. It was here where she, her nephew, five strangers (Dymphna, Old Bertha, Polly, Titan, and Wally), and her estranged ex-husband had first learned of her father's crazy scheme to send them all to Fat Chance to give each of them a shot at capturing the American Dream.

Cleo had known it would never work. She'd counted the days until she could leave Texas. She knew she didn't belong there. And yet she'd felt at home as long as she'd been in Fat Chance—and now she didn't feel as if she belonged anywhere.

Her nephew was a different story. He was sure he belonged in Fat Chance. Professor Elwood Johnson was in love with Dymphna, that girl who was raising Angora goats. Dymphna was a nice enough young woman, but Elwood didn't have much experience with women and he shouldn't settle for a . . . farmer. Once Cleo was gone, all the money and responsibility of the Johnson fortune would be his. Cleo fancied he'd do better meeting a fellow professor or other learned professional—maybe a lawyer. She shot a glance at Wesley, who was demonstrating a new golf swing he'd learned. Even though he was in his fifties, Wesley knew lots of smart young women. Perhaps he'd help her find a suitable match for Elwood.

The thought of having a worthwhile task ahead of her made Cleo perk up. She tuned back into the conversation.

"How is that new associate of yours, Wesley?"

"Kimberly Goodman?" he asked, stopping mid-swing. "She's doing a great job. Why do you ask?"

"I was just curious. I've been thinking of starting a mentoring program. And I thought I'd start with her."

"Mentoring for what? She graduated third in her class from UCLA and is now an associate at one of the most well-respected law firms in the city. She seems to be doing all right for herself."

"There's more to being successful in this town than good grades and a prestigious job, Wesley," Cleo said—although she couldn't really think what those things might be. "But if you don't think she needs my help . . ."

"I'm sure she'd be delighted," Wesley said, backtracking.

"Good," Cleo said, feeling a bit more like her old self. "Let's meet here tomorrow—about seven o'clock?"

"Tomorrow?" Wesley frowned. "That isn't much notice."

Cleo lifted a non-Botoxed eyebrow to full effect.

"I'll have to check her schedule, of course," Wesley said. "But I'm sure Kimberly will be grateful you're taking such an interest in her."

"One does what one can."

* * *

"Is that you, Elwood?" Cleo called.

One of the problems with living in a twenty-thousand-square-foot mansion was that it was hard to pin another person down without, well, stalking them.

"Yes, Auntie," he said, his voice echoing in the marble-tiled foyer.

"I'm in the dining room," Cleo called back.

She'd been sitting for an hour, hoping to have a chat. She knew the servants must find her pathetic, but she had other concerns. Top on her worry-list was: Did a grant come through today? Would he be leaving for Fat Chance tomorrow?

The defeated look on Professor Elwood Johnson's face told her that the grant still eluded him.

Cleo walked a fine line with Elwood. She had cultivated an attitude that she was not interested in parting with her money—and to some degree that was true. The last thing this family needed was for the last of the Johnson heirs to go off half-cocked to Texas. This was not *Downton Abbey*—there wasn't a male successor conveniently lurking in the next mansion. And it certainly worked to her benefit that Elwood refused to ask for monetary assistance. He was determined to get to Fat Chance on his own merits. Luckily for her, the university moved at such a glacial pace that she had time to distract him.

"I saved you some dinner," Cleo said, ringing a dinner bell as Elwood sat heavily at the table. "I can tell by the look of you—you haven't eaten."

As Elwood sat down, a sturdy middle-aged man arrived carrying a tray.

"Thank you, Jeffries," Elwood said wearily as he placed a napkin in his lap. He looked over the perfectly balanced meal before him. "I know the kitchen staff retired over an hour ago. I appreciate this."

"I'm sorry things are taking so long with the grant," Cleo said.

"It is what it is." Elwood shrugged.

Cleo blinked in surprise. It wasn't like Elwood to use banalities. She attributed this new habit to his association with the inhabitants of Fat Chance. She knew he missed the girl and the dog, but if he was stooping to clichés, it was time for some subversive tough love.

"I'm having a little dinner party tomorrow," Cleo said cautiously. "Wesley and his protégée are coming over. I would like you to be there, to round out the party, if you don't have any other plans."

"Whatever," Elwood murmured.

If he knew about her matchmaking plans, he would resist. As long as he didn't ask any questions, Cleo didn't have to make excuses. This was all for his benefit. Never apologize, never explain.

"Whatever" indeed!

CHAPTER 8

Dymphna and Thud were up bright and early, she feeding, he terrorizing, the chickens. The goats, having been shorn the day before, appeared to accept their baldness. As she raked the barnyard, Dymphna caught a slight whiff of something . . . delicious . . . coming from town. Any aroma that could permeate the barnyard was noteworthy. But whatever she was sniffing was downright heavenly. Thud smelled it too. He stood with his front paw on the fence, looking down the hill to Main Street.

"What is it, boy?" she asked, patting Thud's head and tousling his wrinkles.

She stood with her hands on her hips as she watched Polly and Old Bertha walking toward the café from the Creakside Inn. Powderkeg, Titan, and Pappy converged on the café from the other side of town. She sniffed again. The delectable smells were certainly emanating from the café, which must mean that Fernando had decided to stay! Clearly everyone in town knew. Living up on the hill, Dymphna was often out of the loop. Would it have been too much for someone to come over yesterday afternoon to let her know something this momentous had transpired? She felt her cheeks flush as she thought back to yesterday's feverish shearing of the goats with the handsome vet.

Perhaps it's best that nobody from town came by.

"Who wants breakfast?" she asked Thud, as she opened the gate. The chickens let up a collective squawk and she looked back at them. "You've had your breakfast already."

Dymphna's stomach was rumbling by the time she reached the café. Thud had raced ahead of her and was sitting with his massive head on Titan's thigh. Dymphna stood in the doorway, looking at

everyone. Just like old times, they had pushed all of the tables together to make one communal eating area. The tabletop had three jars
of wildflowers grouped together in the center. Two baskets flanked
the centerpiece, heaped with something lumpy. *Biscuits? Scones?*
The possibilities were enticing. A huge, dented coffeepot and three
small bowls of jam were also on the table.

Since her own homemade jams were the only ones around, Dymphna
knew they had to be hers. She felt a little flutter of anticipation, wondering if they met with the great Fernando's approval. As Dymphna took a
seat, the scene around her made her misty eyed. It made her miss Professor Johnson. She looked to see if Thud was feeling the same way. Thud
looked over at her, heaving a sigh from Titan's lap. He looked very
sad. But he was a bloodhound. Bloodhounds always looked sad.

Dymphna sat next to Old Bertha, who was inspecting the contents
of the basket. She held it up to Dymphna's nose. "Smell."

Dymphna inhaled deeply.

Heaven! There were scones and tiny muffins.

"Stop worshipping them and pass them down," Polly called from
the other end of the table.

"You have your own basket down there," Old Bertha said, stacking two scones and a mini-muffin on her plate.

"That's what you think," Polly said, frowning as she held up an
empty basket.

Dymphna took a quick look at Pappy and Powderkeg's plates, which
were heaped with muffins. Titan had just one scone and he was sharing it
with Thud. Dymphna took a muffin and walked the basket over to Polly,
as it didn't seem safe sending it through the enemy lines of the hungry
men. She returned to her seat and savored the sight of the golden-
topped muffin on her plate. She hadn't realized how much she missed
Cleo's food. She considered herself a true artist when it came to making her knitted angora creations, and even with her canning and jam
making. But when it came to cooking a tasty meal, well, Dymphna's
strengths lay elsewhere. She took a small scoop of her strawberry
jam and slathered it on the muffin. As she bit into it, Old Bertha held
up the coffeepot and waggled it at Dymphna, who nodded. As the
smell of fresh coffee filled her nostrils and the tang of the strawber-
ries and sweet muffin hit her tongue, Dymphna closed her eyes, sa-
voring every moment. Old Bertha broke her reverie.

"I don't know why he decided to stay, but if that man comes to his senses and tries to leave, I'm going to hog-tie him," Old Bertha said, popping half a scone in her mouth.

Fernando came out of the kitchen carrying an enormous pile of fluffy pancakes in one hand and a new basket of breadstuffs in the other. He plunked the breadbasket down in front of Titan and Polly. Pappy put his hands in the air, ready to grab the tray of pancakes. Fernando held it away from him.

"Were you raised by wolves?" Fernando snapped at Pappy. He bowed to Old Bertha and Dymphna. "Ladies first."

"Hey! What about me?" Polly asked. "I'm a lady. You could have started with me."

Fernando held the tray as Old Bertha took two pancakes and put them on her plate.

"Age before beauty," Pappy said, winking at Old Bertha across the table.

Old Bertha looked up, fork poised over the pancakes. Fernando glared at Pappy, who looked confused.

"Don't help," Fernando said.

"That's not a compliment," Titan whispered to Pappy.

Pappy frowned as he grabbed another muffin from the basket Polly was trying to hoard.

"These are delicious," Dymphna said, saluting him with her second helping from the breadbasket.

"Honey, you ain't seen nothin' yet," Fernando said, passing the pancakes around. "I need to get into that town . . . Spoonsville."

"Spoonerville," came a chorus from the table.

"OK, Spoonerville," Fernando said. "Anyway, I've made an extensive shopping list. There wasn't much to work with here."

"Your shopping list can be as extensive as you want," Powderkeg said. "The store in Spoonerville isn't exactly Harrods."

"Well, one can dream," Fernando said, winking at Powderkeg.

"You can always order supplies," Pappy said. "We'd have to pick them up from Dodge's store and bring them around by the creek. Or if we take the Covered Volkswagen, we can carry them down the trail, since we obviously don't have a working road."

"Yeah," Fernando said, grabbing a cup of coffee and sitting next to Dymphna. "Let's talk about that."

There was silence in the room as everyone stared at Fernando.

"Talk about what?" Polly asked.

"The lack of a working road," Fernando said.

"What about it?" Pappy asked.

Dymphna could see tension building in Fernando's features. She wished there was some way to just speed up the settling-in process. Pappy had been in Fat Chance so long, he'd forgotten how extreme the place appeared to a newcomer.

"Why isn't there one?" Fernando asked.

The inhabitants of Fat Chance looked at each other, shrugging their shoulders and shaking their heads.

"There just isn't," Dymphna said.

"Hasn't anyone ever thought it might be *nice* to have a road into town?" Fernando spoke slowly, as if to children.

"Of course it would be *nice*, young fella," Pappy said. "And it would be *nice* if the buildings stood up straight and we had cell phone reception from one end of Main Street to the other, but that's just not the way it is. You Hollywood types want everything done instantly."

"First of all, I was raised in Napa Valley, so I'm not a 'Hollywood type,'" Fernando said. "And secondly, it looks like there hasn't been a road down the hill for about a hundred years—"

"Twenty," Pappy said, cutting him off.

"Excuse me, twenty." Fernando sat back in his chair. "I can see how you wouldn't want to rush things."

"The thing is," Titan said softly, "we're doing what we can with what we've got. It's the only way to be happy here."

Everyone at the table looked at him, including Fernando.

"Good to know," Fernando said. "More pancakes, anybody?"

A year of living in Fat Chance, Texas had not diminished the preparation required for a trip to Spoonerville. Because there was no road and Pappy's Covered Volkswagen was the town's only official transportation, the townspeople had settled, by silent agreement, that Pappy would drive over in the VW bus with Old Bertha, and the younger people would walk over to the store with Pappy's mule, Jerry Lee. Everyone would buy their supplies, Pappy would load up the van and the mule, and then the parade back to Fat Chance would begin.

Fernando arrived in the middle of Main Street with his shopping list, ready to join the procession. He could see Pappy and Old Bertha climbing up the trail toward the Covered Volkswagen. Powderkeg and Polly were wearing steel-framed backpacks and Dymphna was kneeling in the dirt, tying saddlebags to Thud. This group was ready to *shop*.

Titan had a firm grip on a halter worn by an old mule. The mule was also wearing saddlebags.

"This must be Jerry Lee," Fernando said.

"He's very friendly for a mule," Polly replied.

Fernando stretched out his hand to pat the animal, but Jerry Lee nipped the air in front of Fernando's fingers. Fernando retracted them instantly.

"I thought you said he was friendly," Fernando said accusingly to Polly.

"For a mule. I said he was friendly for a mule."

Powderkeg looked down at Fernando's feet and shook his head. "I'm a leather-worker, so I know those are quality boots. But you won't make an eight-mile round trip in anything that new—not to mention that's a stacked heel, not a flat heel. More for show than for any real work. And not exactly perfect for hiking."

"Pappy told me the same thing yesterday." Fernando stared at his feet as if they were a complete surprise. "Maybe I could ride with Pappy and Old Bertha?"

"You could," Polly said. "But you'd still have to walk back. The VW gets pretty full. Supplies have to last us a week or more."

"Got any sneakers?" Powderkeg asked.

"I don't want to arrive in a real cowboy town in *sneakers*," Fernando huffed. He saw the confusion on Powderkeg's face.

"What size shoe do you wear?" Titan asked.

Fernando looked at Titan's feet, encased in well-worn but gorgeous red cowboy boots. "A ten," he said gloomily. It was obvious that Titan wore at least a thirteen.

"Powderkeg, don't you wear a ten?" Titan asked.

"Eleven and a half," Powderkeg said.

"Well, he's right. He can't show up in sneakers," Titan said. "It's hard enough to make a good impression over there."

"Should I just give you the list and wait here?" Fernando asked.

"No," Titan said. "News travels fast. They'll want to get a look at you."

"You're scaring me," Fernando said.

"You said you wanted a taste of the Old West," said Powderkeg. "Well, Spoonerville is as authentic as it gets."

"I have an idea," Dymphna said, giving a final tug to Thud's saddlebags. "Wear your sneakers as far as the Rolling Fork Ranch entrance, then change into your boots."

Fernando looked relieved and headed back to the Creakside Inn, silently giving thanks that he'd thrown his athletic shoes in his bag at the last minute.

"What a great idea, Dee," Titan said to Dymphna as he turned toward the forge. "Hang on, I'm going to get my sneakers too."

"Why?" Powderkeg asked. "Your boots are broken in just fine."

"They still hurt like hell," Titan said, lifting the hem of his jeans to reveal a two-and-a-half-inch stacked cowboy heel. "Eight miles is a long walk in heels, no matter how long you've been wearing them."

"Didn't you ever see women changing shoes at the last minute?" Polly asked Powderkeg. "Flats on the street and then power heels for the office?"

Powderkeg shrugged. "I never worked in an office. Titan and Fernando are going to change shoes at the last minute to make the right *impression* in *Spoonerville*? Do I have that right?"

Dymphna and Polly nodded simultaneously.

"Think of it this way," Dymphna said. "The right tools for the job."

Powderkeg smiled and gave her a thumbs-up and a wink.

When Titan and Fernando had returned in their running shoes and stowed their cowboy boots in Thud's saddlebags, the group headed down the creek toward Spoonerville. The mule and Thud clearly knew their way, although Titan did keep a hand on Jerry Lee's halter to keep him moving.

"Thanks for giving us a chance," Dymphna said to Fernando. "I have to admit I was surprised."

"I have some money socked away," Fernando said. "I guess I just saw something here that made me think I'd give it a shot." *But I'm not telling you what it is, in case I'm wrong*, he thought. *I don't want to get anybody's hopes up, let alone my own.*

Fernando and Titan pulled on their cowboy boots once they were under the arch that proclaimed they'd arrived at the Rolling Fork Ranch. By the time they had walked the last half mile, Fernando was glad he had listened to Powderkeg.

Strutting around in unbroken-in cowboy boots was not for sissies.

CHAPTER 9

Although there was a hitching post, Titan tied Jerry Lee to the bumper of the Covered Volkswagen, which sat at the bottom of stairs that led to the Spoonerville store. Dymphna clipped a leash to Thud's collar, walked up the steep steps, and looped the leash around the leg of an ancient bench. The bloodhound thumped his tail piteously and Dymphna gave him a kiss on the head.

"Sorry, Thud," she said. "You know Dodge doesn't like dogs in the store."

Dymphna watched Fernando, Polly, Powderkeg, and Titan go into the store. She patted Thud again, stalling for time. She didn't want to admit it, but she was hoping she might run into Tino, the vet. He did say he was back working on the ranch, didn't he? She realized she was being silly. After all, he'd worked on the ranch for the entire first six months she'd been in Fat Chance, and she'd never once run into him before, so what were the odds that she'd see him now? A million to one? A billion to one? Guilt washed over her as she realized Professor Johnson could probably calculate the odds for her. She kissed Thud again and finally walked into the store.

There, talking to Titan, was Tino. Dymphna couldn't hear what the two men were discussing, although she could see Titan was telling Tino a story using elaborate hand gestures. Titan extended one muscular, ebony arm as if in flight, while dangling the other at an angle. He must be talking about Fancy!

Titan suddenly grabbed the doctor's hand and pumped it up and down. Apparently deciding this did not express his feelings to their full extent, he grabbed Tino in a bear hug and lifted the man off his feet.

Dymphna caught Tino's eye while he was still dangling in the air. When he was back on the ground, he motioned her to join them.

"Did you know that this . . ." Titan paused, trying to keep his emotions under control. "This great man saved Fancy's life years ago?"

Dymphna blinked in surprise. With her broken wing and one eye, Fancy must have been quite a warrior at one time. In theory, Dymphna had always known that the old buzzard must have a backstory, but she never thought she'd ever hear it.

"I didn't actually save her life," Tino said. "I just gave her a fighting chance, that's all."

Polly joined the group, carrying bottles of water for all of them. It had become a ritual to down a bottle of cold water after the long walk to Spoonerville. Polly brought an extra one for the vet. Tino accepted the bottle and cracked open the cap.

"Fancy . . . that's what you call her?" Tino asked, taking a long drink. "She didn't have a name back then. She was a fearless bird. A lot of people on the ranch tried to drive her out, but she'd staked her territory."

"Why would they want to drive her out?" Titan asked indignantly. "Vultures don't hurt people."

"No, but she was aggressive," Tino said. "She'd get too close to the barn or the ranch house or the store. You could practically watch her daring people or other animals to mess with her."

"That's my girl," Titan said proudly.

"Well, one day I found her by the side of the road," Tino said. "At first I thought she'd been hit by a car, but after looking her over, it was clear she'd been in a fight with some other animal. I took her back to my office. I knew she'd never fly again, but I just had a feeling I could patch her up and she'd be OK. I never met a bird like her before or since."

"How did she end up over in Fat Chance?" Dymphna asked, humming with admiration for the man who would save an ugly old buzzard.

"I don't know," Tino said. "She escaped from her cage one night. I looked for her, but lost her tracks down by the creek. I figured she was ready to be free, so I just let her be. I'm happy she's got a home with you, Titan."

Titan looked modestly at the floor.

"Hey, Titan!" came a booming voice from the doorway. "You bring me those horseshoes for Molly?"

Dymphna didn't recognize the man. There seemed to be an end-less supply of strapping men at the Rolling Fork.

"Yes, yes," Titan said. "I have them in the VW bus. I'll be right out."

Titan turned to the doctor and spread his arms for another hug, but Tino put out his hand to shake. Dymphna stifled a giggle—she knew Titan's hug could knock the wind out of you.

"Thanks again, Doc," Titan said.

"I'm happy she made it," Tino said, patting the giant man on the shoulder as Titan went out to conduct his business.

"Hey, Titan," came Dodge's gravelly voice from behind the counter. "I understand you saved my bull last night."

"Who told you?" Titan asked.

"Rocket." Dodge sneered.

"He did?" Titan asked, eyes wide.

"No, of course not," Dodge said. "He's a damn longhorn."

Dymphna and Tino exchanged a look. Animals could tell you lots of things, if you just listened.

"Powderkeg told me," Dodge said.

"Oh," Titan said. "Well, you're welcome."

Titan headed out the door. Polly puffed her cheeks in disgust.

"Dodge is such a jerk—he didn't even say thanks," Polly said to Tino and Dymphna. Then, to Dodge, "You got a lot of help from Fat Chance, Dodge, first from Thud and now Titan. One of these days, you might just admit how awesome we are!"

Dodge turned his back on her without a word. Old Bertha was standing at the counter waiting for service—and Old Bertha never waited long without complaining.

Polly smirked. "Well, I guess he's not going to register our awe-someness today." Dymphna tried to will Polly to leave. Polly looked like she was about to start a new conversation, but was interrupted by Old Bertha's voice.

"Polly!" Old Bertha barked. "Get over here! Dodge says you or-dered a bunch of strip nails. You planning on some remodeling you haven't told me about?"

"Strip nails? Why would I do that?" Polly rolled her eyes and went to do battle with Dodge.

Tino and Dymphna stood in awkward silence as they watched Polly pour a handful of flat-head nails into her hand and hold them under Dodge Durham's nose.

"Nail strips, Dodge, not strip nails! For a manicure! What am I supposed to do with these?"

Dodge, a tall man with an impressive belly, didn't back down.

"Listen, you guys order the weirdest stuff! How am I supposed to keep it all straight?" he said. "Fine, I'll keep the strip nails, but you're on your own with the nail strips. I ain't orderin' 'em."

"We're always in trouble here," Dymphna said to Tino. "Dodge doesn't really like any of us."

"Don't take it personally," Tino said. "Dodge doesn't like anybody."

Dymphna heard the unmistakable buzzing of a cell phone.

Tino reached into his back pocket and pulled out his phone. He stared at the screen and frowned. Meeting her eyes, he said, "Damn. I have to take this. Will you excuse me a minute?"

Dymphna nodded. She was having cell-phone-reception envy. If only phones would ring like that in Fat Chance! As he answered the phone, Tino stepped out onto the porch. Dymphna wasn't sure if "Will you excuse me a minute" meant "I'll be right back" or "This conversation is over." She looked around the store. If Tino wanted to find her, it wouldn't be difficult. She decided to just go about her business and hope for the best.

She noticed Dodge, from his vantage point at the checkout stand, glancing out the window, looking at Thud. She felt as if Thud should be allowed in the store, given that he'd once saved Dodge's life. But she knew Dodge did not like being reminded of that day, and Thud's rattlesnake-skin dog collar, custom-made by Powderkeg, was the colossus of reminders.

Dodge returned his attention to the checkout line. Fernando looked down at his foot-long checklist stretched out on the counter.

Dodge looked at Fernando quizzically. "What's hoisin?" he asked suspiciously.

"It's Chinese," Fernando said. "It's a strong glaze with mashed soy beans in it, among other things."

"And what about this?" Dodge pointed to the list. "Liquid smoke."

"It adds a smoky flavor to meats," Fernando said.

"I've never ordered most of this stuff on here," Dodge said. "Cleo never ordered Boston butt or rapini. What are you going to be cooking over there?"

"Just the best barbecue you and your cowboys have ever tasted," Fernando said loudly.

"Really?"

"Really. I thought about it and decided what this area needs is a decent barbecue restaurant. We need a place to feed hungry men."

The store was crowded, not only with most of the inhabitants of Fat Chance but several ranch hands as well. Everyone had stopped what they were doing and listened intently to Fernando.

Polly, who had two boxes of cereal cradled in her arms, looked wide-eyed at Dymphna. Dymphna shrugged. This was the first she was hearing about this.

"Where's Pappy?" Old Bertha rasped to Powderkeg. "I'll bet he'd be very interested to hear *this*."

Dymphna looked around the store. Exactly where *was* Pappy? She remembered he'd said that Dodge had a special delivery for him, but she hadn't seen him since they'd arrived.

Dodge and Fernando bent back over the list. Apparently, if barbecue was at stake Dodge was going to take this order seriously.

Dymphna was so intent on the proceedings at the cash register that she didn't notice Tino returning to the store. Trying desperately to act casual, she grabbed two cans of chicken noodle soup and popped them into her basket as he approached. As he got nearer, she gasped when she realized what she'd done. She was a vegetarian. She just had time to pop the cans back on the shelf before Tino was standing beside her.

"Sorry about the interruption," he said.

Dymphna continued to study the soup cans. Talking to Tino up at the farm was easy; talking around soup seemed nearly impossible.

"What are you looking for?" Tino asked.

"Um . . . ," Dymphna said, trying to think of any vegetarian canned soup. "Tomato?"

Tino reached out his hand to the tomato soup cans right in front of her nose and handed one to her.

"Thanks." She flushed as she tossed the can into her basket. She knew her cheeks were probably the same color as the tomato soup on the label.

"That call I just took," he said, looking outside where he'd been standing. "It was a local farmer named Meriwether—she lives about six miles from here. Her horse has barbed wire stuck in its tail and she needs some help getting it out. I've got to get over there. My truck is outside. I was wondering if you'd like to go over there with me."

"Wouldn't I be in the way?"

"I wouldn't ask you if that were the case," Tino said seriously. "I saw the way you calmed your goats yesterday, and I think you'd be a big help. I know this horse. She can be skittish. If you could keep her distracted while I work on the tail . . ."

"I'd be honored to help," Dymphna said. "Let me give this basket to my friend. I'll meet you at your truck."

Dymphna found Polly and gave her the shopping basket and some money.

"Will you take Thud back with you?" Dymphna asked. "I'll pick him up at the inn when I get back, but I don't know how late I'll be."

"No problem. I'll make sure he gets dinner," Polly said, then lowered her voice to a whisper. "I'm so jealous!"

Dymphna sprinted outside. Why would Polly be jealous of a trip to help a horse? Thud lumbered to his feet, but Dymphna gave him a quick kiss on the head, said the name "Polly" very distinctly so he would understand his immediate future, and then ran to Tino's battered green Ford F-150 truck, which he'd pulled up in front of the store. They sped away in a cloud of dust.

Dymphna looked at Tino's hands on the steering wheel. They were simultaneously the hands of an artist and the hands of a working man. She felt him look her way and she met his gaze. There were those beautiful green eyes again.

She suddenly realized why Polly was jealous.

CHAPTER 10

After distributing his horseshoes, Titan returned to the group outside the store, a huge smile on his face.

"From that smile, I'm guessing the ranchers and their animals were happy with the results of your labor," Powderkeg said.

"Not only that, I met Mr. Honeycutt!" Titan said.

"You did?" Polly said, obviously impressed. "I didn't think he was actually a real person."

"Who is Mr. Honeycutt?" Fernando asked.

"Just the owner of the Rolling Fork," Old Bertha said.

"He offered me a job," Titan said. "He wants me to move to the ranch."

The little group stared at him.

"Congratulations," Dymphna said, her voice quavering. "We'll miss you!"

"It's hard to imagine Fat Chance without you," said Old Bertha. "But you deserve this."

"You do," Powderkeg said solemnly, shaking Titan's fist.

"This hurts me," Fernando said. "I mean, I know I just got here, but . . . well, the place won't be the same without you."

"Are you guys crazy?" Titan asked. "I'm not moving to the ranch! What would I do without you guys—and what would I do with Fancy?"

The group let out a collective whoosh of relief.

Old Bertha leaned back against the passenger door of the Covered Volkswagen, feeling as if the town had dodged a bullet. It would not have been the same without Titan's calming presence. The van had been loaded to the rafters with supplies, as were Thud's and Jerry

Lee's saddlebags. Evening was in the air. But Pappy was nowhere to be found. Old Bertha waved the other Fat Chancers on their way, dismissing protests that they should stay with her until Pappy showed up.

"Where is he?" Powderkeg asked Bertha.

"How should I know?" Old Bertha said. "We rode over together. That doesn't mean we talked. By the way, did you order more fan belts?"

"I did. How did you know about that?"

"Pappy told me."

"So you *did* talk on the way over," Powderkeg said, beaming broadly.

"You're a regular Columbo," Old Bertha said.

"I'll just hang with you. Just in case."

"Just in case . . . what?" Old Bertha asked.

"I don't want any cowboys getting fresh with my girl," Powderkeg said, winking at her.

"I think I can handle any excitement that might be coming my way," Old Bertha said, knowing full well no excitement was coming her way.

"I think Powderkeg is hoping to run into that lady pilot I told you about," Titan whispered to Fernando. "He made a terrible first impression."

"Hard to imagine," Fernando said dryly.

Reluctantly, Powderkeg left with the little band of Fat Chancers heading for home.

"Fernando," Polly said. "Let's have it."

"Have what?"

"Why did you decide to stay?"

"For the waters," Fernando said.

"You've been misinformed," Titan said.

Polly and Powderkeg traded a confused look. Fernando and Titan exchanged a high five, as if they were part of the brotherhood of the traveling *Casablanca* quoters.

"But seriously," Titan said, "I'd like to know too."

"Last night, while trapped . . . while *sitting* in my room, I found a novel on the bedside table and started reading. It was the story of a gambler in the Old West who rode around Texas challenging cowboys to poker games on payday. Cowboys had money in their pockets and were bored out of their minds. Easy pickins'," Fernando said. "So I started thinking. If this were the eighteen hundreds, why were they coming here? What would the townspeople have had going for themselves in Fat Chance, Texas?"

From the little Polly, Powderkeg, and Titan had learned about the history of Fat Chance, there didn't seem to be much. The town's claim to fame was that it had been destroyed by a tornado not once, but twice.

"Nothing?" Titan volunteered.

"That's what it looks like, right? No hot springs, no gold, no coal," Fernando said. "But *something* brought people to town. I don't know what. I'm no historian."

"Yeah," Powderkeg said. "We're a little low on historians now that Professor Johnson is gone."

"That doesn't matter," Fernando said, "because we don't need to know *what* brought people to town, we only need to know that they came. My challenge is to find something that will bring them back."

"And you think barbecue is going to bring people to Fat Chance?" Polly asked.

"Exactly," Fernando said. "Once I start cooking, just let that crappy road stop them from coming to Fat Chance."

"You seem pretty confident," Powderkeg said.

Oh, honey. You have no idea, thought Fernando.

Old Bertha was starting to get annoyed. Finally, she saw Pappy heading toward the Covered Volkswagen. He seemed to be leading a large, shaggy dog. She frowned. She'd never been much of an animal person, and Fat Chance had far too many already, as far as she was concerned. Fancy, the buzzard, pretty much kept to the forge. Buzzards seemed to have an instinct that they were not fit company for humans, thank the Lord. Old Bertha shivered to think what Fancy did to keep herself fed, but she'd learned long ago to just not think about things that made her uncomfortable. Thud was practically the town mascot. While Old Bertha didn't love the fact that the dog was allowed in the café, she knew she was alone. In her dreams, the inhabitants of Fat Chance would one day make something of their town—and then the health department would swoop in and make things right. Dymphna had her menagerie of goats and chickens up on the Fat Farm, but Old Bertha never found reason to get up there, so she just ignored them. Pappy's mule, Jerry Lee, could have been the poster boy for stubborn animals. She had once called Jerry Lee "obstinate" to

Pappy's face and had to endure a lecture on the intelligence of mules. But of course, Pappy was as stubborn as Jerry Lee.

Two peas in a pod.

In the early days of Fat Chance, Old Bertha learned more about mules than she'd ever wanted to know. She'd heard that mules were sexless, but to her horror, on her first trip to Spoonerville with the Fat Chance gang, she spied Jerry Lee mounting a female mule. One of the ranch hands saw her astonishment and let her know that sexlessness in the mule world was a common misconception among city people. The truth was, the animals were male and female, they were just sterile.

And rude.

As Pappy got closer, the animal at the end of the tether didn't appear to be any breed of dog Old Bertha had ever seen. Of course, out here, that didn't mean anything. There were lots of weird-looking mutts running around Spoonerville and the Rolling Fork. Even the ugliest dogs were elevated to the lofty rank of "cow dog." Old Bertha squinted into the sun. Whatever this was coming at her, it was the strangest-looking dog she'd ever seen.

Pappy arrived at her side.

"This is Elvis." He beamed, patting the animal's neck. "Elvis, meet Old . . . I mean, Bertha."

"What is it?"

"A mule," Pappy said. "A miniature mule! Isn't he a beauty?"

"He's awfully small."

"I know." Pappy stared down at Elvis. "That's why he's called a miniature."

"Is he yours?" Old Bertha prayed that not another beast was headed to Fat Chance.

"No," Pappy said. "He's *yours*."

"What am I gonna do with a miniature mule?"

"I thought he could keep you company down at the Creakside."

"I *have* company down at the Creakside," Old Bertha said. "In case you forgot, Polly, Powderkeg, and now Fernando are all paying guests! I have a full house."

Pappy loaded Elvis into the only available space in the Covered Volkswagen, the space between the two front seats.

"You have a full house of *people*," Pappy said. "That is not the same as having a miniature mule."

Old Bertha got in on the passenger's side. She hugged the door but could still feel the mule's breath on her arm.

"You got me there," she said.

Dymphna gently caressed the horse's muzzle. She winced as she felt a gentle tug ripple up the horse's spine.

"You are such a good horse," she murmured to Rosie as Tino lightly coaxed the barbed wire out of her tail. "Such a brave girl."

"Almost there, Dymphna," she heard Tino say. "How is she doing?"

"I was just telling her what a good horse she is."

"You're both doing great," Tino said. "Just keep her still a few minutes longer."

Dymphna continued to soothe Rosie, who seemed to understand that they were there to help. Dymphna thought back to breakfast, when Titan told the story of releasing that longhorn from a tree's branches. That poor bull was lucky that a human being was around to rescue him. And, while Rosie was lucky too, Dymphna couldn't help but feel the farmer should have taken better care of her barbed wire. Animals were such a responsibility; you had to be accountable to them!

But then Dymphna chastised herself immediately. She'd met Rosie's owner, Meriwether, who was an elderly widow. Perhaps the farm was getting to be too much for her. The people Dymphna had met in Texas in this last year were proud, and she knew better than to judge this woman's choices. People like Meriwether, who held their ground, were an inspiration to Dymphna, who sometimes felt overwhelmed by her little farm back in Fat Chance.

Dymphna looked around the barn. It was definitely in need of some repair, but it was clean and well cared for. As she stroked the horse's neck, she felt that Rosie was calming her down as much as she was calming Rosie.

She could suddenly feel the tension leave the horse and she knew without being told that Tino had completed his mission. She peeked around Rosie to see Tino holding up a tangle of barbed wire. Rosie had lost some hair from her tail, but that seemed to be the extent of the damage. As soon as the procedure was complete, Meriwether tiptoed into the stall.

"Is Rosie going to be all right?" Meriwether asked Tino in a shaky voice.

"She'll be fine," Tino said, as they made their way to the truck. He tossed the barbed wire into the truck bed. "But I think you need some help around here, Meriwether. This could have been a lot worse."

Meriwether hung her head, as if being scolded by the school principal.

"I'm sure you could find a ranch hand from the Rolling Fork who needs a little extra cash," Tino said. "Put a sign up at the Spoonerville store where everyone can see it."

"Or maybe one of the guys from Fat Chance would want to help out," Dymphna said, well aware that everyone in Fat Chance was always looking for a way to make a few dollars.

"That would be wonderful." Meriwether brightened. "Everybody around these parts has heard of your little community. Do you think one of the men would like to come over and help a few times a week?"

"I can't actually speak for any of them, but I'll bet one of them would!" Dymphna said.

"Wonderful!" Meriwether said.

"Sounds good," Tino added.

"Just don't send Pappy," Meriwether said, her voice suddenly sounding much stronger—and full of venom.

CHAPTER 11

As the Volkswagen lurched toward the turnout above Fat Chance, Old Bertha pretended she was riveted by the view out the passenger window, scenery that she saw every week on the trip back and forth to Spoonerville. She didn't want to turn around and have to acknowledge Elvis, who was still breathing down her neck and occasionally nibbling her sweater.

What the hell am I going to do with a miniature mule? she thought.

"These mules are as easy as dogs to have around the place," Pappy said, as if reading her mind.

Old Bertha turned to face him and was met with Elvis's velvety muzzle.

"Awww," Pappy said, scratching the mule's back. "He wants a kiss."

"I hardly know this dang mule. He's not getting a kiss," Old Bertha said. "I don't know what you were thinking, Pappy. I don't know anything about mules."

"I can help you take care of him. He really only needs a fenced yard and some hay."

"I doubt that," Old Bertha said. "Has he had his shots?"

"Yep."

"What about his hooves? Are they trimmed?"

"I thought you said you didn't know anything about mules," Pappy said.

"Titan has bored us all to tears with talk about hooves. I know more than I want to know."

"His hooves are trimmed. And don't worry about that. When the time comes, I'll just trim him up when I do Jerry Lee's."

"Can I just ask you why you bought him for me in the first place?"

"I know a bunch of guys who rescue miniatures," Pappy said. "Horses, mules, donkeys, pigs. People in the cities don't know what they're getting themselves into, and when the animal is full grown, even if it's small, it's bigger than people had in mind. Then people just want to get rid of it."

"Somebody wanted to get rid of Elvis?" Old Bertha involuntarily reached out and patted the mule on the head. "That's terrible."

"It is," Pappy agreed. "He's from Memphis—which probably goes without saying. Anyway, when the guys heard they had a mule named Elvis, they contacted me. They thought I might like him for a companion for Jerry Lee."

"That sounds like a good idea."

"But Jerry Lee already has a companion—me," Pappy said. "And I've got Jerry Lee. It got me thinking. You don't have a companion. It just seemed to fit."

Old Bertha stared at Elvis. He stared back with his liquid brown eyes. He had a tuft of white hair that shot straight up between long ears that almost touched the ceiling of the VW. He prodded her with his muzzle.

When you get to be my age, she thought, *I guess you don't get to be too fussy when it comes to companionship.*

"Crap!" Pappy suddenly shouted, as he pulled the VW off the road.

"What's wrong?" Old Bertha asked as Elvis fell onto her lap.

"There's smoke coming out the back," Pappy said. "The damn fan belt must have broke."

"We're at least three miles from the turnout."

"I know."

Old Bertha eyed Elvis. "Can I ride him?" she asked, as she helped the miniature mule out of the bus.

"No!" Pappy said. "He has a hundred-pound weight limit. Maybe he could support someone . . . uh . . . maybe Polly or Dymphna. But definitely not you."

Old Bertha bristled. "What exactly does that mean?"

Pappy opened his mouth, but she cut him off.

"Never mind," she continued. "It's getting near dark. What are we going to do?"

"Maybe we'll have to sleep in the van," Pappy said with a leer.

"It's full of supplies, in case you forgot!"

"We can move everything outside."

"Maybe somebody will come along and we can flag them down," Old Bertha said.

"Maybe," Pappy said. "Let's get Elvis out there as a decoy—maybe some Good Samaritan will take pity on the poor guy. Then we'll jump out of the bushes and say we're with him. It's an old hitchhiking trick."

"I know. Cutthroat and I used to do that. I was the decoy. When someone would stop, Cutthroat'd be in the car before the driver knew what was up. Of course, that was years ago."

"Cutthroat Clarence hitchhiking?" Pappy said. "Hard to picture."

"It was way back in the fifties, when I was working for him in his hardware store," Old Bertha said. "He was always broke, so his car was always breaking down. I thought it was because he was putting every penny into the business, but after he died, I found out he was saving for my engagement ring."

"Cutthroat as romantic fool," Pappy said. "Equally hard to picture."

"Well, don't strain your imagination too far," Old Bertha said, suddenly sounding bitter. "He took the money for the ring, sold the hardware store, and bought a restaurant, leaving me without a job."

"And with a broken heart?" Pappy asked.

"Now who's being a romantic fool?" Old Bertha snapped. "Anyway, I can always be a decoy if you need it."

"Thanks," Pappy said. "But I think we'll have better luck with Elvis."

The little band that had walked back from Spoonerville stood in front of Cleo's Café. Dymphna had returned from her trip with Tino to Meriwether's farm. He'd left her at the turnout above Fat Chance, and as she walked home, she thought about the time they had spent together. She had mixed feelings about their . . . what would she call it? Helping a veterinarian take snarled barbed wire out of a horse's tail probably wasn't exactly a date—but this was Texas, so who knew? And Tino had asked if he could see her again.

While she was happy to help Powderkeg and Titan distribute the supplies from Jerry Lee's pack, Dymphna couldn't wait to see Pappy and find out exactly what Meriwether had against him.

"Looks like you bought out the whole store," Titan said, handing four loaves of bread to Fernando.

"You ain't seen nothin' yet," Fernando said. "Wait until Dodge gets that list ordered. We're going to put Fat Chance on the map. We'll be known for miles around for barbecue and *plats d'accompagnement*."

"*Plats du* what?" Titan asked.

"Side dishes," Dymphna said.

"You really think that's going to happen?" Polly asked.

"I'm going to make it happen." Fernando grabbed three jars of hot sauce from Powderkeg. "So, listen, Powderkeg. I'm going to need a new sign. 'Cleo's Café' just doesn't sing."

The inhabitants of Fat Chance just stared at him. Fernando was going to change Cleo's sign? Powderkeg furrowed his brow; he wasn't quite sure he wanted to take down Cleo's sign, which he had designed and executed with particular care.

"You want a sign that *sings*?" Powderkeg asked.

"I think he means something that will grab people's attention," Dymphna said.

"Like what?" Powderkeg asked.

"I don't know," Fernando said. "I was leaning toward 'Cowboy Up.'"

"Do you even know what that expression means?" Dymphna asked. Fernando shook his head.

"That means getting back up after a disaster," Polly said. "I think you should keep thinking."

"Oh!" Fernando said. "It was the only saying I could think of that had the word 'cowboy' in it. What about 'Cow Chips?' Maybe have a little chipmunk on the sign?"

"Not sure that would have the crowd stampeding either," Powderkeg said.

"Stampede?" Titan offered.

"I don't want any negative connotations," Fernando said.

"It's not as negative as 'Cow Chips,'" Powderkeg said.

"What message are you trying to get across?" Polly asked. "In the simplest terms."

"I want to get the word out that this will be a great place for cowboys to find amazing food."

"Then how about..." Dymphna took a deep breath. "'Cowboy Food'?"

Fernando stared at her, blinking. "It's perfect! It's genius," he said, and threw his arms around her in a big hug. "I love, love, love it!"

"If breakfast this morning is any indication, I'm sure the cowboys will be tripping all over themselves getting here," Titan said.

The little group continued to distribute the supplies they'd brought back from Spoonerville. Jerry Lee let out a whinny that ended in a sad-sounding hee-haw.

Titan patted the mule. "What's up, Jerry Lee? You miss your Pappy?"

"Hey," Powderkeg said. "Where are Pappy and Old Bertha? They should have been back long ago."

"I hope that stupid old bus didn't break down again," Polly said.

"Speak of the devil," Dymphna said, pointing up the trail. "And who is that with them?"

"Is that Mikie?" Titan asked.

"Are you blind?" Polly asked. "That's a woman."

Titan and Powderkeg exchanged a look.

"Her name is Mikie," Powderkeg said. "But I wouldn't mention it if I were you."

"They're walking some kind of animal," Dymphna said, spotting the small brown and white creature being led down the uneven trail.

Jerry Lee and Thud, experts at traversing the trail, ran to greet Pappy and Old Bertha. Jerry Lee took one look at the four-legged newcomer and bolted back down the hill. Thud served as the welcoming committee, barking excitedly at the little mule that couldn't seem to find his footing. Pappy scooped him up and carried him the rest of the way down the trail to the blessed flat surface of Main Street.

"Where have you been?" Powderkeg called to them. "We were about to send a search party!"

"We were?" Titan asked, but Fernando shushed him.

"There is something afoot," Fernando whispered to Titan while studying Powderkeg. "And I'll bet it has something to do with that lovely lady."

"Mikie's a pilot," Titan said. "I wonder what she's doing here?"

"And I wonder who her little friend is," Dymphna said, taking in the marvel that was Elvis.

"The damn fan belt broke," Pappy said. "Mikie was driving by and towed the bus to the turnout. We're dead in the water until Dodge gets the new belts, I guess."

"Don't worry about it," Mikie said. "I can always help out."

"Bertha," Pappy said, "I know I should take Elvis over to the inn so you two can get to know each other, but right now I think I should just bring him with me and Jerry Lee and get him fed and watered. It's been a long day."

"That's fine," Old Bertha said, looking tired.

No one said anything as they watched Pappy lead the two mules away.

"His name is Elvis?" Polly finally said. "Really?"

"So we've got Jerry Lee and Elvis?" Titan said.

"Is Elvis a baby?" Polly asked. "He's so cute."

"He's a miniature," Old Bertha said.

"So now we have two mules in town?" Powderkeg asked.

"Three, if you count Pappy," Old Bertha said.

Thud barked and wagged his tail.

"Not you, Thud," Fernando said. "You ain't nothing but a hound dog."

Everyone groaned.

"Mikie," Powderkeg said, "I know I speak for all of us when I say we're grateful you returned our seniors to us."

"Who are you calling a senior?" Old Bertha snarled.

"I mean—Thanks for returning our . . ."

He looked at Old Bertha, who stared at him, hands on hips, as if daring him to come up with an inoffensive description. He gave up and his sentence drifted into the wind.

"No problem," Mikie said. She turned to Titan. "I just came down the trail to let you know that Rocket got loose again."

"Oh no!" Titan said.

"Yeah." Mikie shook her head. "It's been too windy to take the plane out. I've been driving around but haven't spotted him. Thought you'd like to know."

"How can a longhorn escape?" Powderkeg said. "Twice!"

Mikie bristled. "Longhorns are very smart animals." She turned to Titan. "Keep an eye out for him, would you?"

"Of course," Titan said.

"I don't understand how a white bull with a freckled face and two enormous horns can hide where nobody can find him," Powderkeg said.

"I guess you'll just have to ask him when you find him," Mikie said, turning on her heels and heading back up the trail.

"What did you ever do to her?" Polly asked.

"What do you mean?" Powderkeg asked.

"It's obvious she can't stand you," Polly said, as they watched Mikie disappear up the trail.

"Oh, Polly, you are so young," Powderkeg said, engulfing Polly's head like a melon and shaking it. "That's all an act. She craves me."

"And people accuse *me* of having an ego," Fernando whispered to Dymphna.

CHAPTER 12

Cleo surveyed the dining room table. Her orders to the staff had been carried out to the letter. A crisp white linen tablecloth spilled perfectly over the curved edges of the mahogany table. The Wedgwood Colonnade dishes and the heirloom silver glimmered in the shafts of sunlight that trickled through the French doors. Elwood had gotten home an hour ago and sped straight to his room. Jeffries had gone up and extracted a promise that he would come down for dinner at the appointed hour.

Elwood can be so difficult to help, thought Cleo.

She heard the doorbell chime exactly at seven o'clock. Jeffries headed toward the foyer, but she cut him off. Cleo had come to the conclusion that the younger generation was not impressed with the trappings of wealth—she'd noticed that her nephew seemed to have an absolute aversion to them. She'd also had a bit of research done on Wesley's associate Kimberly Goodman, who, while a scholar and possibly a budding legal superstar, came from Silicon Valley money. Cleo had heard that Kimberly's father, the CEO of a burgeoning cyber-space empire, worked out of a cubicle so he'd have his finger on the pulse of his company. You could never predict how those people would react to a butler.

Cleo answered the door herself.

Wesley and Kimberly had obviously come from the office. Wesley had tried to affect an informal look by leaving his tie in the car. Kimberly was wearing the skirt from an Armani suit, but had followed Wesley's nod to 'casual' by not wearing the jacket. Cleo remembered the days when women felt they had to dress like miniature versions of men in order to be taken seriously, arriving in law offices wearing boxy pantsuits, shapeless blouses, and billowy silk ties.

Those days were clearly a thing of the past, Cleo thought as she studied Kimberly. Ally McBeal, not Hillary Clinton, was clearly this woman's role model. Kimberly's skirt was at least three inches above her knees, her black pumps hovered around four inches, and her blouse revealed ample cleavage. Her lustrous black hair cascaded down her back instead of being tied back.

Wesley, Kimberly, and Cleo were still in the foyer when they heard footsteps. Cleo now studied her nephew as he descended the stairs. He had not changed his clothes and appeared every inch the distracted university professor that he was.

Is he really coming to dinner in acrylic?

Wesley made the introductions.

"Oh, please call me Cleo," Cleo said after having been introduced as Ms. Johnson-Primb.

"Great," Kimberly said. "I'm Kimmie."

Kimmie? Could one take an attorney seriously whose name is Kimmie?

"My aunt calls me by my given name—Elwood," Professor Johnson said as he shook Kimberly's hand. "But I am more comfortable being addressed as Professor Johnson."

"I totally get it," Kimberly said. "If my name was Elwood, I'd go by Professor Johnson too."

"I'm glad we understand each other, *Kimmie*," Professor Johnson said.

"Dinner smells delicious," Wesley said. "Do we have time for a cocktail beforehand?"

"Of course," Cleo said.

She always built cocktail hour into any occasion that included Wesley. She led everyone into the library. Jeffries was at the bar; now that Cleo had proven herself a woman of the people by answering the door herself, she could at least let the house return to its natural rhythm.

"Hello, Jeffries," Wesley said. "I'll have the usual."

"Scotch neat, sir?" Jeffries asked, although he didn't wait for an answer.

"Wesley, where are your manners?" Cleo scolded playfully. "Ladies first! Kimmie?"

"At the office, it's partners first," Kimberly said. "I'll have a scotch neat as well."

Cleo smiled a tight smile. So, it was the old game of drinking what the boss drank, was it? Kimmie might as well be wearing a boxy suit.

"Madam?" Jeffries asked.

"I think I'll have scotch on the rocks," Cleo said, tapping a long fingernail against her lip as if having to decide. She and Wesley were creatures of habit, especially when it came to their liquor.

"Professor Johnson?" Jeffries said. "May I offer you something, sir?"

"Do we have tomato juice?"

"Dear"—Cleo tried to keep her voice light—"Bloody Marys are for brunch, not as an aperitif."

"I don't want a Bloody Mary," Professor Johnson said. "I want tomato juice."

Wesley raised an eyebrow in Kimberly's direction—a glance that Cleo interpreted as "I told you he was a weirdo." The slight nod from Kimberly confirmed her suspicions.

Cleo endured a half hour of small talk about Kimberly's law school achievements and law firm ambitions before Jeffries announced that Cook was ready to serve dinner. Cleo dispatched her guests to the dining room as quickly as possible. She took Wesley's arm and he escorted her to her seat. Cleo caught a glimpse of Elwood and Kimberly coming in behind them. Elwood had his hands in his pockets, but he did hold out his hand in a sweeping gesture to allow Kimberly to precede him into the room.

At least he's remembered something.

When casual-but-elegant-with-no excess-staff-so-we-don't-appear-ostentatious was the order of the day, Cleo found a buffet was just the ticket. She thanked her lucky stars the room accommodated a ten-foot sideboard. Cleo had asked the staff to set the sideboard with a selection of what she called "the lows and the frees"—low calorie, low cholesterol, low carbohydrate, dairy-free, gluten-free, nut-free, and meat-free offerings.

After each of them had made their selections—Cleo noticed that Kimberly scooped up more of the "frees" than the "lows"—Wesley took it upon himself to pour the wine. Cleo appreciated the gesture. If she worked any harder at appearing to be one of the proletariat, she would burst.

Cleo, Kimberly, and Wesley chatted easily through the meal, but Cleo couldn't seem to bring her nephew into the conversation. She appreciated the fact that he'd even agreed to come to dinner as he was so painfully shy. Although she hesitated to bring up the subject, she knew it was the only way to get Elwood to feel like talking.

"Elwood," Cleo said to her nephew, who appeared to snap out of a trance when he heard his name. "Why don't you tell Kimberly about our little adventure last year."

"Did you travel?" Kimberly asked, clearly thrilled to get a conversation going at long last.

Cleo had to give the girl points for trying.

"Yes," Professor Johnson said. "My aunt and I went to Texas."

"Texas?" Kimberly asked doubtfully, shooting Wesley a panicked look. "I've heard Austin is wonderful."

"I'm sure it is," Professor Johnson said. "But we didn't go to Austin. We went to Fat Chance."

"Fat Chance, Texas," Kimberly said. "I don't believe I've heard of it."

"That's because it doesn't really exist anymore," Professor Johnson said. "It's a ghost town."

"That is exciting," Kimberly said. "May I ask what took you there?"

"It's complicated," Professor Johnson said.

"But interesting," Wesley said, responding to a plea for help delivered as a kick under the table from Cleo. "Complicated but interesting. More wine?"

As Wesley poured more wine, Professor Johnson filled Kimberly in on his grandfather's scheme to return the chance to pursue the American Dream to five strangers, two family members, and Cleo's estranged ex-husband.

"This doesn't make any sense to me." Kimberly looked around the room. "You two clearly don't need to pursue anything."

"My grandfather left all his money to my aunt and his philanthropic interests," Professor Johnson said.

"In all fairness, Elwood," Wesley added somewhat defensively, "that was according to your own wishes."

"I know. I'm not complaining. I'm just explaining that I'm not a rich man."

"Not yet, Elwood," Cleo said, as much to reassure Kimberly that money was coming his way as it was to her nephew. "But when I die, everything I have is yours."

"Let's not even think about that," Wesley said gravely. "That's a long way down the road."

Cleo took a sip of wine. Unlike her father, she couldn't stand Wesley's fawning.

"OK," Kimberly said eagerly. "Your father, Cleo—and your grandfather, Professor Johnson—left a ghost town to all of you to pursue the American Dream. Did it occur to any of you that the American Dream is dead?"

"Of course," Professor Johnson said. "But that was beside the point. In order to get the pot of gold at the end of the rainbow, we had to fulfill the terms of the contract."

"Well said." Wesley saluted Professor Johnson with his wineglass.

"Who were the other people?" Kimberly asked. "Why them?"

"Apparently, of all the people my grandfather screwed over in his lifetime," Professor Johnson said, "these were the people he remembered. It was sort of a random sampling."

"I'd love to hear about them and what it was your grandfather did to screw them over." Kimberly settled back in the dining room chair. She looked wide-eyed at Cleo. "No offense!"

"None taken." Cleo was happy to see that the young woman was finding something interesting about Professor Johnson—even if it really was about Cutthroat. "I'll just get these plates out of here and bring in dessert." She picked up her dinner plate and silverware.

"You will?" Wesley was clearly surprised.

"Yes," Cleo said tightly. "And you will help me, Wesley."

It took a few minutes for Wesley and Cleo to remove the plates. It was painfully obvious that neither of them had ever done anything remotely like clearing a table. Finally they were gone, having broken only one piece of stemware between them.

"That . . . ," Professor Johnson said, looking toward the door that led to the kitchen, "was excruciating."

"It was sweet." Kimberly smiled a sultry smile as she poured them each another half glass of wine. "I think they were leaving us alone so you could tell me the story of Fat Chance in private."

"Or they were both bored."

He saw Kimberly's smile fade.

"Oh! Not by you!" he said. "I mean . . . well, they know the story. Very well. By heart, even."

I'd be very interested to hear it myself," Kimberly said, but in a more professional tone.

"What do you want to know?"

"Everything," Kimberly said. "It all sounds so crazy."

"It was crazy. We were all out of our leagues. But it turned out to be the most incredible experience of my life—and I don't think I'm the only one who feels that way."

"If it was so incredible," Kimberly asked, "why didn't you stay? You said your grandfather left you three years' salary. That would have seen you through for a while—just like the rest of them."

"I'm a college professor," he replied. "I don't have a skill that lends itself to entrepreneurship. I couldn't make a life for myself until the town was big enough to house a university."

"Which doesn't sound like that will happen anytime soon." Kimberly smiled.

"No, not anytime soon." Professor Johnson smiled for the first time since coming down the stairs. "Besides which, I already spent the money my grandfather left me."

"You did?" Kimberly looked startled.

"Yes. I realize my aunt would keel over if she heard me discussing money with a stranger, but you do work for our law firm."

"*Your* law firm?" Kimberly arched an eyebrow. "I thought it belonged to Wesley."

"Point taken." Professor Johnson sneaked a peek at the closed kitchen door. "Sometimes my environment gets the better of me."

"It's fine," Kimberly said. "I was just teasing. Anyway, you were saying?"

"I can't actually have a career as a professor in Fat Chance. But I have an idea to create a museum there. I've spent my money investing in the museum, I guess you would say."

"Oh!" Kimberly said, sounding surprised. "Well, I guess you'll be filling a niche."

"I hope so. I think I've made a wise investment. Now I just have to get a grant, so I can get back there."

"It sounds like a very special place."

"It is. A special place with special people."

Cleo opened the kitchen door and popped her head in. "Coffee?" she asked.

"No, thank you, Ms.... no, thank you, Cleo," Kimberly said. "We've still got some wine."

Cleo disappeared back into the kitchen.

"You were saying?" Kimberly asked.

"I don't know," Professor Johnson said. "What was I saying?"

"Something about special people. I would love to hear about them."

Professor Johnson proceeded to tell her all about the eccentric inhabitants of Fat Chance. Story after story poured out of him. Kimberly listened intently, raising her eyebrows and shaking her head from time to time, but never interrupted him.

He stopped abruptly when he noticed she was out of wine.

"I must be boring you." Elwood poured her some more wine. "Going on about people you don't even know."

"Don't be silly."

"I know that the whole thing really does sound insane."

"I can just imagine Wesley's reaction when your grandfather announced this great plan of his. I would have loved to have heard *that* conversation." Kimberly chuckled. "Anybody else I need to hear about?"

There was one person.

"Yes," Professor Johnson said. "There's a wonderful woman named Dymphna. She had a few sheep grazing in Malibu, and my grandfather sold the land out from under her. He gave her a little farm with some Angora goats. She has a special kinship with animals. And she knits."

"Raising sheep in Malibu?" Kimberly said. "She sounds like a crazy person."

"She's optimistic," Professor Johnson said. "She's also the most amazing woman I've ever met. And she has my dog with her. "

"Oh," Kimberly said. "So it's like that."

Professor Johnson met her gaze. "Yes," he said. "It's like that."

"Do you have any pictures?"

"Uh, yes, I do!" He reached for his cell phone and scrolled through it. He held the phone out to Kimberly.

"She's very pretty," Kimberly said, looking at a picture of Dymphna sitting on a stack of hay. Dymphna's hair was blowing in the breeze and she was laughing as she tried to keep a long, curly strand out of her face. "But I meant pictures of the dog."

"Oh." The professor scrolled again—this time much faster. He held the phone out again. "Here he is. This is Thud."

"Oh, he's a real beauty," she said. "He looks very smart."

"He is. And fearless. I know I'm not objective. But I really think he is the greatest dog in the world."

"I bet he is." Kimberly moved closer to Professor Johnson and looked at the phone. "Do you have any more pictures of him?"

CHAPTER 13

Titan couldn't think where else to look for Rocket. He'd gone up and down the creek, through all the clusters of trees in the area, up behind Dymphna's farm, and looked over his own thirty or so acres that fanned out behind the forge. Nothing. He returned to the forge, dispirited and hopeless.

"Poor Rocket," Titan said to Fancy as he entered. "He must be terrified out there—and he might be tangled in branches, or caught his hoof—who knows?"

Titan heard a rustling of feathers coming from Fancy's perch.

"What's the matter, Fancy?" he asked the buzzard, turning up the lights.

To the untrained eye, Fancy looked as she always did, glaring through one angry-looking orb. She was sitting on the perch Titan had welded for her when he first arrived in Fat Chance. He may have been bequeathed the forge, but he'd also inherited the bird, who, due to her injured wing, could no longer climb a tree in which to roost at night. The perch was primitive, as it was one of Titan's first ironwork efforts. After months of honing his craft, Titan presented Fancy with a more spectacular effort—a majestic stand full of curlicues and graceful curves. Fancy had turned her back on it immediately, hopping to her original perch where Titan had tossed it in the back of the forge. She climbed up and stared at Titan fiercely. This perch was her home and she wasn't about to abandon it. Titan returned her new perch to the forge, added a few flat sleeping areas to the filigree model, and sold it as a cat tree.

But Titan knew the bird's moods. Right now, she was agitated, swaying from side to side.

"What is it, girl?" he asked again, stepping up and looking her right in the eye.

Fancy let out a loud squawk, jumped off her perch, and lurched into a darkened corner of the forge. Titan stared after her. Titan had taught Fancy how to climb up onto his wrist; Powderkeg had fashioned an arm-guard out of leather so he could handle her without her powerful claws digging into his skin. He wondered if he should pick her up.

Titan headed toward the front of the forge to retrieve the arm-guard when he heard it. A faint knocking at the front door.

"Hello?" Titan asked.

He stepped closer. The sound came again. More like a thumping than a real knock.

"Hello!" Titan called out.

Another thump, this time more insistent. Titan could hear the flapping sound of Fancy's one wing behind him. Titan took a deep breath and swung the double doors open with one quick pull.

"Rocket?" Titan stepped aside as the longhorn plodded into the forge, gracefully tilting his horns to fit through the doorway. Fancy squawked in panic, but the bull appeared completely calm. Rocket looked at Titan and snorted.

Titan walked carefully around the bull, pulling the arm-guard onto his wrist.

"Hi, Rocket. Thanks for coming by. I'm just going to put old Fancy back on her perch and I'll be right with you."

Titan had never felt silly talking to Fancy, but this conversation with a bull whose horns practically touched the walls felt a little awkward. Titan had to duck under one of the horns in order to get to the buzzard, who was spinning in circles in the corner. Rocket stood quietly as Titan coaxed Fancy out of the corner.

"Fancy, come on now. We have a guest! Where are your manners?"

He managed to nudge Fancy onto his wrist, but only under protest. She darted her beak at the bull as Titan carefully put Fancy on her perch.

"We were really worried about you, weren't we, Fancy," Titan said, trying to calm the buzzard by including her in the conversation.

The bird seemed to settle. Titan now turned toward the bull, who was still watching him carefully.

"This . . . This really *is* a surprise."

Rocket snorted calmly.

"I'm not sure what to do with you." Titan looked around the forge. "As a matter of fact, I'm not sure there's enough room for you to turn around and go out the way you came."

As if longhorns always stopped in after dark, Titan casually ducked under the horn again and walked to the back of the shop.

"I think if I cleared a path you could walk straight out the back," Titan said to Rocket. "The door isn't quite as wide as the double front door. But if you'll let me help you, I think we can manage it."

It took about an hour for Titan to clear a path through all the metal scraps of all sizes, tools, and several projects he was working on. He strained to open the enormous barn door at the back of the forge. It had never worked properly, but in the past, he'd only needed to push it far enough to the side to let himself in and out. He chided himself for not having worked on the door sooner. But he cut himself some slack. Who expected a longhorn to come visit?

Titan slowly guided Rocket out the back of the shop. He patted the coarse hair between the massive horns.

"You're a good boy." Titan stood stroking the bull's side. He didn't know what to do with Rocket, now that he'd gotten the longhorn out of the forge. He couldn't just turn the bull loose. It was dark and those tree branches would be more menacing than ever.

"I'm going to take you back to Dodge in the morning," Titan said. "You can stay here tonight. I'll get you some water, but I don't have any . . . hay? Do you eat hay? I'll ask Pappy in the morning."

Titan went over to the pump at the side of the forge. He grabbed the rusted handle and pumped several times. Water splashed into a trough at the base of the pump. Titan may not have gotten the barn door in working order, but he kept the trough clean, so Jerry Lee, Fancy, and Thud could stop by for a drink whenever they were on his side of the street. Before the trough was full, Rocket had wandered over.

"Here you go, buddy," Titan said.

He jumped free of the horns as the bull lowered his mighty head to the trough. Titan thought about finding a rope, to tie the bull to a hitching post for the night, but instinct told him that Rocket wouldn't go anywhere. Titan gave Rocket another resounding pat on the ribs.

"Good night, big boy. I'll see you in the morning."

Titan went back into the forge. He closed the back door but left it slightly ajar, so Rocket would know he was not alone.

Fernando had been stocking the kitchen for hours. He was shocked to see night had fallen when he decided to take a break before working out the morning's breakfast menu. He walked to the dining room, sat down and stretched out his legs. He had just closed his eyes when he heard the front door squeak open. Leaping to his feet, he saw Polly standing there, looking alarmed.

"I'm so sorry!" Polly said. "I saw the light on and just thought you might like some company."

"Oh, honey, you scared me to death." Fernando grabbed his heart. "I thought I'd locked the door."

"Oh, none of the locks work around here," Polly said. "I mean, what's there to steal anyway?"

"Want some peach brandy? It was the only thing of any interest I found at Spoonerville. I bought the place out." Fernando headed toward the kitchen. He turned back toward Polly. "You are twenty-one, right?"

"Yes." Polly smiled. "I'm actually twenty-three. Had my very first real birthday party right here."

"Must have been a blow-out," Fernando yelled from the kitchen.

"It actually was," Polly yelled back. "It was before all the guys left."

Fernando returned with the peach brandy and two juice glasses.

"I think there might be some real brandy snifters in Professor Johnson's bar," Polly said, pointing through the archway into the darkened saloon. "If you're a purist."

"I don't think we need to be purists when we have screw-top brandy." Fernando twisted off the bottle top. "I'm thinking I might be able to make some fruit wines and brandies. I hear Dymphna has a ton of fruit growing up on her farm."

"She does," Polly said. "And I know she can only make so much jam. Her cellar is already full of the jams and jellies from last year's crop. She might be happy to hear of other things to do."

"Good to know," Fernando said. "I'd be happy to make some sort of deal with her."

"That's the way it works here. We're very big on the barter system."

He poured them each two fingers full. They toasted, and then Polly stared first at the pinkish liquid and then at Fernando.

"This was your idea, dude" she said. "You first."

"Dude?" Fernando raised an eyebrow.

"One of the guys who left—Wally?" Polly shrugged. "He was one of my sort-of-boyfriends for a while. He called everybody 'dude.' I guess I picked it up."

"*One* of your sort-of-boyfriends?"

"Yeah," Polly said. "The good old days. So are we drinking this stuff or what?"

Fernando smiled and saluted her with his juice glass.

"Is brandy always this thick?" Polly asked, staring into her own glass at a liquid the consistency of warm honey.

"I'm not a connoisseur of screw-top peach brandy, I'm afraid." Fernando knocked back the brandy in one gulp. He closed one eye in a painful squint. "Lord Almighty, this is sweet. It must be half sugar."

"Really?" Polly said. "That's awesome!" She took a sip. "Hmmm, I love it. My idea of a good alcoholic beverage is one that would taste good over ice cream."

"It's always refreshing to come across a sophisticated palate," Fernando said, getting up.

Polly bit her lower lip. Had she offended him?

"Did I bum you out?" she asked. "Where are you going?"

"Back to the kitchen," Fernando said. "To get ice cream."

He came back with two bowls full of vanilla ice cream. He picked up the brandy bottle and toasted Polly.

"*Salud*," he said as he poured the brandy over the ice cream. The alcohol danced across the top of the ice cream scoops, then tumbled down the sides like a tipsy volcano.

He handed one of the bowls to Polly.

"So, it seems you and I are on the same page," he said. "How to get some good-looking cowboys to visit Fat Chance."

Polly licked her spoon clean and held it up. She and Fernando clicked silverware.

"I'll eat to that," she said.

CHAPTER 14

Fernando's head was already spinning with ideas for his new restaurant as he rang the chuck wagon triangle that hung on a post outside Cleo's Café. The townspeople had made sure Fernando knew of the existence of the triangle. They were serious about their breakfast.

He watched as Old Bertha, Polly, and Powderkeg headed over from the Creakside Inn. He was disappointed that they were all heading over as a group. He wanted to talk to Old Bertha alone. His room was on the top floor, and trying to leave the inn at 5:30 a.m., walking over stairs that groaned with each step as if they were being murdered, made it a tense way to start the morning.

The women were bent over some paperwork in Powderkeg's hand. Every so often, Powderkeg would look up and point at the café.

What's going on with those three? Fernando wondered.

As they approached, Polly waved. "Dude, wait till you see Powderkeg's design for your sign!"

"It's still pretty rough," Powderkeg said, "but I think I'm on the right track."

Fernando took the drawing as the three reached the boardwalk. The pencil sketch was of a sign similar to those that hung over each of the stores on the boardwalk. The words "Cowboy Food" were carved in letters that appeared to have been weathered. All the O's were lassos.

"*J'adore cette*," Fernando said.

"Knock it off," Old Bertha said. "We've got enough problems around here with everybody speaking Texan. We don't need you throwing around your third-grade French."

"High school French," Fernando said. "Get inside, my lovelies. I'll clang again for the latecomers."

Before he struck the triangle, Thud leapt onto the boardwalk, followed closely by Dymphna.

"Sorry we're late," Dymphna said. "I was spinning yarn and was . . . just in another world. I guess I'm just like Cinderella."

"Sleeping Beauty," Fernando said.

"Are you sure?"

"Trust me, darling," Fernando said. "I know my Disney princesses."

Thud ran into the café. But Fernando caught Dymphna's arm and held her back.

"Hey," he said. "I want to talk to you about the fruit up at your farm. I'm thinking about making wine and brandy to go with your jams and jellies. Interested in a partnership?"

"That sounds great." Dymphna beamed. "Last year I had a ton of all kinds of berries and some peaches left over, even after all the canning. Actually, I have a bunch of it in cold storage in the cellar, if you want to experiment with them."

"You make me sound like a mad scientist," Fernando said. "Which, come to think of it, might be about right. Yeah! That sounds perfect. I can play around with the frozen stuff until this year's harvest comes in. Thanks."

"Thank *you*," Dymphna said.

"What the . . ." Fernando looked down the street.

Dymphna turned, her jaw dropping at the sight.

Titan ambled down Main Street, Fancy hopping along with her ungainly gait on one side of him as usual. Rocket followed them, his horns glistening in the morning sun. Titan had a lead rope in his hands, but the bull was untethered.

"I love a parade," Fernando said. "But this is one for the books."

Everyone looked up as Mikie's plane buzzed overhead. Titan waved. The plane's wings dipped in greeting, then Mikie sped off.

"I see you found Rocket," Dymphna said to Titan.

"More like he found me." Titan turned around to pat the bull. "He spent the night out back of the forge. I thought I'd see if Pappy had something for him to eat."

"I already have a regular old mule and a miniature mule," Pappy said, stomping up the boardwalk. "What do you think—I'm made of hay?"

"I have nowhere else to turn, Pappy," Titan pleaded. "It's just breakfast! I'll have him back to Dodge's by lunch!"

"Do bulls have three squares a day?" Fernando whispered to Dymphna.

"You know he's fine just grazing," Pappy said. "That's what cattle do. They graze."

"Isn't that what mules do, too?" Dymphna asked innocently. "Especially now. It's so green around here."

"Fine," Pappy said. "He can have some hay. Just bring him around back."

Dymphna smiled. She never knew Titan to be duplicitous, but he did use his powers for good, not evil, when it came to animals. Everyone in town knew Pappy spoiled Jerry Lee by giving him a little alfalfa with molasses mixed in, even when the fields were abundant with green grass. It was the mule equivalent of a doggy treat. Rocket was going to score!

"Go with Pappy," Titan said to Rocket, slipping the rope around Rocket's enormous neck and handing the lead to Pappy.

"Come on then," Pappy said, turning on his heels.

The longhorn followed, but stopped and looked back at Titan from time to time before turning the corner of the boardwalk.

"Those eyes just kill me," Titan said. "It breaks my heart that he hates living with Dodge."

"From what I've heard about Dodge," Fernando said, "can you blame him?"

Fernando opened the door and piloted Dymphna and Titan into the dining room, where they joined the others. Fancy started her long waddle back to the forge. Fernando was relieved that the buzzard wasn't expected to join them for breakfast.

Dymphna and Titan stepped over Thud, who was sleeping in a patch of sunshine. The trio from the inn sat rigidly—and guiltily—in their seats.

"Nice try, people," Fernando said. "I saw all of you looking out the window."

Fernando headed into the kitchen. No one seemed particularly sheepish that they'd been caught.

"It appears, Titan, that you have a new fan," Powderkeg said.

Titan shrugged and reached for the breadbasket Old Bertha was offering. He was never comfortable being the center of attention.

"Looks like we've got bran today," Old Bertha said, nibbling on a muffin with a glazed top. "Hmm, I think he's got honey in this!"

Titan passed the breadbasket. Fernando returned with a platter of scrambled eggs on his forearm, carrying a tray of bacon in one hand and a pot of coffee in the other.

"Let me give you a hand with that," Polly said, jumping up from the table.

"Thanks, dude," Fernando said.

Polly giggled, which made everyone at the table stop and stare. Polly was *not* a giggler. Dymphna remembered that Suzanna had said Fernando had that effect on women. She thought Suzanna had said *older* women, but apparently his magic could work on any female.

Pappy stomped in and sat down. The inhabitants of Fat Chance waited for some snappish comment, but he appeared mesmerized by the food. Fernando really was a magician!

Polly looked at Dymphna. "I haven't seen you since you went out to help that horse yesterday."

"It was an amazing experience," Dymphna said.

"I'll bet." Polly wiggled her eyebrows at Dymphna.

"Where'd you go?" Powderkeg asked. "Anybody we'd know?"

Old Bertha snorted. "Do we know *anybody*?"

"Actually, it wasn't anybody I'd even heard of," Dymphna said. "She's an older lady and she knew about us."

"Awesome," Polly said between bites of eggs. "I love that we're rock stars."

"That's probably a bit of an overstatement," Titan said. "But what did she say about us?"

"Just that she'd heard of us," Dymphna said. "And that she was looking for someone to help with the farm. She's a widow."

Everyone but Old Bertha stopped eating and looked at Dymphna.

"A paying gig?" Polly asked.

"I think she's looking for a man," Dymphna said.

"Who isn't?" Fernando said as he made his way around the table with another round of coffee.

"I could use the cash," Powderkeg said.

"So could I," Titan said.

"Maybe we should both go," Powderkeg said. "I mean, I'm not as young as I used to be, but I'll bet she needs some carpentry work. If she's got a horse, she'll need shoes."

"That sounds fair," Titan said. "We'll go as a team."

"Maybe I'll tag along," Pappy said. "Couldn't hurt to check the place out."

"Oh! Sorry, Pappy, I forgot." Dymphna paused, realizing there was no good way to pose her next statement. "She said she didn't want you to come by."

Conversation stopped for a second time. Old Bertha's head jerked up with interest.

"What is this widow's name?" Pappy asked, taking off his glasses and wiping them clean.

"Meriwether," Dymphna said. "Meriwether something . . . I actually didn't catch her last name."

"Meriwether McMurphy." Pappy cleared his throat and put his glasses back on. "When I first got here, we had a thing."

"A thing?" Old Bertha asked.

"Yes, a thing," Pappy said.

"That's sweet," Titan said.

"What kind of thing?" Old Bertha asked.

"Do I need to spell it out for you?" Pappy asked.

"Might as well," Old Bertha said.

"A T-H-I-N-G," Pappy said.

Old Bertha looked annoyed, but Dymphna couldn't help but see Pappy in a new light. She knew he had 'a thing' for Old Bertha, but it had never occurred to her that he had had any sort of romantic life before the beneficiaries of Cutthroat Clarence came to town. She never thought that Pappy had had any kind of life before they came to town.

"She was a widow, a really sweet gal," Pappy said. "I might have taken advantage of her good nature, if you get my drift."

"Pappy!" Polly said, her eyes widening. "You dog!"

"Hey, I was young . . . well, younger. And she lived on a farm. She knew about the birds and the bees. I just might have let her think I was right on the verge of marriage, that's all."

"A Lothario," Old Bertha said. "I knew it."

"I thought you were a hermit until we got here," Dymphna said.

"There are hermits and there are hermits," Pappy said vaguely. "It depends on your definition."

"Somebody who doesn't live in society," Titan said. "Someone completely antisocial."

"I wasn't that kind of hermit," said Pappy.

Old Bertha snorted. "Obviously. Although you clearly led that poor woman to believe your intentions were honorable."

"Why are you making me out to be the bad guy? I'm telling you, our—"

"Relationship?" Polly interjected.

"Yeah. Our relationship was mutual," Pappy said.

"But based on a lie." Old Bertha crossed her arms across her ample chest.

"Of course it was based on a lie," Pappy said. "How do you think men got laid in those days?"

Old Bertha, Dymphna, and Polly collectively gasped while the men all nodded their heads in understanding.

"Hey, it's all water under the bridge," Pappy said. "I haven't seen her in years. I lost track of her after she got remarried. She must have taken over her father's farm. I didn't even know she was still there."

"And now she's a widow again," Dymphna said.

"Maybe I should look in on her," Pappy said.

"I suggest you leave the poor woman alone," Old Bertha said. "She obviously wants nothing to do with you."

"I think you should go with us, Pappy," Powderkeg said. "She might change her mind when she sees you."

Fernando nodded toward Powderkeg and whispered to Titan, "Is that man delusional? He doesn't seem to know *anything* about women."

"Don't let him hear you say that," Titan said, stifling a giggle.

The door to the café swung open. Mikie burst in, looking swiftly around the room. Dymphna watched as Powderkeg stood up, a smirk on his face.

"Hi there, Lacey," he said, playing to the crowd. "Can I help you?"

"I came to see Titan," Mikie said. She looked at Titan. "I flew over Fat Chance this morning and saw Rocket following you down Main Street. I told Dodge what I thought was good news, but he went ballistic. He thinks you stole his bull!"

"Rocket came to see me last night," Titan said.

"The wand chooses the wizard," Fernando whispered to Dymphna.

"He's on his way over," Mikie said. "And he's mad as a hornet. I'm so sorry, Titan. If I had known . . ."

"It's not your fault." Titan stood up and embraced Mikie, who melted into his arms.

"Shit," Powderkeg said under his breath. Polly was sitting to his left and he asked, "What am I doing wrong?"

"Uh . . . everything?" Polly said.

The unmistakable murmur of an ATV moving closer let the townspeople know that Dodge was on his way. Everyone froze when the noise suddenly stopped outside the door. The café door swung open again, this time so forcefully that it nearly came off its hinges.

"Hey, settle down, tough guy," Fernando said, banging down the coffeepot and stomping over to Dodge, who was glowering at everyone. "If you haven't come for breakfast, you can take your business outside."

Dodge looked down at Fernando. He narrowed his eyes. "I could squash you like a bug."

"Try it," Fernando said.

"My beef is not with you." Dodge looked over Fernando's head. "It's with Titan."

Titan was still standing, but he had pushed Mikie behind him for safety. "There's no need to be rude," he said. "I'll be happy to speak to you outside."

Dodge took a menacing step forward, but Fernando halted him with a poke to his copious belly.

"You hard of hearing?" Fernando said. "I said outside."

"Fine," Dodge said without taking his eyes off Titan. "Let's go, Titan."

Dodge turned around and stomped out the door. Powderkeg and Pappy stood up, but Titan held up his meaty hand.

"Thanks," he said. "But I'd rather handle this alone."

"We're going to be watching from the window," Pappy said. "You just let us know if you need backup."

Titan nodded and headed out into the street.

Fernando staggered to a chair and sat down. "Oh my god, oh my god. I'm hyperventilating!"

"Go get him a paper bag," Old Bertha said.

Mikie ran into the kitchen, returning with a large crumpled brown bag. Powderkeg and Pappy stood at the window, alternately looking at the street, then back at Fernando, who breathed into the bag over and over.

"OK," he said, handing the bag to Dymphna, who patted his back. "I'm OK."

"I'm blown away! The way you stood up to Dodge was amazing," Polly said.

"I *know*, right?" Fernando said. "I just love being a cowboy!"

CHAPTER 15

Cleo drove her new Mercedes E500 through the canyons of Beverly Hills. She'd had an early morning meeting with one of her charitable organizations. She'd tried to pay attention, but these meetings had all begun to blur. As hard as she tried not to think about it, this life she was leading felt silly after she returned from Fat Chance. On the one hand, she knew that it was her duty to continue her father's good works. But on the other hand, she didn't actually need to be here. The money would work just as well without her.

She needed to find something to hold her interest, but couldn't think of what it could be. She'd bought new clothes, a new car, had an outdoor kitchen built on the back lawn. Nothing was working. On top of which, she couldn't tell Elwood that she and Wesley had eavesdropped on every word of his conversation with Kimberly. At breakfast, she just wanted to scream at him "What could you possibly have bought for a museum that doesn't even exist?" and after breakfast, wanted to write Kimberly a thank-you note. Cleo was very impressed with Kimberly's shrewd maneuver, asking about Thud and then moving in closer to look at endless pictures of that ridiculous dog. She'd convinced herself that things were going well enough that she could arrange for Elwood and Kimberly to have another rendezvous.

Professor Johnson considered himself a Renaissance man. He knew his way around a university, the latest technology in his field, and a lazy student defending a defenseless dissertation. But he couldn't outsmart his aunt. As he drove down the Pacific Coast Highway, he wondered how it was that he found himself headed to the Getty Villa in Malibu to meet Kimberly. One minute, he was vaguely listening to his aunt Cleo discussing new events at the museum, and the next, he had two tickets and a date to listen to a talk on ancient flora.

Professor Johnson knew that small talk was not his strong suit. With his PhD in natural sciences, he was perfectly at ease lecturing on campus about cell organization or biosynthesis. But ask him which team he hoped would win the soccer tournament and he'd go into a social panic. He looked at his watch. If his calculations were correct, he would be at the museum at least an hour before Kimberly arrived—enough time to get a snack and look around the place by himself. He'd done some research on the museum before he left Beverly Hills, but didn't everyone? If he had time to poke around before they met at the outdoor theater, he might pick up an interesting tidbit or two about ancient Rome to toss around should conversation lag. He was fairly certain that conversation would lag.

He parked in the enormous parking structure, took a picture with his cell phone so he'd remember where he left his car, and headed down the walkway to the museum. As he threaded his way toward the entrance, a rabbit leapt out of the bushes, stopping in front of him. The rabbit stood still in the middle of the path and looked Professor Johnson right in the eye. Professor Johnson stared back. The rabbit didn't budge. Professor Johnson glanced around. There were no other people on the pathway. He looked back at the rabbit, which continued to block his path. He remembered a discussion he'd had with Dymphna at her farm, where she'd informed him that her spirit animal was a rabbit. As a man of science, he certainly didn't believe in the concept that one's totem represents one's traits. But Dymphna could make you at least entertain ideas you previously would have dismissed.

There was no dismissing *this* rabbit; that was certain. It twitched its nose and continued to stare at him. Professor Johnson looked around the grounds again. He was still the only human being on the walkway. He looked down at the rabbit. He realized the air was so still he could almost hear the rabbit breathing.

"Do you have a message from Dymphna?" he whispered.

"Professor Johnson?"

Professor Johnson and the rabbit both leapt into the air. As the rabbit skidded into the shrubbery on the opposite side of the path, he spun around to see who had addressed him—and caught him talking to a rabbit.

It was Kimberly.

Of course it was Kimberly.

"I didn't mean to startle you," Kimberly said, reaching out to adjust Professor Johnson's glasses on his nose.

"No no," Professor Johnson said, gasping. "It was nothing. There was a rabbit . . ."

"Yes, there was."

"You're early, Kimberly," he said, switching gears.

"I guess I am." Kimberly looked at her watch. "And it's Kimmie."

"Right! Kimmie."

"Wesley said you usually got to your destination an hour ahead of schedule, so I thought . . . what the hell, I'll get there early too, so he doesn't have to walk around alone."

"Yes," Professor Johnson said, trying to hide his rising panic. "What the hell. Exactly."

Kimberly stood as still as the rabbit, looking at him.

"Did you know that since 2005, the Getty has returned almost fifty antiquities to Italy and Greece, acknowledging they were products of illegal excavations?" Professor Johnson blurted.

"Yes, I did know that." Kimberly laughed. "Wesley's law firm is very active in the arts community. Where do you think we got the tickets to this lecture?"

"I hadn't thought about that."

Kimberly spun Professor Johnson around, took his arm, and started walking toward the largest garden at the Villa. The scent of bay laurel wafted around them as they made their way to the famous 220-foot-long reflecting pool.

"I suppose you know that these statues"—Professor Johnson pointed to the bronzes that studded the garden—"are replicas of statues found at the Villa dei Papyri, a private home in the ancient Roman city of Herculaneum, which was covered in volcanic ash in AD 79."

"I knew that as well," Kimberly said. "I guess I was looking at the same website you were."

Professor Johnson stopped in front of the reflecting pool, took off his glasses and wiped them on his shirttail. Kimberly touched his hand.

"Just relax," Kimberly said. "Seriously."

"Am I that obvious?"

"Uh . . . yeah."

"I'm just not very good with people."

"No shit, Sherlock."

"I hope you don't feel as if you were forced into a date with me."

"I don't!" Kimberly said. "Not at all."

Professor Johnson felt himself unwind.

"I feel like I was forced into a lecture about ancient flora," she said.

"Oh." Professor Johnson's face fell. He'd actually been looking forward to the speech.

"I'm kidding," Kimberly said. "Seriously. I can't wait to hear about all the poison plants those Romans kept around for the occasional murder."

"I never know when you're kidding."

"That's part of my charm," Kimberly said. "Let's get a glass of wine before the lecture. They have a great selection here—for a museum, I mean."

As Professor Johnson followed Kimberly to the bistro, he refrained from pointing out the purple foxglove growing in the garden, which was rumored to be quite the favorite poison in its day.

Professor Johnson was just getting out of his car as Cleo pulled into her impeccably manicured circular drive.

"How was your date with Kimberly?" she chirped.

"It was very informative," Professor Johnson said. "Although she goes by Kimmie and it wasn't a date."

He went into the house, leaving his aunt staring after him. Cleo sighed. Should she look for another woman? That seemed a little tasteless. She wasn't a pimp!

If I can't make myself happy, why am I so sure I can arrange happiness for him? she thought.

Jeffries appeared at the front door, but Cleo waved him away. Retail therapy might not give her the rush it used to, but it certainly kept her mind occupied in a pinch. She still loved the fact that Tiffany's would have a manager meet her before regular store hours for a bit of private shopping.

She took her latest purchase into her father's old office. Her father's taste was old-school in every sense of the word. The desk was mahogany, the chair tufted leather, the safe tucked away behind a portrait of Napoléon. Her father never actually used the safe, but after Cleo took over the room, she had decided to keep some of her per-

sonal treasures in it. Any burglar worth his salt would have researched
the house and known that there was a state-of-the-art vault on the
premises, but she felt fairly sure a bad guy would leave this room
alone.

She lifted the portrait of the Little Corporal off the wall and placed
it on the ivory and brown Kashan rug. Her fingers had muscle memory for the combination, and the safe was open in a flash. Cleo took
the diamond cuff out of the blue Tiffany box and snapped it on her
wrist. The cuff, with its impressive 35.7 carats of diamonds, caught
the sunlight and shot prisms around the room. There was no denying
it was a stunner, but now that she had it home, Cleo wondered if she
didn't already have something very similar in her collection. No matter, now she'd have two. Cleo put it back in the box and shoved it into
the safe. Her eye caught sight of a small gray ring box against the
wall of the safe, almost as if in hiding. She pulled the box out and
stared at it. She hadn't remembered that she'd kept it. With a lump in
her throat, she opened it. Inside were her engagement and wedding
rings from Marshall. She smiled when she thought of her ex-husband
living in Fat Chance, now going by the name of Powderkeg. The engagement ring was a sweet little silver twisted-vine band with a mod-
est star sapphire in the center. Cleo had never really thought about the
ring before. But now she realized that while Powderkeg had made the
ring himself, creating the tender turns of metal, he must have used all
his savings to buy the little sapphire. She remembered how she had
cried when he gave it to her. She put the ring on her left ring finger. It
still fit, but Cleo was shocked at how much her hand had changed
since she took the ring off so many years ago. Her eyes welled up
with tears.

Her wedding ring was a different animal altogether. Her father
never approved of her marriage, but he'd had to put on a public show
of support. He insisted that his daughter wear a ring worthy of *his*
station. Cleo slipped the platinum ring, with its four carats, onto her
right hand. She wondered if accepting the ring from her father had
been the first step toward her divorce.

She held both hands up to the light and studied them.

Should she have turned her back on everything but love?

Cleo made a decision. She was going back to Fat Chance. And Elwood was going with her.

* * *

Dodge continued to berate Titan, who just stood quietly, letting Dodge's words bounce off him. Powderkeg and Pappy made their way silently onto the boardwalk, followed by Polly, Dymphna, Old Bertha, Fernando, and Mikie. A silent message seemed to pass between them. If Dodge made one move toward Titan, he'd find himself in the middle of a Fat Chance sandwich.

Powderkeg put a comforting arm around Mikie's shoulder, but she shrugged him off, shooting him a scowl.

"If you've finished," Titan said when Dodge took a breath, "I'll go get Rocket for you."

"Now that you've been caught red-handed!" Dodge said. "This isn't the Old West, but we still don't take kindly to cattle rustlers."

"Rocket came to see me," Titan said. "Forget it, you're not even listening."

"What the . . . ?" Dodge looked down the street.

Titan turned around to see what had gotten Dodge to shut up for a second. Everyone on the boardwalk turned too.

"This is impossible," Pappy said. "I had him tied to a hitching post and had that gate secured."

Rocket-the-escape-artist had done it again. He came walking up the middle of Main Street, his lead dangling from his ears. Jerry Lee and Elvis followed behind. Thud raced out the café door and joined the other animals for an impromptu parade down the street. Rocket continued his slow pace toward Titan, but as they approached the forge, the other animals raced off.

"Elvis," Old Bertha said to Pappy as a cloud of dust rose up in the street, "my donkey's escaping."

"He's a mule," Pappy said patiently. "He knows where the food is now. He'll be back."

"He better be," Old Bertha said.

"So now you want him?"

"Maybe."

"Would you two can it?" Powderkeg growled. "This showdown ain't over."

All eyes returned to Titan and Pappy. Titan took the rope and started to lead the bull to Dodge. Rocket planted both of his front hooves and wouldn't budge.

"Come on, Rocket," Titan said. "Time to go home."

Dodge stormed over to the longhorn.

"Come on, Rocket," Dodge said, pulling the lead out of Titan's hand. "I don't have time for this."

Titan stood calmly by, with his hand on the longhorn's rump, as Dodge tried to pull the bull forward.

"I don't think he wants to go with you," Titan said.

"He's a bull," Dodge said, panting. "I don't care what he wants."

"It doesn't look like he's going to go with you, Dodge," Titan said.

"I can see that. You make him come with me."

"I probably could make him go," Titan said. "But he'd just come back."

"So what do you suggest? I just leave him here?"

"No," Titan said. "I'd like to buy him, though."

The onlookers on the boardwalk looked at each other. There was no way Titan could pay for a prized stud. Even receiving three years' salary from Cutthroat couldn't have given him that much of a nest egg. Before moving to Fat Chance he'd been a freelance Vegas burlesque dresser, and he'd been living off his windfall from Cutthroat for the last six months.

"Do you have any idea what this bull is worth?" asked Dodge.

"No," Titan said. "But I'm guessing I'm about to find out."

"He's worth sixty thousand dollars," Dodge said. "But I'll tell you what. Since Rocket seems to like you and all, I'll sell him to you for forty thousand."

"I don't have that kind of money," Titan said. "But I could pay you a little at a time . . ."

"Oh?" Dodge let out a spiteful laugh. "You mean from the money you make on your *jewelry*."

"And my horseshoes."

"Your horseshoes, huh?" Dodge said. "That gives me an idea. I heard old man Honeycutt offered you a job on the ranch."

"He did."

"Well, it's always smart to stay on his good side, so I'll make a deal with you. I'll let Rocket stay with you for a month. If you can come up with the forty grand, we're square. And if you don't, you accept Honeycutt's offer—and I'm a hero."

Powderkeg took a step forward, but Pappy held him back.

"I accept," Titan said. He put out his hand, but when Dodge offered his own to shake, he pulled his away. "I don't want to shake your hand. I just want Rocket's lead, please."

Dodge handed over the lead, then turned to the assembly on the boardwalk. "Show's over, folks," he said. "Mikie, I wouldn't spend too much time here if I were you." Dodge got back on his ATV and roared away toward Spoonerville.

"What a jerk," Fernando said.

"Welcome to my world," Mikie said.

"You really should go," Dymphna said to Mikie. "This isn't your fight."

"Look, Dodge isn't my boss," Mikie said. "Mr. Honeycutt is. If there's anything I can do . . ."

"We'll be fine," Polly said. "But thanks."

"OK, I have a full day's work ahead of me, so I better head out," Mikie said. "But the offer stands!"

"Your truck up at the trailhead?" Powderkeg asked.

"Yep," Mikie said.

"What's it to you?" Old Bertha asked.

"Thought I'd walk up that way, check on Pappy's fan belt situation," Powderkeg said with a devilish grin.

"I don't have a 'fan belt situation,'" Pappy said. "I've got a busted fan belt."

The devil in Powderkeg's grin was replaced by a sheep.

"I'll see you guys," Mikie said, stopping to hug Titan again.

He returned the hug with one arm, the other still holding the lead to his new longhorn.

Cleo sat in the library, having a light lunch by herself. She chose the library because it looked out onto the driveway and she'd be able to see Elwood arrive. She didn't know his schedule, but Cook did. Cook had looked warily at her when she'd asked for the particulars. Cleo could guess what she was thinking: "Couldn't an aunt take an interest in her nephew's life? Even after thirty years?"

While she waited, Cleo continued to binge watch *The Sopranos*. She used to watch the HBO hit with her father every Sunday night. Her father would watch Tony brutally murder some poor enemy and point out to Cleo how tough it was to be a boss.

"Nobody understands what it takes to keep things together, Cleo," he'd say as Tony's lackeys rolled another body into the ocean. "Sometimes you've got to do what you've got to do."

For her part, Cleo related to Meadow, the average daughter of the Mafia kingpin, who went along as if nothing unusual funded her charmed life. Now that Cleo was older, she related more to Carmela, who only tried to *appear* as if she was an average rich housewife.

Elwood's Suburu Outback pulled into the driveway. Cleo smiled and clicked off the TV. She looked out the window as the green SUV took its customary spot. Elwood had driven a Toyota Prius for years, but turned his latest one in for the green SUV as soon as they'd returned from Fat Chance. They never discussed it, but she knew it was a sign that he intended to return to the Hill Country. It was his Texas car.

Cleo hoped to discuss her change of heart. She wanted to get back to Fat Chance and she certainly didn't want to go alone.

She really did feel alone. She'd had a stormy relationship with her father, but—for good or for ill—he always had an opinion about what she should do or how she should do it. In her younger days, she'd had her mother, a lovely, quiet woman who never really stood up to Cutthroat but who clearly loved her kids. Cleo's eyes stung with tears as she recalled her own brother, Elwood's father, long dead now. Cleo had taken in her smart, serious nephew Elwood when he was just a kid. She did everything she could to raise him and make him feel secure and happy.

No, I didn't. I gave him everything money could buy, but that's not the same thing.

She even missed her father's trusted attorney and adviser, Sebastian Pennyfeather, who had disappeared in a boating accident more than thirty years ago. Wesley, then a young partner, took his place and had done a wonderful job with the law firm. He was a dear and trusted friend, but he wasn't the father figure Uncle Sebastian had been.

Now that she had decided to go back to Fat Chance and see if she could make a new start with Powderkeg, there was no one to fight, to concede to, or to consult.

She was alone.

She watched through the window as Elwood pulled his backpack onto his shoulder and clicked the alarm. The set of his jaw told her everything she needed to know. No good word had come from the university today. She raced to the library door and swung it open just as Elwood appeared in the foyer. He looked surprised to see her.

"Hello, Auntie," he said. "I didn't expect to see you."

"I had an easy day," Cleo said, realizing she sounded like the Queen of England, happy to skip out on a ribbon cutting. "Come into the library. I thought we might chat."

"Chat?"

"Yes," Cleo said, faltering. "You know. Have a conversation."

"I do know the definition of 'chat,'" Elwood said. "But thank you."

He followed his aunt into the library. She motioned for him to take a seat.

"Shall I have Cook prepare something for you?" she asked, dabbing at her lip gloss before turning on the video monitor to the kitchen. "It's no bother."

"No, thanks," Elwood said. "I ate at school."

"Oh well"—Cleo sat opposite Elwood—"I just thought it's been so long since we've had a real chance to . . ."

"Chat."

"Yes," Cleo said, wondering why this was so difficult. After all, they were family. "So, you first. Tell me something."

"I had coffee this morning with Kimmie," Elwood said.

"Kimmie?" Cleo asked. "You mean Kimberly? Wesley's Kimberly?"

"Yes. The attorney with whom you set me up. We've seen each other once or twice."

Good Lord! Whip-smart Elwood fell for the old "Show me pictures of your dog" trick.

"Perhaps that was a mistake," Cleo said. "I mean, if your heart is set on Dymphna, so be it. You know the old saying, 'the heart wants what it wants.'"

"Of course I know it," Elwood said. "Emily Dickinson. But I recall you were quite incensed when Woody Allen quoted it as an excuse to marry his stepdaughter."

"That was your grandfather who was incensed," Cleo said, relieved that they seemed to be conversing comfortably. *We're bonding!* Going for broke, she added, "I believe what your grandfather said about Woody Allen was 'The dick wants what it wants.'"

Wrong move. Elwood blinked at his aunt.

Cleo wondered if she'd ever get it right.

Perhaps I should have said "penis."

"Anyway," Elwood said, "I'm surprised to hear you say . . . any of this. I assumed the point was to get my mind off Dymphna."

"Well, it *was*," Cleo said. "But I've changed my mind. Is that so hard to believe?"

"Yes."

"That just shows you what you know. I change my mind all the time."

"Name one time you've changed your mind this year," Elwood said.

Besides the fact that I now want to go back to Fat Chance?

"Just last month, I ordered a new pair of trousers with the hem measured to my instep," Cleo said. "When I got home, I called the tailor and changed it to ankle length."

"I stand corrected."

"Did you have a nice time with Kimberly?"

"I did," Elwood said. "That is to say, she's a very smart woman. We could . . . chat. But she isn't Dymphna."

Who is?

"I just keep thinking, Auntie," Elwood said in a rush, "what if I never get my funding? What if I never get back to Fat Chance? What if Thud and Dymphna are doing just fine without me? Maybe I should just accept that possibility. Maybe if I keep myself distracted, it won't hurt as much when the ax falls."

"Darling," Cleo said, reaching across and squeezing Elwood's arm. "I know I haven't been very forthcoming or supportive or . . . well, that's enough, but now that I'm just changing my mind right and left, I think I might as well go for broke. I'll give you the money and you and I can both go back. I can be your investor! Now, don't say anything just yet . . ."

"No, thank you," Elwood said promptly.

"I asked you not to say anything just yet." Cleo retracted her hand. "Can't you just think about it?"

"There's nothing to think about. Grandfather set up the entire Fat Chance experiment so we could see what we could achieve on our own. If I take the family money, it's exactly the opposite of what he had in mind."

"Darling, I don't mean to be harsh, but your grandfather is dead."

"But he was right."

"Now who's refusing to change his mind?" Cleo tried to keep the rich-girl-pout out of her voice.

"That would be me." Elwood stood up. "It was very nice spending this time with you, Auntie. But there is nothing you can say. If the university doesn't give me the funding, I'm stuck in Los Angeles."

Cleo watched as Elwood walked out the door, closing it behind him.

That did not go well at all.

She sank back and clicked on *The Sopranos*. It was one of her father's favorite episodes. Meadow was in the throes of applying to colleges, and her mother, Carmela, gets the idea to put pressure on a powerful alumnus of Georgetown University to write a letter of recommendation for Meadow. Carmela brings the woman a ricotta pie and gently reminds the woman who Carmela's husband is. The alum refuses to be intimidated, but Carmela leaves the ricotta pie and requests that she "return the plate when you're done." The plate is returned and Meadow's acceptance letter is in the mail.

"So subtle," Cutthroat would say and shake his head in appreciation. "Carmela is a velvet steamroller."

Cleo sighed. If only real life were as easy as it appeared on TV. She closed her eyes, but before she fell asleep, they suddenly flew open. Jumping to her feet, as if struck by an electric shock, Cleo clicked off the TV, lathered on another coat of lip gloss, and pressed the video intercom button. Cook appeared on the screen, standing in front of an immaculate white and marble kitchen.

"Yes, Miss Cleo?" Cook asked.

"Cook"—Cleo's hands were on her chest to steady her thumping heart—"do you have a recipe for ricotta pie?"

"*Sí*," Cook answered. "Mr. Clarence gave me a *Sopranos* cookbook a long time ago. There's one he liked in there."

"Excellent!" Cleo said. "I need one right away. Take extra care."

"Yes, Miss Cleo."

"Oh!" Cleo said, almost as an afterthought. "And Cook?"

"Yes, Miss Cleo?"

"Put it on one of our best pie plates."

PART TWO

CHAPTER 16

Powderkeg and Pappy sat in Cleo's Café, now officially renamed Cowboy Food. They tried peering into the kitchen, but Fernando slammed the door on them.

"Sure smells good," Powderkeg said.

"I came here to eat, not smell," Pappy groused. "I can smell it from my place."

Now that Fernando had perfected his sauce, he invited the men to try his latest smoked pork tenderloin. Fernando had invited Titan, but since Titan had adopted Rocket, he'd sworn off meat. The fact that out of the seven townspeople two were now vegetarians concerned Fernando, but Pappy dismissed the notion.

"Giving up meat isn't a trend among cowboys," Pappy said. "You'll be fine."

Fernando reckoned he had no choice but to believe him.

He felt guilty about not inviting Old Bertha and Polly to the tasting. But this was "men's work." He knew Polly was his main cheerleader in filling the town with men in jeans and cowboy hats, but Powderkeg and Pappy were his target audience. He salved his guilty conscience by sending the women a gooey dessert—he could certainly use their opinions on that! Dymphna was supportive of his efforts—and he appreciated the fact that she was nonjudgmental about the aroma of smoked meats that wafted over town. She wasn't big on sugar either, so the dessert-bribe angle was out. He'd contented himself with sending his brandy experiments up to the farm. He certainly felt he owed Dymphna for all the fruit she cheerfully sent his way.

Fernando pushed the door to the dining room open with his butt. His two diners turned and watched the heaping plates of food being set before them with worshipful glances. Fernando sat down with them. The men just continued to stare at the food.

"What are you waiting for?" Fernando asked. "Eat!"

Pappy took the first bite. He looked at Fernando's hopeful face. "It needs bread."

Fernando dashed to the kitchen and returned with a loaf of sliced homemade bread.

"Good idea, Pappy," Powderkeg said, stacking the meat on a slice of bread, then closing it in with another. He watched the barbecue sauce and the juice from the brisket soak into the bread. "That's what I'm talkin' about!"

Fernando watched each of the men chew, but said nothing. When he was the pastry chef at the tea room, his friend Suzanna had hated it every time he demanded to know how she liked this scone or that biscuit. He held his silence until each man had eaten half a sandwich.

"Let the praise begin," he said.

"Dude," Powderkeg said. "You've got this."

Fernando put on his practiced humble face and bowed his head. He looked up through his lashes at Pappy, who was shaking his head.

"What's the matter?" Fernando asked, alarmed.

"The bread is all wrong," Pappy said.

"What are you talking about? That bread is great!"

"It *is* great," Pappy said. "But not for barbecue. Barbecue needs plain old white bread. Sliced in a plain old slicer—none of this hand-carved crap."

Fernando turned to Powderkeg for backup.

Powderkeg kept eating and shrugged. "Sorry, Fernando," he said. "But I think Pappy is right. You want the guys from the Rolling Fork to feel right at home, right?"

"Yes," Fernando said. "But I also want to redecorate the home. Give it a whole new vibe."

"They don't want the home redecorated," Pappy said. "Great meat, spicy beans, tangy slaw, white bread . . . don't make me tell you twice."

Powderkeg waggled a thick slice of Fernando's homemade bread and said, "You can use this for bread pudding."

Fernando gasped.

"He's kidding," Pappy said. "Although it would make great bread pudding, now that you mention it."

"You two are cretins." Fernando picked up the plates and headed toward the kitchen.

"How are the brandy experiments going?" Powderkeg called into the kitchen.

"Yeah," Pappy yelled. "We'd be happy to give you opinions on that too!"

"You can't come in," Old Bertha yelled out her back door. "I mean it, Elvis."

She turned back to the kitchen, letting herself down into a chair at a small, scarred table. She looked over at Polly, who sat with her wet hair wrapped in a towel turban.

"That damn mule will be the death of me," Old Bertha said.

"He doesn't want to be outside by himself," Polly said, contemplating a tower of apple cobbler teetering on a wobbly plate between them. "I don't know why you won't let him in. It's not like he's going to wreck the floor."

"I'm just not much of an animal person."

"You're not much of a people person either," Polly said. "But you're doing all right."

The back door rattled again.

"I swear, Elvis," Old Bertha said. "I'm going to send you right back to where you came from if you don't settle down."

"Come on, Bertha." Polly broke off a piece of cookie. "Let him in."

"You let him in."

"Do you mean it?" Polly looked up in surprise, the giddy anticipation barely hidden on her freshly scrubbed face.

"You better hurry before I change my mind."

Polly sprang out of her seat and raced to the back door. Elvis stuck his head in and looked around. When he caught Old Bertha's eye, he pulled his head back outside.

"You said you wanted to come in," Old Bertha said to the miniature mule. "Well, come on in then."

Elvis put a hoof on the kitchen floor. He stood for a moment, looking up at Polly.

"It's OK, Elvis," Polly said, as if talking to a baby. "Who is the good little boy?"

"Hey!" Old Bertha said. "He can come in, but no baby talk. Now sit down and have some of this cobbler."

Polly gave Elvis a quick pat and sat back down at the table. Old Bertha dug a spoon into the cobbler and scooped up a heaping serving. Polly watched, mesmerized, as ribbons of vanilla sauce stuck to the serving spoon. "What kind of cobbler is that?"

"You'll have to ask Fernando," Old Bertha said. "He said he made it from apple fritters and cornmeal."

"I love being Fernando's guinea pigs." Polly took a bite. She rolled her eyes in appreciation. "But I'm not going to fit in my jeans if he doesn't settle on some recipes and open the restaurant."

"Genius can't be rushed," Old Bertha said.

"I know." Polly took another bite. "Fernando said the same thing."

"Where do you think I heard it?" Old Bertha said, serving herself another helping.

Titan had taken to leaving the back door of the forge open so Rocket could look in whenever he felt alone or stressed out. Unlike Fancy, whose moods Titan could read, Rocket was a closed book. Titan figured if Rocket hung around, he must be happy and Titan left it at that. Fancy begrudgingly accepted the fact that Rocket was now part of the household, but she gave the bull a wide berth.

Titan was exhausted. Since making his deal with Dodge, he worked every day, often with the help of Powderkeg, Pappy, and Fernando, making sure his acreage was properly fenced. It wasn't that he expected any fence to hold Rocket, but he felt he should at least make a show of being a proper caretaker.

Titan had built a bedroom for himself in the loft of the forge. He'd also built a platform that extended outside from the loft, so he could sleep outside when the forge refused to cool in the evening. From his perch, he could watch Rocket wander over to the back door and get screeched at by Fancy. If Titan wasn't on the ground floor, Rocket would look up and spot Titan looking down on him.

Titan had no game plan when it came to Rocket's future. If he had to move to the Rolling Fork Ranch, would he still "own" Rocket, or would he have to return the bull? Rocket would probably always find a way to get away from Dodge Durham. Titan put that thought out of his head. That was just being egotistical. Although he had to admit, the bull really did seem to like him. And if he did have to move, what would happen to Fancy? Would Mr. Honeycutt want a lame buzzard moving onto the ranch? Would Fancy be safe there? The more he thought about the future, the less clearly he could see it. He took one more look at Rocket, who snorted his good-night. The sun was still on the horizon and Titan told himself he was only going to rest his eyes. He closed them and was asleep in minutes.

CHAPTER 17

Dymphna replayed her less than satisfactory phone conversation with Professor Johnson over and over again in her mind. It was bad enough that she had to live out her romance in the middle of Main Street, with Old Bertha pretending not to listen, but this afternoon's reception was particularly bad. She mostly had to guess at what he was saying. Finally, in frustration, Professor Johnson said they should just give up. Dymphna tried not to worry. Surely he just meant give up on the phone call?

Thud suddenly let out a long, yowling bark. When Thud started barking, it never really narrowed down what was happening on the farm. It could be the chickens were chasing each other around the yard or the goats were close enough to the farmhouse to cause Thud umbrage. When Dymphna first arrived in Fat Chance, the blood-hound suddenly staggering to his feet and howling used to terrify her, but now his theatrical alerts were just one more noise she associated with the farm.

Dymphna was putting the final touches on a jerry-rigged repair job to her spinning wheel when Thud let out another long caterwaul. She paid no attention to him. He ran to the door and continued barking furiously. She knew that he could let himself out the back, so she continued to concentrate on why her yarn was not winding onto the bobbin. Yesterday, in desperation, she'd had Powderkeg take a look; with his carpentry skills, he was the closest thing she had to an expert, but he was as stumped as she. Thud leapt up on the door and started whining. This was a new sound, and it got her attention. She could hear footsteps on her porch. She went to the door and stood there, grateful to have the big dog by her side.

Dymphna leapt back as a low knocking sound came from the door. Was someone trying to kick the door in? Thud barked happily again, lunging at the door, wiggling his entire back end. Dymphna tightened her grip on Thud's collar, to steady her nerves.

The low knock came again, more forcefully this time.

"I have a dog!" Dymphna blurted.

"There's a rumor going 'round to that effect." Tino's voice came through the door. "Open up, my hands are full."

Dymphna let out her breath, which she hadn't realized she was holding.

"Keep hold of Thud," Tino said through the door. "I can't have him jumping on me."

Dymphna could feel her heart race. Was he hurt? With one hand on Thud's collar, she turned the handle and jerked the door open. Tino stood there, a lopsided grin on his face. In his arms was cradled a little yellow duckling, bobbing its head out of an old plastic Tupperware container with what looked like a shredded cotton T-shirt in it.

"Can we come in?" Tino asked.

"Of course." Dymphna tried to keep Thud from jumping up and slobbering all over her new fluffy guest. She reached for the baby duck. "May I hold it?"

"That's why I'm here." Tino carefully transferred the duckling to Dymphna's waiting arms and shrugged out of a large backpack. "This baby needs a new mama."

"What happened?"

Tino shrugged. "I don't know. I just found him down by the creek all by himself."

"*Him*self?" Dymphna asked. "Is he a boy?"

"Beats me. I'm a good vet, but I'm not *that* good. You can't tell when a duck is this little. It just looks like a he to me."

"How little is he?"

"I think he's about eight weeks old," Tino said. "He's already got his feathers, which is lucky for him. It means he's waterproof. They aren't when they're really young."

Thud came over to investigate. Dymphna lowered the container so the bloodhound could take a sniff.

"You have to be very gentle, Thud," Dymphna said.

Thud sniffed carefully at the duckling, who looked up at Dymphna with sad eyes. The little creature didn't seem to be particularly afraid of the dog—perhaps its duckling brain was on fright overload already.

Tino started unpacking the backpack. "I brought you some chick food to get you started. Although this guy will probably be ready to fend for himself pretty soon."

"You mean he'll fly away?" Dymphna asked, already missing the duckling.

"Not yet. He's too small."

"But eventually?"

"Maybe. But maybe not. If he bonds with you, he'll stay. I mean, you've got the creek and the little pond."

Dymphna nodded, trying not to get her hopes up. "What should I do with him right now?"

"Best thing is to put him in the bathtub," Tino said. "In the morning, you can start introducing him to the other animals . . . see how he does. But don't force it. The chickens might be territorial at first."

Dymphna nodded again, taking it all in. The duckling started to struggle in the Tupperware container. Dymphna wrapped the duckling in the T-shirt and cradled him in her arms. The duckling was stronger than she anticipated. She really had to keep a grip on him.

"Can he walk . . . waddle?" she asked, trying to hold on to him.

The duckling suddenly wrenched himself free, landing on the ground, startling Thud, who barked, then climbed onto the sofa. Dymphna and Tino watched as the duckling raced through the living room, quacking. He ran into the empty fireplace, where he crashed into the bricks. The impact showered the duckling with soot. Dymphna managed to retrieve him, wiping away black grime with the T-shirt.

"I'll wash this shirt for you," Dymphna said apologetically.

"That's okay," Tino said. "I sort of figured I'd seen the last of it when I offered it to this guy as a security blanket."

"I'm going to name him Crash," Dymphna said, continuing to clean the duckling and watching Thud gently investigate the newcomer. "He sort of named himself. And I like the way Thud and Crash sound together."

Tino smiled at her and she felt her cheeks flush. She hadn't seen Tino in the two weeks that had passed since they worked on Rosie together at Meriwether's farm. She was touched that he'd thought of her when he saw another animal in distress. She hoped the glow that she was feeling inside wasn't showing.

"I hope you don't mind that I brought him here," Tino said. "You know, for a small town, it's pretty unusual to find two people as good with animals as you and Titan. But Titan has Fancy and now that longhorn. So I figured . . ."

Dymphna's glow started to dim.

I'm just a safer haven than a forge with a buzzard and a bull.

Tino saw Dymphna's cheeks fall.

"But if you don't want him, I'm sure Titan . . ."

"No no," Dymphna said. "I do want him. And I think if he decides he likes it here, the pond will be a great place for him."

"That's good!" Tino said. "I guess I can cross this little guy off my list."

Dymphna had no idea how to take that.

As if reading her mind, he explained. "Now I don't have to worry about him."

Dymphna smiled. "Can you stay for a little apple-peach brandy? Fernando has been experimenting with fermenting fruit in peach brandy—this is his first jar."

"A *jar*?"

"This is what's left after he strains the fruit and cans it. Better to call it a jar rather than runoff, he says."

"Sounds horrible."

"It is! Fernando says when he makes his own brandy from scratch, things will be better, but he did save a bunch of fruit from going bad, so I can't complain."

"Why not?" Tino said. "I'm off duty. I'll get Crush . . ."

"Crash."

"I'll get Crash set up in the tub and I'll be right out."

Tino came out of the bathroom and closed the door firmly behind him. "I think he'll be quiet tonight. He's had a big day. Just make sure Thud keeps his distance for a while."

"I will. Should I look in on him during the night?"

"Could I stop you?" Tino asked, grimacing as he took a sip of brandy. "I hope Fernando's barbecue is better than his brandy."

"He's still experimenting with both," Dymphna said. "He brought a smoker into town yesterday."

"Smoked brandy." Tino held up his glass. "Couldn't be worse than this."

Dymphna laughed. "How is Rosie?"

"The horse? I guess she's fine. I haven't heard."

Dymphna studied Tino. What *was* his attitude about animals? One minute, he and she seemed to be of one mind, that animals were an almost sacred part of the earthly experience. And then the next, he seemed all business.

Of course, animals *were* his business.

"Shall we go sit on the porch?" Tino asked. "We've been getting beautiful sunsets lately."

"Sounds wonderful," Dymphna said. "But I won't be able to hear Crash."

"Crash will be fine. Trust me."

Dymphna allowed herself the cosmic display of the picturesque sunset, but she left the front door open, in case a plaintive peep should come from the bathroom. She relaxed when Thud, rather than sit on the porch with the humans, stationed himself at the front of the bathroom door, lying on the floor like a rumpled sentry.

"Thud will let me know if there's a problem," Dymphna said.

Tino chuckled.

"What?"

"I think it's cute how you anthropomorphize animals the way you do."

"You don't think animals have emotions?" Dymphna asked, startled.

"To a certain degree. I know Thud is a loyal—not to mention brave—dog, who feels protective of his owner. But are those emotions or instinct?"

"You could ask that question of humans as well."

"True," Tino said. "But do I think Thud is evolved enough to be watching over Crash so you won't be worried about the duckling? No."

"I think you're not listening."

"To you?" Tino asked, surprised.

"To Thud," Dymphna said. "To the universe. You'd be surprised what is going on in the animal kingdom if you'd pay attention."

"You might be right. But you need to cut me some slack. I'm a veterinarian. Just like an MD, I have to keep a professional distance from my patients."

"Is that instinct or emotion?"

"It's survival." Tino tossed the rest of his brandy into the dust. "OK, Fernando has some work to do. I can't drink any more of this."

Dymphna giggled. "That's one thing we can agree on." She stood up and hurled the remains of her own glass off the porch as well.

She suddenly realized that the two of them were standing very close to each other. Dangerously close. She could feel her heart beating faster. She knew that if she didn't back away, they would be in each other's arms in another instant. But she couldn't make her feet move. A movement from inside the house distracted her. She turned to see Thud shambling out of the house onto the porch. He wedged his massive bulk between Dymphna and Tino, looking out at the night sky, bookended by the two humans.

The spell was broken.

CHAPTER 18

Fernando poured Powderkeg and Pappy each another jelly jar of wild blackberry brandy.

"This tastes like peaches," Powderkeg said.

"Just go with it," Fernando said.

"These fruit brandies are awful sweet," Pappy said, taking a sip. "But it makes me think I should start making wine with my grapes."

"You have grapes?" Fernando perked up.

"Not a lot. I've got a small arbor out back. Just for fun. Makes shade for Jerry Lee. You can sit around watching the bees get drunk. You know, that sort of thing."

"Now working with grapes—that's something I know how to do," Fernando said as he took a small sip of the brandy. "I was really hoping that the fermented fruit might add to the taste of the crappy brandy just as much as the crappy brandy would add to the taste of the fruit, but I guess I'll have to chalk this up to a failed experiment."

"Don't say that," Powderkeg said, taking another sip. "I don't mind telling you, this grows on a person. If Professor Johnson ever gets back here, he can sell this in his saloon."

"'If' being the operative word," Pappy said. "Sometimes I think Fat Chance is jinxed when it comes to love."

"Here's to Pappy, our Hill Country philosopher." Powderkeg saluted Pappy and Fernando before throwing back his brandy.

"I'm serious," Pappy said. "Professor Johnson and Dymphna are trying to hold it together, but he's in Los Angeles. Polly couldn't hold on to any of the boys. And poor old Powderkeg got left in the dust by Cleo."

"Not to mention Old Bertha won't give you the time of day," Powderkeg retaliated. "No offense."

"No offense taken," Pappy said glumly. "It's a fact."

"And even after giving her Elvis, a token of love if ever there was one," Fernando said.

"The woman has a heart of stone," Pappy said.

"I, for one, am moving on," Powderkeg said, pouring himself more brandy. "I've got my eyes set on Lacey Carmichael."

"You got a death wish, man?" Fernando asked, sipping from his own jelly jar.

"What do you mean?" Powderkeg sounded a bit slurry.

"From what I've seen, Mikie isn't exactly interested," Fernando said.

"She's interested," Powderkeg said. "She's just fighting her natural attraction to me, that's all."

"Huh," Fernando said.

"What does that mean?" Powderkeg asked, sitting up straight.

"What does what mean?"

"Huh?" Powderkeg said. "What did you mean by 'huh'?"

"I meant, I think you're crazy," Fernando said. "I was trying to be polite, but since you called me out . . ."

"Yeah," Powderkeg said. "You're probably right. But I'm going for it anyway. I'm the first to admit, I'm an acquired taste."

"Like this brandy," Pappy said, lifting his glass. "More power to you."

The men toasted.

"I guess we should be thanking our lucky stars that all we're worrying about is women," Pappy said.

"And men," Fernando said. "And barbecue."

"Right," Pappy said. "What I mean is, things could be worse. We could be in Titan's boots."

"Isn't there anything we can do to help him?" Fernando said. "I've only been in town a little while—but it's pretty obvious Titan struck a bad deal with Dodge."

"Titan is too naïve for his own good," Pappy said. "He thinks everything will work out just fine. Well, I'm here to tell you, that's just not true."

"Could we all put our money together—you know, take up a collection, and buy the bull?" Fernando asked.

Pappy and Powderkeg shook their heads.

"First of all, we're all on limited funds here. Time is ticking on this town, whether we want to admit it or not," Powderkeg said. "And secondly, Titan would never take it."

"How do you know?" Fernando asked.

"We already offered," Pappy said.

"Isn't there anything we can do for Titan? For that steer?" Fernando asked.

"He's not a steer, he's a bull," Pappy said. "A steer is neutered. The bull is still . . . well . . . he's still the baby daddy, if you get my drift."

"That's what makes him so valuable," Powderkeg said.

"It's all about the family jewels," Pappy said.

"Isn't it always?" Fernando poured more brandy.

"You know what we should do?" Without waiting for an answer, Powderkeg continued. "We should turn that bull into a steer. Problem solved." He paused. "Until Dodge got wind of it."

"What's he gonna do, sue us?" Fernando asked, indicating the grandeur that was Fat Chance, Texas.

Powderkeg snickered. "Point taken. Too bad nobody here knows how to neuter a bull."

"Speak for yourself," Pappy said, draining his glass. "You don't live in Texas for thirty years without learning a thing or two."

"Let's move it on out," Fernando said. "OMG! I've always wanted to say that!"

The three men finished their brandies and walked out of the café. They stopped at Pappy's and picked up a tool that looked like giant pinchers.

"Ouch," Powderkeg said.

"It's not gonna be a day in the park for old Rocket," Pappy said. "But it's for his own good. This way he can stay with Titan and they both can live in Fat Chance."

Powderkeg, Pappy, and Fernando made their way over to the forge. They stood quietly at the front door, listening. A snort echoed into the night.

"Unless Titan is a snorer," Powderkeg whispered, "that's Rocket, and he's around back."

"Watch out for that damn bird," Fernando said, looking around.

"Fancy is asleep," Pappy said.

"How do you know?" Fernando asked as the men inched their way through the darkness into the area behind the forge.

"You trust him to castrate a full-grown bull, but you're questioning what he knows about buzzards?" Powderkeg whispered.

"Shut up, you two," Pappy said as they reached the corner of the forge.

They peeked around the corner and there stood Rocket, drinking water out of an old bathtub that Titan had made into a water trough. His white, freckled coat was visible in the tiny sliver of moonlight.

"Holy crap, he's big," Powderkeg said.

Rocket stopped drinking and looked toward the men. They retreated behind the building.

"No turning back now." Pappy took a step forward.

"Why is there no turning back?" Fernando asked.

"You think if that bull gets even a whiff of our intention, we got any room for negotiations?" Pappy asked.

"For what it's worth . . . I rode a bull once and I know a couple of things about keeping the animal under control," Fernando said.

The men turned to look at him in surprise.

Good, he thought. *I've got their attention.*

"Of course I didn't ride him for long. Damn thing threw me in two seconds, but you can learn a lot about a bull, bouncing around on his back like that."

Powderkeg and Pappy were staring at him as if they couldn't believe what he was saying, but he swore that it was God's honest truth.

"So what happened?" Powderkeg asked.

"Well, the music was so damn loud, I couldn't . . ." Fernando slurred.

"Music? What music?" Pappy said. "What are you talking about, man?"

"The bull," Fernando insisted. "The mechanical bull I rode."

For some reason Fernando couldn't quite understand, both men lost interest in his story at the same moment. Apparently they had no appreciation of how hard it is to stay on a bucking, ten-ton metal bull. Fernando's feelings were hurt.

"We've got to do what we've got to do," Pappy said. "We have to save our friend . . . and his bull . . . and this is the only way. Fernando, did you bring any more of that brandy along? I could use a little touch of courage right this minute."

Fernando admitted that he didn't think to carry brandy on a field trip to castrate a bull.

"But, seriously, if you think about it," Fernando whispered, "if somebody said that the only way to save you was to cut your nuts off, would you really, really, really want to be saved?"

"That's a good point, Pappy," Powderkeg said. "Now that I'm feeling a little more sober, maybe we should rethink this."

"Lily-livered chickenshits," Pappy said. "I'll handle this myself."

"We who are about to die, salute you," Powderkeg said to Pappy's back.

Pappy shook his head and turned to head back toward Rocket.

Rocket, hearing the noises coming from the corner of the forge, decided to investigate. He met Pappy halfway around the building. Pappy was nose to nose with the immense animal, which startled them all.

The men screamed and the bull roared. Rocket lowered his head, the points of his horns catching the moonlight.

"What's going on?" Titan yelled as he rappelled himself down a rope from his second story perch. He swung down as Rocket took a few steps back, head still lowered.

"This doesn't look good," Fernando said. "Titan, talk to him!"

"Rocket, chill out," Titan said calmly. "These are our friends."

"We are!" Pappy said as he shoved the pincher in his waistband, under his Hawaiian shirt. "We come in peace."

Rocket lifted his head and snorted. He ambled over to Titan, who scratched the bull's head.

"What are you guys doing here so late?" Titan asked sleepily.

"Just making sure Rocket is doing OK," Pappy said. "We know he's had a hard road."

"Aww," Titan said. He turned to address the bull. "You see, Rocket, everyone loves you here."

The bull snorted. The threesome exchanged guilty glances.

"Now that we know he's OK," Pappy said, "we'll be going."

"Are you sure? I could invite you in—I have some of Fernando's brandy . . ."

"No!" Powderkeg said, cutting him off. He took a deep breath. "I think we've all had enough brandy, thanks."

"OK," Titan said. "I wouldn't really want to wake Fancy anyway."

"God forbid," Fernando said, pulling at Pappy and Powderkeg.

The men breathed a collective sigh of relief as they headed down Main Street.

"Do you think Rocket knew why we were there?" Powderkeg asked.

Pappy shrugged.

"Do you think he really would have charged us?" Fernando asked.

"Maybe." Pappy shrugged again. "Or maybe not."

"If he wasn't going to charge us, that bull is one drama queen," Fernando said.

CHAPTER 19

"Auntie," Elwood called out in the foyer of Cleo's mansion. "Where are you?"

Cleo came out of her second story bedroom and looked down the curved staircase. "I'm up here, darling."

"You will not believe what happened today!" Elwood called up, climbing two stairs at a time.

"The university came up with the funding?" Cleo asked. She realized her mistake as soon as she'd said it. Elwood stopped dead in his tracks.

"Yes," he said. "How did you know?"

"Wild guess," she said, then quickly changed the subject. "That is wonderful news. Have you told Dymphna yet?"

"I tried calling, but you know what the phone service is like out there. I'll send a text and e-mail, but there isn't any guarantee she'll get them."

"Well then, what are we waiting for? I'll have Jeffries . . . Donald . . . get the plane ready."

"I can't leave right this minute," Elwood said as he climbed the rest of the stairs. He swung his backpack off his shoulder and started rummaging around in it. "I've got to finish my classes. I can't leave the kids hanging."

"Of course," Cleo said.

Damn Elwood. Always thinking of others.

"And I won't be taking the plane—I have to bring the Outback. It'll be good to have some backup in case the Covered Volkswagen gives up the ghost."

Cleo grimaced. Of course Elwood would want to drive! This every-man attitude of his could be so annoying! She thought about taking the plane herself and meeting him there, but she just couldn't envision arriving in Fat Chance alone. She'd have to go with him.

If he'll take me.

"Would you mind some company?" she asked hesitantly.

"I hadn't really thought about it." He put his backpack on the floor, knelt, and continued to look through various compartments in it. "Who did you have in mind?"

"Me," Cleo said in a small voice.

Elwood looked up in surprise. His glasses slipped down his nose. Cleo hoped she didn't look as pathetic as she felt.

"You?"

"Yes. I mean, I did tell you I had changed my mind about Fat Chance."

"Yes, but I assumed that was just a weak moment." Elwood finally stopped digging. "The provost himself came out of his office to wish me well. He shook my hand and said to give this to you."

He stood up and handed his aunt a pie plate.

Pappy stood in the middle of the street with his cell phone up to his ear. "Good to hear," he said. "OK, I'm losing reception."

He pulled the phone away, shook it, and returned it to his ear. "I said I'm losing reception," he yelled. "I'll see you at the store in two hours."

"Could you keep it down?" Powderkeg rasped as he jumped off the boardwalk onto Main Street. "I could hear you from the shop."

"Sorry," Pappy said. "I'm still nursing a hangover myself from that infernal brandy."

"Next time we should stick with fruit smoothies," Powderkeg said. "Leave the brandy for the heavy hitters."

"Not sure if there'll ever be a next time," Pappy said.

"Lucky for Rocket." Fernando seemed to appear out of nowhere. He turned to Pappy. "Did I hear you say you were heading to Spoonerville?"

"Yeah," Pappy said. "Jerry Lee and I are heading over there."

"I'll go with you," Fernando said. "I have a couple things on order that must have come in by now."

"No more peach brandy, I hope," Pappy said.

"I'll pass," Powderkeg said. "If we could take the damned Covered Volkswagen. But no fan belts means walking."

"That's why I'm going," Pappy said. "That was Mikie on the phone just now. The new fan belt is in."

"I'm not a gambler," Old Bertha said from the boardwalk, where she sat with Elvis in front of the grocery store. "But if I were, I'd bet that Powderkeg is about to change his mind."

"If the innkeeper-grocer thing doesn't work out," Powderkeg said to Old Bertha, "maybe you could go into fortune-telling. Pappy, count me in."

Before the trio headed out, Fernando asked Pappy if he could fill Jerry Lee's saddlebags on the way to Spoonerville.

"On the way *to* Spoonerville?" Pappy asked. "Usually supplies only go one way."

"I know," Fernando said. "I have my reasons."

"Knock yourself out," Pappy replied.

Fernando, Powderkeg, and Pappy headed out to Spoonerville with Jerry Lee outfitted with his fully packed saddlebags. By unspoken agreement, the three decided not to mention the excursion to Titan. It seemed a little coldhearted to ask him to face Dodge, especially since not one of them thought Titan had a chance of coming out ahead in their arrangement.

As the store came into view, the men stopped so Fernando could change out of his sneakers and into his boots. Mikie's biplane flew overhead, close enough to the ground that the men could see her wave to them before the plane disappeared from view.

"Maybe Mikie'll rush over to the store now that she knows we're here," Fernando teased as the group headed into the final stretch of their journey.

"Count on it," Powderkeg said.

Pappy tied Jerry Lee to the hitching post, then grabbed Powderkeg's sleeve as an older woman in jeans and a plaid shirt, her white hair in a tousled bun, walked up the stairs. A tall, lean cowboy was at her side.

"Powderkeg!" Pappy rasped. "I think that lady is Meriwether Mc-Murphy!"

"Your old flame?" Fernando asked, straining to get a look at the woman.

"Yes!" Pappy said.

"'My old flame,'" Fernando sang. "'I can't even think of her name.'"

"Yes, I can," Pappy said. "I just told you—Meriwether McMurphy! What's gotten into you, Fernando?"

Fernando just shook his head.

"I haven't seen her in thirty years! She looks old."

"Thirty years will do that to a person," Fernando said.

"What's she doing here?" Pappy asked.

"I guess now that she has somebody to help her, she gets round a little more," Powderkeg said.

"I guess I better go say hello." Pappy ran his fingers through his wild hair.

"Don't you go cheating on Old Bertha," Powderkeg said.

"Old Bertha might just have to get in line," Pappy said. "Let's see what today brings."

"You two are delusional," Fernando said as he unpacked Jerry Lee's saddlebags. "You know that?"

"When you live in a place like Fat Chance, Texas, that can be a good thing," Powderkeg said.

The three men climbed the stairs to the store. Fernando, carrying a small box, opened the door, and with a sweeping hand gesture, ushered his compatriots inside. The store was packed with cowboys.

"Must be payday," Fernando said gleefully. "Just like in the novel I read."

"I thought they were gambling in the novel," Pappy said.

"They were spending M-O-N-E-Y," Fernando whispered. "That's the important thing. Now—watch and learn."

Fernando wandered over to the cashier's stand, Dodge was ensconced in his usual place behind the counter.

"Hey, Dodge." Fernando placed the box on the counter. "My order come in?"

Dodge ducked his head under the desk and came up with a filled paper bag. He passed the bag to Fernando without comment.

"What do I owe you?"

"A hundred and twenty dollars," Dodge said.

"Wow," Fernando said, playing to the patrons of the store, some of whom were eavesdropping. It wasn't every day that someone spent over a hundred dollars at the Spoonerville general store. "Well, you've got to spend money to make money. Isn't that what they say?"

He turned and looked at Dodge, as if waiting for him to answer.

"I guess that's what they say," Dodge said reluctantly.

"Let me see if I have my credit card with me." Fernando patted his jeans and shirt pockets. "Nope. Maybe it's in here."

Fernando opened the box he'd been carrying and set it on the counter. Inside was a thick towel. He lifted the towel—and the intoxicating aroma of barbecue filled the store. Murmurs of appreciation bounced off the walls as cowboys and ranch hands followed their noses. Fernando was waiting for them—brisket and toothpicks in hand. Fernando caught Powderkeg's sly thumbs-up signal as he started to pass out samples of the tender meat.

"This is fantastic," one man said, trying to spear another sample.

Fernando slapped his hand away. "One sample per person," he said, handing another ranch hand a toothpick.

"This is the best barbecue for a hundred miles," another man said.

"Only for one hundred miles?" Fernando said.

"Well, maybe . . ." The man looked around for support.

"The world?" Fernando offered. "The universe?"

It was as if Fernando had turned the store into a party. Everyone was smiling and chatting about the food.

"Where can we get more?" a woman asked.

"In three weeks," Fernando said dramatically, "I will be opening my new restaurant. You're all invited to the grand opening in Fat Chance."

There was a confused silence as the patrons looked at one another.

"Fat Chance?" a cowboy asked. "You mean . . . the ghost town?"

"Yeah! That's right, I heard about y'all," a cowboy said. "You guys still trying to keep that town going?"

"We *are* keeping the town going," Fernando said. "Don't forget, in three weeks, my grand opening. I'll keep you all posted. Come for a visit, stay for the Cowboy Food."

Everyone clapped, with the exception of Dodge. The party atmosphere dissolved with the last bite of brisket. Fernando turned back to Dodge.

"That will be a hundred and twenty dollars," Dodge said. "In case that slipped your mind during your little show."

"Oh! Here it is!" Fernando said as he pulled his wallet out of his back pocket. "It was here all along."

"What a surprise," Dodge said, running the card.

"I hope we'll see you there, Dodge." Fernando returned his card and sales receipt to his wallet.

"I'll probably stop by," Dodge said. "Three weeks? It will almost be time to take Rocket back. Might be good to see how he's doing."

Pappy had managed to wander over toward Meriwether during Fernando's performance. He studied her. Thirty years ago, Meriwether Murphy was a sturdy, tanned, spirited widow. The woman in front of him seemed not only physically frail, but fragile as well. Maybe that's what a second widowhood did to you. Pappy started to speak, but hesitated. They hadn't parted on bad terms, but they didn't exactly part on good terms either. Pappy had just disappeared into Fat Chance. Until Cutthroat's beneficiaries came strolling into town last year, he'd almost been a hermit. It wasn't personal, his bailing on Meriwether. But he wouldn't be winning any awards for breakup etiquette. He'd tried to carry off his surprise that she was so hostile toward him all these many years later, but he was dismayed to hear how antagonistic she actually was. He certainly would never admit it to any of the men in town—except maybe Titan—but he actually was happy to have a chance to speak to her. To apologize. He couldn't explain his actions, but he could apologize for them.

He stood looking over her shoulder as she read the ingredients on a jar of peanut butter.

"Still eating those peanut butter and banana sandwiches?" Pappy asked, smiling.

Meriwether looked up and tilted her head to the side.

"Do I know you?" she asked.

Pappy's smile faded. "Uh, well . . . ," he stammered.

"You look sort of familiar," she said. "I take that back. You don't look anything like the man I'm thinking of. He was much younger and didn't look like a bum. But you sort of sound like somebody I used to know."

"Now come on, Meriwether. You know damn good and well it's me."

Meriwether put the peanut butter back on the shelf. "To answer your question," she said without looking at him, "no, I don't eat peanut butter and banana sandwiches anymore. I made a concerted effort to give up things that weren't good for me."

She brushed by Pappy, then looked around. "Hank?" she called out. "Where are you?"

The young man who had accompanied Meriwether into the store appeared from another aisle.

"Yes, ma'am," he said. "You ready to head back to the farm?"

"I am."

"Did you get your peanut butter?" Hank asked, noting her empty hands. "I thought you came in for peanut butter."

Meriwether slapped at Hank's shoulder and strode out the door, the confused young cowboy at her heels.

CHAPTER 20

After Fernando's little show, Powderkeg wandered outside. He sat on a bench on the general store's porch, his long legs stretched out and feet up on the railing. He took a long draught of a Big Red. Closing his eyes, he put his head back. His hangover was wearing off, but his brain still felt as if toy army men were marching through it, poking into its recesses with their plastic rifles.

He opened one eye to see Meriwether and her young ranch hand leave the store. Hank was beside her as Meriwether muttered something about seeing "that damn fool." Apparently Pappy had made contact. Powderkeg pulled his hat over his eyes.

When he opened them, he looked down the steep stairs, expecting to see Jerry Lee waiting patiently for the Fat Chance crew to retrieve him. Instead, he saw Mikie scratching Jerry Lee's ears. The mule looked like he was in heaven.

Who wouldn't be?

Powderkeg stood up and made his way down the steps. "Hey, Lacey. I mean, Mikie."

"Hey back," Mikie said, focused more on the mule than the man. "Thought you guys would be gone by now."

"Fernando and Pappy are still conducting some business," Powderkeg said. "I saw your plane go by earlier. You flying an Annie?"

"What do you mean?" she asked.

Powderkeg knew he had her attention now. "An Annie," he said. "An Antonov An-2? Russian plane? Sold cheap after the Cold War ended? Ring any bells?"

"Yeah," Mikie said, pushing her baseball cap back to get a better look at Powderkeg. "How did you know that?"

"I was in the Air Force in 'Nam. Took down an Annie in a Huey."

"I'm impressed." Mikie regarded Powderkeg solemnly. "I gotta say, you don't look old enough to have fought in Vietnam."

"I barely was. Squeaked in by the skin of my teeth."

"Thank you for your service," Mikie said, catching Powderkeg off guard.

"Oh! Well. My pleasure."

"And thank you for leaving enough Annies in the sky so Mr. Honeycutt could buy one for the ranch. She's a clumsy bird, but I love her."

Powderkeg turned to look up the stairs. Pappy and Fernando were heading down with their supplies.

"You know anything about Annies?" Mikie asked. "Their engines, I mean."

"A little something. Yeah."

"I wouldn't mind a second opinion on something. I mean, if you can spare the time."

Pappy and Fernando joined them before Powderkeg could answer.

"Hey, Mikie," Pappy said as he started to load up Jerry Lee's saddlebags. "What's happening?"

"Not much. Thinking about having Powderkeg here take a look at my plane, if you can spare him."

"I don't know about that, Mikie," Pappy said, casting a devilish grin in Powderkeg's direction. "I got this new fan belt that needs installing."

"I'll run him over in the truck before dark, I promise," Mikie said. "This won't take long."

"That's what she said," Fernando said under his breath.

Pappy and Fernando finished packing the saddlebags and headed back to Fat Chance as Mikie and Powderkeg split off toward the east of the Rolling Fork Ranch. The conversation between Powderkeg and Mikie was easy, smooth, and flirtatious.

When they arrived at the plane, Mikie swung easily into the cockpit. She turned over the engine.

"Do you hear that missing in the engine?" she yelled.

"Yeah," Powderkeg said. "I think you might want to check your fuel lines."

"I will." She turned off the engine. "Thanks. It's always good to have backup when you're making decisions about an old plane."

"Why an An-2?" Powderkeg asked. "I'm not an expert on vintage war machines, but this old girl is expensive to run, I know that much."

"True," Mikie said. "But there are trade-offs. She flies low and slow, which is perfect for chasing strays on a ranch."

"You feel safe up there in this thing?" Powderkeg peered doubtfully at the nine-cylinder radial engine.

"Very," she said. "I was born to be up there."

Powderkeg stopped looking at the plane and looked at Mikie instead. "I used to say that same thing," he said.

"What happened?"

"Life." He shrugged. "I guess."

"Life has a way of going full circle," Mikie said, looking up at the clear sky.

"I guess maybe you're right."

"I know I'm right." Mikie leaned against the leading edge of the lower wing, her hands in her jeans pockets. "I'm always right."

"Good to know."

"Hey, it's getting late. I better get you over to Fat Chance."

"Right again," Powderkeg said.

"So you were Air Force," Mikie said. "That's cool. I like a man in uniform."

"I'm not in uniform anymore."

"That's OK," she said, stepping closer. "I like a man out of uniform too."

Dymphna was standing in the yard, the sun casting late afternoon shadows. The goats were playing a Capra-esque version of tag, scattering the chickens as they chased each other. Usually Thud joined in, but this afternoon, he stood quietly by Dymphna's side, shaking his wrinkled coat anytime a goat got too near. Dymphna, holding the duckling, reached down and petted the dog.

"Are you protecting Crash?" Dymphna asked. "Who's the good dog?"

Thud looked up with his permanently melancholy expression and wagged his tail in the dust, as if to say "That would be me."

Dymphna sat on the ground, holding Crash in her hands. He was surprisingly strong and tried to wiggle away from her.

"Hang on, little guy. Let me introduce you to everybody before I put you down."

"Think he's ready for gen pop?" came a voice behind her.

She didn't need to turn around to realize it was Tino. She could feel the smile spreading across her face and nuzzled into the duck's down to hide it. Thud was already demanding his attention as she stood up, duck in arms, and faced him.

"Gen pop?" she asked.

"General population," Tino said. "You know, like in prison."

Dymphna's smile froze. *Prison?*

"I've never heard that term," she said. "I've never been to prison."

"You also don't watch much TV, I guess." Tino smiled easily. "That's where I get all my tough-guy lingo."

Dymphna relaxed. She loved the fact that talking to Tino was effortless. She held up the duck for inspection.

"When I went into the bathroom this morning, he was sitting in the sink," she said. "Obviously he no longer wants to be a tub duck. I thought I'd see how he does with the other animals and decide what to do then."

"He might try to escape, you know," Tino said. "He still can't fly—but he doesn't know that."

"I know. I'll watch him." Dymphna kissed the wiggling Crash in her arms. "But the day will come when he *can* fly—and I'm ready for whatever he decides. He's welcome to stay but free to go."

"You really mean that too, don't you?"

"Of course I do," she said, startled. "Is that unusual?"

"Apparently not in Fat Chance. Mind a little professional help?"

"No! I'd love it," Dymphna said, "I was flying by the seat of my pants and hoping for the best."

"I'm sure Crash will be fine, but I might start him out with the chickens and work up to the goats."

"Sounds good." Dymphna turned to Thud. "Thud, get the goats into the barn, please."

Tino watched in amazement as the bloodhound started barking happily. He bounded around the yard, ears swinging. The goats stopped their game and looked at him. As if on cue, the goats pranced into the barn.

"That's amazing," Tino said. "I mean, bloodhounds are bred to hunt, not to herd."

"Thud's a lover, not a fighter," Dymphna said, walking to the barn. Tino followed.

The goats looked up at them. She handed Crash to Tino. The duck-

ling took this as an opportunity to attempt an escape, but Tino knew
what was coming and held on securely as Dymphna closed the barn
door.

"Sorry, guys," Dymphna said to the goats, who looked solemnly
at her as the barn door closed. "This won't take long."

She turned to see Tino smiling gently at her with those emerald
eyes. She suddenly felt shy. It was a familiar feeling; she'd been shy as
long as she could remember. Life in Fat Chance had given her much
more confidence, but she had to admit that shyness wasn't completely behind her. She felt it in Spoonerville or when she took her
knitted accessories to the co-op artisan shop in Dripping Springs.
She still felt shy when trying to have a conversation with Professor
Johnson, but she thought she'd probably get over that when—if—he
ever came back. And now, here was Tino and his disconcerting eyes.
Thank God there was Crash to discuss.

"OK," she said, trying not to sound breathless. "Goats are secured! Now what?"

"What about Thud?" Tino asked.

Dymphna and Tino turned to look at the bloodhound panting up at
them.

"What about him?" Dymphna asked.

"He's a big guy. You might want to put him in the house."

"Oh no. Thud will be fine."

"I know *Thud* will be fine," Tino said, holding the duck up. "I
meant he might scare Crash."

"He won't." Dymphna took Crash from Tino.

She placed the duckling in the center of the yard. Crash shook himself and scratched his back with his bill. He looked up at Dymphna and
Tino and let out a little peep. Thud sat panting. Tino looked concerned.

"Thud will behave, I promise," Dymphna said.

The chickens took Crash's introduction into the yard as a non-
event, but Waddle, the rooster, marched over. Crash seemed to sense
aggression from the fierce red comb and black beady eyes headed his
way. Dymphna held her breath. Tino took her hand and gave it a sym-
pathetic squeeze. If Crash was going to fly away, now would be the
time.

Crash watched Waddle advance. Crash ran, a panicked peeping
escaping his tiny beak. The sound seemed to infuriate Waddle, who
gave chase. Crash circled Thud, who lumbered to his feet but didn't

leave his spot. Waddle slowed as Crash raced between Thud's front paws. Thud stared down at Crash, then over at Waddle. The rooster flapped his wings menacingly, then turned around and returned to his brood. As soon as the rooster was gone, Crash started exploring the yard, stopping at a water pan. Dymphna watched as a few drops of water worked their way down the duckling's throat. The chickens ignored him. He ignored the chickens.

"That went well," Dymphna said. "I think."

"It did," Tino said. "But I wouldn't push my luck. I'd keep Crash inside another night or two if I were you."

"I will," Dymphna said. "Thanks."

Crash continued his exploration. Thud was watchful of his every move.

"That's an amazing dog you have there," Tino said. "You must be very proud."

"I am proud. And he is an amazing dog. But I can't take credit for him. He was raised by my . . ."

Tino raised an eyebrow—and waited.

"He was raised by Professor Johnson."

"Then are you fostering Thud?"

"No, oh no!" Dymphna said, alarmed. Fostering sounded so . . . impermanent. "He's staying with me until Professor Johnson gets back."

"Then what happens?" Tino asked, pushing a strand of hair off her neck.

Dymphna looked up into Tino's emerald eyes.

"I have absolutely no idea."

CHAPTER 21

The delicious smell of breakfast wafted up to the farm. Dymphna tried to ignore the rumble in her stomach as she continued to coax Crash into playing with the chickens. She felt sorry for the goats, who had to stay in the barn while she spent time with the duckling and the chickens. While she had hoped they would all get along, it appeared she would have to settle for them hanging out in different areas of the yard, but at least they weren't attacking each other.

"What do you think, Thud?" Dymphna asked the bloodhound, who was slobbering over Crash. "Time to introduce Crash to the goats?"

Dymphna could read no clues in Thud's furrowed brow, but she felt the time was right. She opened the barn door and the goats came bouncing out. Crash took one look at the animals and jumped into the air. *Not exactly flying, but a valiant effort*, Dymphna thought. The goats came over to Crash to investigate. The older goats circled the duckling, then took a cue from the too-cool-for-school chickens and went their own way. Dymphna sat on the ground with Thud's head in her lap as she watched the two little kids, now christened Lilee and Albert, poke at Crash. The duckling flapped his wings and the kids backed away. As soon as Crash stopped flapping, the kids returned. Crash tired of the game and waddled over to Dymphna. Thud sat up, leaving room in Dymphna's lap for the duckling.

"Okay, you," she said. "That's enough for today. Back in the house."

Dymphna put Crash back in the bathroom, then she and Thud headed into town. From her vantage point on the hill, she could see Rocket grazing on a slope behind the forge, looking content. She could see a tiny black dot moving down Main Street—that must be Fancy heading back to the forge after walking Titan to breakfast. She saw Fernando come out of the café and forcefully clang the breakfast triangle from the porch of the Cowboy Food café. No other townsfolk were headed toward the café, so she guessed that she and Thud were the only missing guests.

On the way down the hill, she thought about yesterday's visit from Tino. On the one hand, she was struggling with her own guilt over her attraction to him and was worried she was sending a confusing message. On the other hand, Tino was sending his own mixed signals. She had been sure Tino was going to kiss her, but the moment faded on the evening breeze. She wasn't sure what she would have done if he had kissed her. She was both grateful and disappointed that he hadn't. She looked down at Thud, who was heading purposefully toward the café, and she wondered if there was someone hovering around the edges of Tino's mind too.

From the porch of the café, Dymphna could hear Old Bertha.

"I think Elvis needs to have his teeth floated."

"No, he doesn't," Pappy said, sounding exasperated. "He's too young. Stop believing everything you read."

Dymphna had no idea what that even meant, but she brightened at the thought of asking Tino the next time she saw him. In any case, Pappy's obvious plan of establishing a relationship with Old Bertha by giving her a miniature mule seemed to be a huge success.

Maybe too much so!

With a smile on her face, Dymphna swung the door open. She blinked as she realized someone was sitting in her designated seat. She looked to Polly, who was ferociously blinking some sort of signal to her. Dymphna looked around the room. Everyone at the table, with the exception of the woman sitting in *her* seat and Powderkeg, turned to look at Dymphna with surprised eyes. Powderkeg and the woman seemed to have eyes only for each other.

Dymphna grabbed a chair and sat next to Polly.

"We seem to have a guest," Dymphna whispered. She peeked down the table at Powderkeg and could only glimpse the long pony-tail of the visitor. "Do we know her?"

"It's Mikie, the pilot," Polly whispered, handing Dymphna a platter of eggs.

Dymphna gasped and Polly shushed her. Both of them tried to stifle giggles.

"Isn't Powderkeg kind of old to have an overnight guest?" Polly whispered.

Titan shot them a withering glance. Dymphna knew he was not the gossiping type. Neither was Dymphna, usually. But Powderkeg and someone other than Cleo?

Well, good for him! thought Dymphna. Cleo left him—twice—with a broken heart. It was nice—if a little surprising—to see him moving on. It was time.

Is it time? Is Professor Johnson moving on? Am I?

She looked down at Thud, nestled at her feet. He let out a sigh and she patted him. She knew Thud would never stop loving Professor Johnson, no matter how long he had to wait.

Powderkeg and Mikie were the first to stand up after breakfast.

"Thank you all for including me," Mikie said. "But I better get moving. I have to get back to the ranch."

"And Powderkeg needs to install that fan belt," Pappy said. "Which he was supposed to do yesterday."

"Sorry, Pappy," Powderkeg said. "I got lucky . . . I mean *busy!*"

Mikie laughed.

Thank goodness, Dymphna thought. She wasn't sure she would have found the comment funny if she'd been in Mikie's shoes. In fact, she *knew* she wouldn't think it was funny. But Mikie must be pretty comfortable around men, and men's senses of humor, working in a masculine world the way she did.

"We hope to see you again," Fernando said.

"I hope so too," Mikie said, glancing quickly at Powderkeg and suddenly sounding very feminine.

Powderkeg gave the signal that the fan belt was fixed. Titan, Polly, and Dymphna met him at the top of the turnout. They all waited for Pappy. Because the bus had been out of commission, the four artisans were late getting their crafts over to Dripping Springs. As they loaded up the bus, Polly took a few pictures with her phone, some with herself having a frantic good time in the foreground, some without. Pappy finally arrived, followed by Fernando, who came staggering up the hill, trying—and failing—to avoid the craters in the trail. Fernando was carrying a box that looked heavy. Pappy was carrying a key ring.

"Now that we're all here," Polly said, "let me get a picture of all of us."

"I don't like having my picture taken," Pappy growled.

"OK, then you take the picture," Polly said, holding out her phone.

"I don't like taking pictures either." Pappy walked right by her.

Polly took a candid shot of him before he knew what happened.

The group secured their crafts onto the back ledge and took their seats. It had become a well-rehearsed routine and everything went smoothly, with a minimum of fuss or conversation. Polly slammed the door and Pappy started the engine.

"Hold it," Fernando called out from the backseat. "We've got a visitor."

Thud bounded up the trail, sending dust and pebbles flying. Dymphna opened the side door and jumped down. She knelt and rubbed Thud's fur.

"I've got to go to Dripping Springs on business, Thud," Dymphna said, her voice trembling. She and Thud were rarely apart. It occurred to her that if she and Professor Johnson officially broke up, he'd take his dog back. She wondered if you could officially break up if you never were officially a couple. She kissed Thud and wondered if women ever stayed with men just because they loved their dog.

"Come on, Dymphna," Pappy growled. "Let's go."

"Okay." She sniffed and turned back to Thud. "You wouldn't like it in Dripping Springs. You'd have to stay in the bus, and we couldn't have that."

Thud looked forlorn, as usual.

"Go on back to the *farm*, Thud," Dymphna said and pointed. "You need to watch the *farm*."

Thud turned around and raced back down the trail. He skidded to a stop and faced Dymphna, who pointed again toward the farm. He hung his head and then tore off again. Dymphna got back in the bus and the group headed northeast to Dripping Springs.

"He's such a smart dog," Titan said. "I don't think I could get Rocket to go back to the forge if I asked."

There was an uncomfortable silence in the bus. Rocket was a touchy subject. The inhabitants of Fat Chance knew that Rocket made Titan very happy and gave him purpose, but the general feeling was that the longhorn represented impending disaster for their friend. Dymphna shot a quick glance at the back shelf of the Covered Volkswagen and the delicate, almost lace-like iron bowls Titan was bringing to Dripping Springs. Each one was a masterpiece, but Dripping

Springs was not New York City or Los Angeles, where he might have been able to sell them at an art gallery—and even then, he'd have to sell them faster than he could make them. Dymphna could feel tears prick her eyes. There was no way he'd ever make enough money to pay Dodge.

"Fernando, whatever you have in that box smells delicious," Dymphna said to lighten the mood.

"More samples?" Powderkeg asked.

"Yep," Fernando said. "Chicken, this time."

"Can I have some right now?" Polly asked, reaching toward the box. Fernando slapped her hand.

"Do *not* open that box," he said. "Chicken is like genius—"

"It can't be rushed," everyone in the bus intoned.

When they arrived at Dripping Springs, Pappy pulled the bus off Highway 290 and into a parking space in front of the gift store called An Outpouring of Love. Titan and Dymphna saw nothing funny in the name; they genuinely liked it. But Powderkeg and Polly could never resist a jab at it every time they came to town. Powderkeg, annoyed at the meager profits they all made, called it An Outpouring of Low Wages, and Polly, who made fun of anything that hinted of sentimentality, called it An Outpouring of Lame Expressions.

Glenannie, the proprietress, a middle-aged mocha beauty in swirling skirts, silver hoop earrings, and a wide embroidered headband that kept her salt-and-pepper corkscrew curls off her face, met the Fat Chancers at the door. Dymphna was always nostalgic when she laid eyes on Glenannie's clothes. She used to dress like that herself before she became a farmer.

"I heard the bus a block away," Glenannie said to Pappy with a bright, toothy smile. "You'll never sneak up on anybody in that thing."

"Sneaking up isn't my style, anyway," Pappy said, enduring a hug from the tiny woman. Hugging was also not his style.

"Come on in. What have you brought me?" Glenannie asked, her eyes shining.

The store was long and narrow and stuffed to the rafters with local crafts: jewelry, beeswax candles, quilts, lamps, clothing, gift cards, and leather goods. Dymphna was always surprised how much local talent there was. She admired everything she saw.

Dymphna watched as Glenannie inspected the new offerings from

Fat Chance. Glenannie wrapped one of Dymphna's new shawls around her shoulders.

"This is beautiful, my girl," she said, studying herself in a full-length mirror. "I'll put this in the window!"

Powderkeg's leather belts were inspected next, along with a three-legged leather stool held together with thick rope. The seat was hand tooled.

"You are getting very good, Powderkeg," Glenannie said. "This stool is exceptional."

Dymphna thought she saw Powderkeg blush at the compliment. He could make fun of Glenannie's store all he wanted, but he knew she had an eye for quality—and also knew they were lucky she'd taken them in.

Next Glenannie took one of Polly's ornate hats and popped it on her head. The hat was brown, with a darker chocolate-colored head-band, a lighter brown ostrich feather, and a smattering of red berries.

"Hmm." Glenannie turned her head from side to side. "What are you trying to *say* with this hat?"

Polly shrugged, showing a hint of the hostile Goth girl she'd been when the group had first arrived in Fat Chance.

"She's trying to say," Fernando piped up, "that this is a one-of-a-kind hat that only *you* could pull off."

Glenannie shot a look at Fernando. They had never met before. Dymphna was about to introduce him, but when Glenannie was in buyer mode, she was all business. Introductions could obviously wait. Glenannie continued to study her reflection.

"Then it's perfect," she said. "Good job, Polly."

It was all Polly could do not to burst with pride.

"And now, Titan," Glenannie said, "let's see what gorgeous things you've brought for me."

Titan laid out his latest editions of bowls and platters on the counter, along with several pairs of carefully executed earrings.

"Always something special with you." Glenannie took out the hoops she was wearing and slipped on a pair of Titan's. "What do you want for the entire collection?" She swept her hand over the counter. "One thousand? Two thousand?"

The Fat Chancers looked at each other in confusion. Glenannie ran a tight ship with limited stock, though she also took pieces on consignment. There had never been the suggestion of an advance payment before.

"I . . . I have no idea," said Titan.

"All right, three thousand, and that's my final offer."

"I can't possibly take that much money," Titan said.

"Of course you can." Glenannie stepped around the counter, wrote out a check, and handed it to him. "I have contacts in a gallery in Sedona. I'm going to send these pieces up there. Maybe they'll catch on and we'll make a fortune. Worth the risk, don't you think?"

"I suppose . . ."

"I can't make any promises, you understand."

"I do! I do understand," Titan said, staring at the check. "Thank you for believing in me."

"I do believe in you, Titan," she said, reaching over the counter and squeezing his forearm. "And I am proud to invest in your future."

Dymphna suspected that there was more going on, but she couldn't put her finger on it.

Glenannie briskly changed the subject. She turned to look at Fernando. "And you," she said. "You, I don't know. But I've heard the rumors. You're the cook who plans on taking over Texas with his barbecue, am I right?"

"Sounds a bit presumptuous," Fernando said. "But, basically, that's the plan."

"Well, let's see what you've got," Glenannie said as Fernando opened the box and lifted two thick towels to expose a casserole dish full of bite-sized chicken pieces nestled in a reddish sauce.

Fernando speared a large piece of chicken with a toothpick and handed it to Glenannie. Dymphna thought that if she had been Glenannie, she would have felt self-conscious with a room full of people staring at her, waiting for her reaction. For that matter, she would have been nervous if she was Fernando, but the two main participants in the drama seemed oblivious to the anxious stares of the Fat Chancers.

"You're good," Glenannie said after tasting.

"I know," Fernando said.

Glenannie speared another piece of chicken and nodded. "OK," she said as if agreeing to something unspoken. "I'll get the word out."

"Thanks." Fernando started to close the box.

Glenannie put her hand on the box. "And I'll keep the chicken."

"Deal," said Fernando.

Glenannie moved on to the artists' favorite part of their visit: their portion of the profits from their artisanship. Although no one had any illusion that selling a few items here and there at a little craft store in a town the size of Dripping Springs was going to make any of them solvent—let alone rich—it was always nice to be recognized financially. As the group concluded their business, Dymphna overheard a final exchange between Fernando and Glenannie.

"Good luck with Titan's stuff over at that gallery in Santa Fe," he said.

"Thanks."

Dymphna saw Fernando lean in to whisper in Glenannie's ear, but she caught the words.

"The gallery is supposed to be in Sedona," Fernando whispered.

Glenannie frowned, but Fernando first put his fingers to his lips in a shushing gesture, then kissed her on the cheek. Glenannie smiled and nodded. Dymphna thought she looked a little chagrined.

Dymphna pulled Fernando aside as the others loaded themselves into the bus. "What was that about? Why did she forget where the gallery was?"

Fernando made sure no one from the bus was watching. "There is no gallery. She's just trying to help Titan meet his goal so he can keep Rocket."

"How did you know that?"

"It was a guess," Fernando said. "But when she said she had heard about me being in town, I'm not so big an egotist to think it was just because I'm so fabulous. She obviously keeps up on the news around here. If she knew about me, then she knew about Titan."

"Wow," Dymphna said. "That's a lot of guessing."

"But I was right." Fernando headed off to the bus.

"Of course you were," Dymphna said, following him.

CHAPTER 22

"Hello?" Dymphna shouted into the phone. "Professor Johnson? Can you hear me?"

"Yes," Professor Johnson said. Dymphna thought she could hear relief in his voice. They had been trying to connect for weeks by phone, but they might have had better luck with the Pony Express. It hadn't occurred to either one of them to post a letter.

"I miss you," Dymphna said, heat rising in her neck.

Did she miss him? She wanted to miss him. She looked down at her feet. The bloodhound looked up at her. She knew Thud missed him, so she added, "Thud misses you."

"Thank you," Professor Johnson said. "And I, you."

"Any word from the university?"

"Yes!" Professor Johnson said. "That's why it's been so frustrating not getting hold of you for so long."

Was he blaming her?

"I got my grant!" he continued. "I should be arriving in a week."

"I couldn't quite hear that." Dymphna changed positions on Main Street and hoped for a better signal. "When will you be here?"

"In a week!"

"In two weeks?"

"One week."

"I can't wait," Dymphna said as the reception faded. "I'll see you in two weeks. I have so much to tell you!"

And so much not *to tell you.*

She told herself she had nothing to feel ashamed about in her relationship with Tino. They definitely had a connection, but there always seemed to be something that stood in the way of them moving forward romantically. She couldn't actually say what it was. Guilt on her part? Thud's looming presence? Something in Tino's past? She'd discussed the situation with Fernando and Polly over another of Fernando's sensational barbecue experiments. Polly had ventured that Tino might be gay, but Fernando dismissed that idea.

"How do you know he's not gay?" Polly had asked him.

"Are you seriously asking me that question?"

"Then what's your take?" Polly asked, as if Dymphna wasn't there.

"They may have friend-zoned each other." Fernando shrugged. He and Polly turned to look at Dymphna with pity.

"I don't know what that means," Dymphna said.

"There's a certain span of time when friendship moves into romance," Polly said. "If it doesn't happen, it gets too weird to have sex."

"So you get friend-zoned," Fernando said. "It happens *all* the time."

"Maybe that's why Powderkeg and Mikie got involved so soon," Polly said. "The deadly friend-zone threatened them."

"I am so over those two," Fernando said. "They act like love-sick teenagers."

"It's only been a couple of weeks," Dymphna said. "Leave them alone."

"Oh, don't listen to us," Fernando said. "We're just jealous."

As Dymphna and Thud climbed the hill to her farm, she thought about the friend-zone concept. It would actually explain a lot about her life. She always took things too slow. She and Professor Johnson had never actually taken their romance further than an occasional kiss, and now she wondered if he might be friend-zoned along with Tino. Fernando said it happened all the time, and he knew everything.

The only saving grace was that she could still very much imagine making love with Professor Johnson—or with Tino. The idea of either one of them in her swaybacked rope bed didn't seem weird at all, so maybe she wasn't doomed. She gasped at the thought.

She tried to think of something else. It was a shame Professor Johnson wasn't arriving for another two weeks. One week from today, Fernando was having his grand opening, and it promised to be huge. Fernando knew how to promote his food—and himself. Farmers, ranchers, cowboys, and townspeople from Spoonerville, Dripping Springs, and beyond were all abuzz with the idea that *great* barbecue had come to their little corner of the world. Every time talk of Cowboy Food settled down, Fernando would show up with more samples and the excitement would begin again.

Dymphna stopped halfway up the hill and looked at the Fat Farm. She could make out the goats playing in the barnyard. Two of the chickens sat on posts, to stay out of the fray. She couldn't see Crash, who, weeks later, was still was too small to fly, although they were getting closer and closer to that particular day of reckoning. In the meantime, Powderkeg had cut a "ducky door" so Crash could come and go at will. The duckling joined the other animals during the day, but opted for the house at night. Thud looked up at her and wagged his tail. She gave him the OK, and he raced toward the farm, braying happily. She stood where she was, taking in her new life. Her berries and fruit trees were still a few months away from harvesting, her tomatoes, carrots, and broccoli were just about ready to burst.

As she got closer, she could see Titan and Rocket on the hill behind her farm. The acreage beyond the Fat Farm was part of Titan's bequest, which was certainly beneficial, now that he had a longhorn who needed plenty of land to roam. Dymphna bit her lip. Hanging over the anticipation of Fernando's grand opening was the knowledge that Titan was going to lose Rocket—and Fat Chance would then lose Titan. As she and Thud walked down the hill every morning for breakfast, she'd see Titan head into the Cowboy Food café, and watch Fancy make her lopsided scramble back to the forge. What would become of that poor bird? Only Titan loved her, and she only loved Titan.

The thought brought tears to her eyes. She wiped them away as she saw Titan wave. She waved back and headed toward him. As she got closer, she burst into laughter. Titan was walking beside Rocket, who shuffled along with Fancy riding on his head between the horns.

"Oh my gosh, Titan," Dymphna said in a quiet voice, though she had no idea why she was whispering. "How did you get Fancy to do that?"

"It was more about Rocket going for it," Titan said. "But I kept trying, and Rocket finally let me put Fancy on his head. They've been walking around like this for an hour. I'm not sure Rocket even remembers she's there."

Dymphna found herself disconcerted to be at eye level with Fancy. Fancy blinked her one good eye, and Dymphna backed away.

She could only hope that somehow Titan could take the bird with him to the ranch . . . but she was fairly sure the ranch hands would not want a one-eyed, one-winged buzzard around.

Dymphna left Titan to continue his slow march around the field. When she arrived at the farmhouse, Tino was waiting on the porch step with Crash in his lap and Thud at his feet.

"He heard me coming and ran right up to me," Tino said, petting the duckling and sounding delighted.

"He must remember you," Dymphna said.

"He's grown." Tino studied the duckling. "He'll be ready to fly anytime now."

"I know. Every day now I brace myself for it."

"He might stay, you know."

"And he might not."

Crash struggled out of the doctor's lap and came to sit with Dymphna, who had joined Tino on the step.

"What brings you to Fat Chance?" Dymphna asked.

"Elvis."

"Again?"

"I swear, Old Bertha is like a new mother with that mule. Elvis can't even sneeze without her sending Pappy to come get me."

"Just be glad she doesn't have Internet service. At least she's limited on what she can research. I want to check on the vegetable garden." Dymphna stood up, putting Crash on the ground. "Want to walk with me?"

Tino stood up without reply. She took that as a yes. They walked to the side of the yard where Dymphna had planted her vegetables.

"They look happy," Tino said, looking over the neat rows of greens.

Dymphna smiled. She liked the idea that her vegetables were happy. Suddenly, without warning, she reached out and put her arms around Tino's neck and kissed him—which wasn't easy, because she had to stand on her toes. The problem was, now that they were kissing, she wasn't sure where she wanted to go from here. Her boyfriend was coming home in two weeks!

Should I even be thinking right now?

"Where did that come from?" Tino asked when they were done.

"I don't know," Dymphna said. "I'm sorry."

"No need to apologize. I can't say this has never occurred to me. It's just that . . ."

"Yes? Am I in the friend zone? Are you married? Gay?"

Every cliché she'd discussed with Fernando and Polly came pouring out.

"Wow! None of those things," he said, and then added, "What's the friend zone?"

"I'm a little vague on it myself," Dymphna said. "But it doesn't sound good."

"Well then, that's not it. Look, Dymphna, it's a complicated, confidential situation. But as soon as I can talk about it, I will. I promise."

"So it's nothing personal."

"God, no," Tino said. "You're the kind of woman a man dreams about. Especially this man." Tino drew her to him again, smoothed her hair back and kissed her gently, both hands cupping her face. "I just don't want anybody to get hurt—you or me. I've got a conference coming up. I'll be gone for a few weeks. When I come back, we'll talk, OK?"

He kissed her again, then turned and walked away from the farm. Dymphna smiled and touched her lips. She saw Thud staring at her and she blushed. Thank God Thud couldn't speak.

Professor Johnson waited for Kimberly Goldman at the Urth Caffé in Beverly Hills with a cup of coffee and a matcha tiramisu. The tiramisu was for Kimberly. He knew it was a bribe, but what could he do? He saw her at the front door and waved her over to their table, which was in front of a fireplace. He found the whole idea of a fireplace in a Southern California coffeehouse exceedingly silly, but there it was. And he had bigger problems. How was he going to tell Kimberly he was going to Fat Chance in less than a week?

As she walked over, smiling, he studied her. She really was a very attractive woman, well dressed, intelligent. He thought about the few but interesting times they had spent together. She had a good mind and could argue her side of any argument effectively. He supposed she'd better be able to do that, given her profession, but it was still a lovely attribute in a dinner partner. She sat and grabbed a spoon.

"A matcha!" she said, taking a bite and rolling her eyes in delight. "Just what I wanted."

Professor Johnson cleared his throat.

Kimberly stopped chewing and looked at him. "What?"

"Nothing . . . really," he hedged.

"Listen," she said, pointing her fork at him, "I make two hundred and fifty dollars an hour, so I don't have time for horseshit. Let me have it."

She must be a very good attorney, Professor Johnson thought. "I may have mentioned that I've gotten a grant," he said.

"Yes, you have."

"Well, I haven't really delved into the ramifications of this with you. But what it means is . . . well . . . I get to start my museum."

"And?"

"And . . . the museum is in Texas."

"So you're leaving?"

"Yes."

"When?"

"In a few days."

Kimberly took another bite of the tiramisu. Professor Johnson watched her for any sign of emotional distress. He wasn't good at reading people—female people in particular—but he didn't think he was registering sadness or hysteria in his dining partner.

"May I have a sip of your coffee?" she asked.

Professor Johnson slid the cup toward her, touching the porcelain to make sure it wasn't hot, should she decide to throw it at him. She took a sip, put the cup back in its saucer, and looked at him.

"So that's what's been going on with you," she said.

"What do you mean?"

"I just thought you weren't that into me."

"No! I think you are a *very* intelligent woman."

"Thank you," Kimberly said, barely containing a smile. "Because I'm pretty insecure about my intelligence."

"Well, there is no need to be."

"Thanks," Kimberly said dryly. "And you did mention that there was that woman."

"Yes." Professor Johnson nodded. "Dymphna."

"Yes. Dymphna. OK . . . well"—Kimberly stood up—"have a good time in Texas."

He stood up and received a kiss on the cheek.

"And thanks for not being a dick," she said before walking out the door.

CHAPTER 23

Wesley poured himself another two fingers of scotch. He looked out at Cleo's circular driveway from the bay window in her library.

"Wesley, darling, you're going to have to turn around and discuss this sooner or later," Cleo said from her seat in one of the wing-backed chairs.

"Fine." Wesley spun around and stalked to the other chair. He sat and faced her. "I think you've lost your mind."

"I can't argue with you," Cleo said, taking a sip of her cocktail. "But I'm miserable here."

"But you said you hated Fat Chance. You hated the Hill Country. You hated Texas."

"That was all very true. But . . . I don't know. I miss it. I miss *me*. I was fabulous in Fat Chance. I made a difference. I made breakfast every morning, did you know that?"

"You could make breakfast *here*."

"Don't be obtuse. It doesn't suit you. I've been keeping my eye on things," Cleo said as she powered up her tablet. "Polly posts once in a while on Facebook."

Wesley and Cleo both put on their reading glasses and stared at the photos. Most were of Polly modeling her hat creations, her pouting duck lips peeking out from under a drawn-down brim. Others featured her openmouthed signature selfie. Very few featured the other townsfolk.

"Who is that?" Wesley asked, pointing to Fernando. "I don't recall him."

"He wasn't one of Daddy's finds," Cleo said, studying Fernando. "He is a friend of a friend, that sort of thing. I think Dymphna knew him or knew of him. I'm not sure. I wasn't paying much attention. He was a pastry chef in a little tearoom in Venice."

"The Rollicking Bun?"

"I have no idea," Cleo said, peering over her glasses at Wesley. "Do you know it?"

"When we lived in Marina Del Rey, I think my second wife used to go there."

"Fascinating. Anyway, he took over the café. He's planning on selling barbecue from the look of things."

"But"—Wesley furrowed his brow—"if he has the café, what are you going to do?"

"I'm going to take the café back, of course," Cleo said, pulling off her glasses and giving him a withering glare. "I'm a classically trained French chef, Wesley. Everyone will want me back."

"The man is making barbecue, Cleo. In Texas."

"Don't worry, Wesley. I have big plans."

She was debating telling him the exciting news that she and Powderkeg were going to get back together, when she noticed Wesley staring at the screen.

"Who is this?" he asked.

Cleo put her glasses back on. She focused on the picture at which Wesley was pointing. The picture showed Polly in front of the Covered Volkswagen, mouth open with green gum wadded in her cheek. In the background was a white-haired man in a T-shirt, Hawaiian shorts, and hiking boots. He had his glasses off and was wiping them on his shirt.

"That's Pappy," Cleo said. "I must have mentioned him."

"You did," Wesley said thoughtfully. "That just . . . isn't the way I pictured him."

"That's him. For good or for ill."

"Are you going to post something about heading back?"

"No." Cleo shook her head. "Elwood already talked to Dymphna— and I don't believe in posting. I just lurk."

"Ah," Wesley said, enlarging the Fat Chance photos with his fingers.

"You have to wish me well, Wesley. I demand you wish me well."

"I do, darling," Wesley said distractedly, as he studied the pictures from Fat Chance.

* * *

Old Bertha looked at herself in the wavy glass of the antique mirror that hung in the Creakside Inn's tiny kitchen. Polly sat sleepy-eyed at the table, a cup of steaming coffee in her hands. Polly sniffed the air.

"Are you wearing . . . perfume?" Polly said, blinking at Old Bertha.

"No, of course not," Old Bertha said, flushing. "Just a touch of toilet water."

"Yikes. Whoever named that should have to go back to Marketing 101."

"It's a perfectly respectable fragrance," Old Bertha said.

"It's really nice," Polly said. "I'm just wondering why you're wearing it."

"Can't a woman wear toilet water without getting the third degree?"

"In Fat Chance? That would be no."

"If you must know, I have some business with Pappy," Old Bertha said.

"Pappy?" Polly asked, now wide-awake. "*Our* Pappy?"

"Do we know another Pappy?"

"Suit yourself." Polly shrugged and went back to her coffee.

"All right, if you must know," Old Bertha said. Polly smiled behind her coffee cup. Feigning noninterest was the best way to get a response from Old Bertha. "I've been thinking about this Meriwether McMurphy."

"Who? Oh! You mean the old widow who hates Pappy? What? Are you guys in a 'who hates Pappy more' contest?"

"That just shows you what you know, junior miss. She showed up in Spoonerville—when Pappy was there—as soon as she could get a ride. You think that was just a coincidence?"

"Um, yeah."

"And they say you kids are wise in the ways of the world."

"I have no idea what you're talking about."

"Meriwether McMurphy made sure she was at the store when Pappy got there," Old Bertha said. "She's a widow now and is trying to lure him back."

"May I point out two things?" Not waiting for an answer, Polly continued. "One: You weren't even at the store when all of this happened; and two: From *all* accounts, she completely shut him down."

"One: I didn't have to be at the store to know what I know," Old Bertha said heatedly. "And two: from *all* accounts? 'All' being Fernando and Powderkeg? They're *men*. You going to listen to them? They wouldn't know a scheming woman if she came up and bit 'em."

"I can't believe what I'm hearing."

"It's true. Meriwether McMurphy is playing hard to get, mark my words."

"You have a crush on Pappy!" Polly crowed.

"I do not. I just don't want to see him fall into the wrong hands."

Polly watched in stunned silence as Old Bertha left the inn.

"I've been looking for you," Old Bertha said as she stormed into City Hall, where Pappy was sweeping. "I think Elvis has a Napoléon complex."

"No, he doesn't," Pappy said.

"He does. He won't behave. He does whatever gets into his head. He comes in when he wants, he goes out when he wants, eats when he wants."

"He's just stubborn. He's a mule," Pappy said. "You know the old saying, 'stubborn as a mule'?"

"No. The expression is 'stubborn as an ox.'"

"That's a different expression," Pappy said. "A mule is intelligent and has a mind of its own. He thinks things through and decides on his own course of action. An ox is dim-witted and needs prodding just to get going."

"So what?"

"So be happy I didn't buy you an ox."

Old Bertha pulled her cardigan over her bosom and started pacing. "Maybe's he's lonely," she said. "I've heard mules are social animals."

"That's true," Pappy said, still sweeping. "If Elvis is lonely—or if he's getting to be too much for you—I'll take him back and he can hang out with Jerry Lee."

"How would Jerry Lee feel about that?"

"Probably wouldn't pay the little guy no mind." Pappy shrugged. "Jerry Lee is used to having me as his friend. But if it would be good for Elvis, we'd be happy to have him."

"I don't know," Old Bertha said. "I was thinking more along the lines of . . ."

Pappy waited. He stopped and looked at her, leaning on his broom. "What?"

"I was thinking about getting another mule."

"You were?" Pappy said, surprise creeping into his voice.

"I think maybe Elvis should have a companion at the inn. I thought maybe you could help me with that."

"I could," Pappy said. "Let me see what I can do."

"I don't expect charity, you understand. I can pay for my own miniature mule."

"Understood."

"Good," Old Bertha said. "So how much is one?"

Professor Johnson had planned very carefully what to pack for his road trip to Fat Chance. One of the reasons he'd selected the Outback was that, by his calculations, it would hold everything he intended to bring to Texas.

He had not counted on his aunt coming with him.

Hence, the U-Haul trailer.

"How are we going to unload all of this, Auntie?" Professor Johnson tried to reason with Cleo. "You know we can't get the car—let alone the U-Haul—down the trail."

"True," Cleo said, absently chewing on her acrylic thumbnail. "Do you think I have time to send a road?"

"No, Auntie," Professor Johnson said. "And I don't think you should go back to Fat Chance and start throwing your money around. You need to act like everyone else."

"But I'm not like everyone else," she protested.

"I am aware of that. But our friends have their pride. In the six months we've been gone, not one of them has asked you for a dime. They are trying to make it work, just like Grandfather hoped."

"You're probably right. I'll behave, I promise."

"We're still going to have to figure out how to return the U-Haul—the closest one to Fat Chance is three hours away."

"The U-Haul is on my credit card. Wesley can handle it."

"What can Wesley do?"

"Don't be naïve, Elwood. He can buy it if he has to."

Professor Johnson let out a sigh. "Are you ready to go?"

"Oh!" she said suddenly. "One more thing. It won't take up any room."

Cleo ran into her father's office, removed the painting of Napoléon, and opened the safe. She pulled out the tiny box with her engagement and wedding rings and dropped it in her Palladino crocodile handbag. She had hesitated about bringing the bag, worried that Dymphna and Titan might not approve of the reptile skin, but decided they wouldn't know real crocodile if they saw it, so she was probably safe. Besides, this would probably be the last expensive handbag she would ever buy. After all, her soon-to-be-reunited-ex-husband made glorious purses.

By the time Cleo had returned to the driveway, Jeffries and Cook were standing beside the car. Cook hugged Professor Johnson. Jeffries shook his hand warmly, and then embraced him. Cleo wondered if they would give her the same fond farewell.

They didn't.

CHAPTER 24

The big day was just around the corner. Fernando had closed the café to the townsfolk as he transformed the interior. Now that the weather had warmed, he served breakfast on the boardwalk. The floors of the café were sanded and stained, the tables and chair legs leveled and the walls whitewashed. Polly had made red and white checked tablecloths and Fernando had ordered a mountain of wax paper and paper towels. Each table had a caddy that would hold three of his hand-labeled barbecue sauces.

Fernando had also taken the liberty of shining up the Boozehound Saloon, scooting Professor Johnson's display cases—the professor's sorry attempt at turning the saloon into a museum—into an unobtrusive corner. The bar gleamed, the copper railings polished, the player piano humming. Fernando also added some more tables to the saloon. He experienced a twinge of guilt that he hadn't run any of this by the illustrious Professor Johnson, but Fernando's motto had always been 'ask forgiveness, not permission,' and he saw no reason to change now.

Most of the townsfolk loved trying out Fernando's barbecued meats, and all of them loved the side dishes and desserts, although Polly worried that her jeans wouldn't fit by the time the town was overrun with ravenous cowboys, and she'd have to wear her fat pants.

Everyone also enjoyed eating on the boardwalk.

"We should always do this," Titan said.

"When the weather's nice," Old Bertha said.

"Duh," Polly whispered to Dymphna.

"Maybe I could add a patio out back, overlooking the creek," Fernando said. "I mean, when people start flocking to Cowboy Food, we can't be taking up the boardwalk with tables."

Fernando's hope of anything but chickens flocking to Fat Chance was always met with polite silence. It had been less than a year ago when they'd all dreamed of a new, energized town. They'd planned a parade to celebrate a new era, but thanks to Dodge Durham, it had been an embarrassing waste of time. No one left in Fat Chance had given up exactly, but they viewed their town with more realistic eyes than the newcomer.

"How many people are you expecting?" Powderkeg asked cautiously.

"The first day?" Fernando asked. "Maybe fifty."

The veteran townsfolk exchanged glances. This was a more sensible estimate than the hundreds they'd hoped would show up to their Fandango-Up in Fat Chance event a year ago. Given the fact that no one except Dodge Durham, Tino, and Mikie had so much as stepped foot in the town the entire time they'd been here, even five guests might be wishful thinking, let alone fifty. But Fernando's zeal would make a believer out of even the most cynical person.

Fernando served eggs and stewed chicken for breakfast, keeping the chicken at the opposite end of the table from Dymphna and Titan. He announced that he needed a slogan for Cowboy Food.

"What about 'Rustle up to the bar and fill your feed bag with Cowboy Food,'" offered Old Bertha.

"That is the worst visual ever," Fernando said. "Not to mention unwieldy."

"How about 'Need feed? Cowboy Food served here,'" Polly ventured.

"Better," Fernando said. "But the whole 'feed' thing is . . ." His voice trailed off.

"Inelegant?" Titan offered.

"Inelegant?" Pappy snorted. "Fat Chance ain't exactly gay Paree."

"Well, I can dream, can't I?" Fernando said.

"'Cowboy Food—the best use of livestock,'" Powderkeg offered.

"I refuse to set one foot in your restaurant if you use that," Titan said.

"No worries," Fernando said. "I won't."

"'Cowboy Food—it'll ring your cowbell,'" Dymphna said quietly.

Everyone stopped eating and looked at her. Dymphna, never one to crave the spotlight, dipped her head and spread jam on a biscuit to escape the attention.

"Ladies and gentlemen," Fernando said, "I think we have a winner."

Everyone toasted Dymphna with their orange juice glasses. Dymphna's cheeks blushed pink in the morning sun.

"Now who will help me paint a banner?" Fernando asked.

The countdown to Fernando's grand opening weighed heavily on Titan. It signaled the end of his time in Fat Chance and his relationship—he never thought of his bond with Rocket as "ownership"—with the longhorn. He'd hoped for a miracle, but none, at least so far, had materialized. He had discussed his situation with his friend Maurice in Las Vegas, on the rare occasions when he could get his cell phone to work on Main Street. Maurice was of the opinion that Titan should just renege on the deal.

"Just give the cow back," Maurice had said. "And refuse to move to Utensil-town."

"He's a bull," Titan said, knowing that Maurice never paid complete attention. "And it's Spoonerville."

"Semantics, darling," Maurice said. "Or just pack it in. Come home."

But Titan thought, *I am home.*

Fancy was out when Titan returned from breakfast. He went out the rear door of the forge to spend some time with Rocket. Although the bull had forty acres at his disposal, he could usually be found in the general vicinity of the forge. Titan knew the longhorn was home too. He approached the bull, who shambled over, horns bobbing. Titan scratched Rocket behind the ears.

"What are we going to do, big guy?" Titan said.

Three days of traveling with his aunt had pushed Professor Johnson's patience to its outer limits. She demanded they stop at every outlet mall between San Bernardino and San Antonio. Cleo had bought so many pairs of cowboy boots they'd had to stop and buy a roof rack. She told him, over and over, about her first road tip to Fat Chance, when she'd insisted Jeffries drive her.

"I thought going to Fat Chance, Texas, was the end of the world," she said. "Literally and figuratively. And now look at me! Heading back there of my own free will."

Cleo never ceased to amaze herself.

With one day left until they arrived at the turnout above Fat Chance, Professor Johnson realized he hadn't mentioned to Dymphna that Cleo was coming with him. He'd pulled into a gas station to fill up the car and called, but wasn't surprised that he didn't reach her. Even though he knew the chances of Dymphna being anywhere near a cell phone when they hadn't prearranged a cyber rendezvous, he often called just to hear her voice on the outgoing message. His breath caught as he listened:

"Hi, this is Dymphna Pearl. I'm not on Main Street right now, but your call is very important to me. I'll try to get back to you just as soon as I can, but who knows when that will be. Have a nice day and remember that you are loved."

Professor Johnson knew that the message was meant for anyone who called Dymphna, but he took her "remember you are loved" very personally.

At the tone, Professor Johnson informed Dymphna that he would be arriving with his aunt in tow.

"I'll see you soon," he said, and then added before he hung up, "Just one more day."

Dymphna saw that she had a message from Professor Johnson. She wished the man had learned to text; phone calls were so sporadic. She could barely make out the message, but took it to mean he was still on track.

"Just one more week," Dymphna said to Polly as they walked down Main Street to the farm, Thud bouncing ahead of them. "He'll be here in one more week."

"Does that freak you out?" Polly asked.

"Why would it freak me out?"

"Because of the Tino thing."

"Oh, that," Dymphna said, looking straight ahead. "I guess."

"You *guess* you're a little freaked out? Most people know."

"I have some things to think about, obviously. But I haven't committed myself to either man . . ."

"*Committed* yourself?" yowled Polly. "What century do you live in?"

"You know what I mean," Dymphna said, cheeks flushing. "When the time comes, I'm sure the universe will send me the answer."

"You have a lot more faith in the universe than I do," Polly said.

"The truth is, I haven't had any kind of real communication with Professor Johnson in six months. As far as Tino goes, we just seem to blow hot and cold. And he's been gone for almost two weeks as well."

"I wish I had your problem. I guess we'll see what happens."

"What else can we do?"

The women had come to the path that led to Dymphna's farm.

"OK," Polly said. "I'll see you tomorrow at breakfast."

Dymphna shook her head. "Fernando said we're on our own for breakfast. He needs to get ready for the grand opening tomorrow afternoon."

The women turned to look down their deserted Main Street and the bright new banner stretched across it: Cowboy Food—It Will Ring Your Cowbell. Powderkeg had volunteered to help with the banner and much to his dismay, Fernando had insisted that he paint both sides of the banner with rustic lettering.

"You've got to see the banner coming *and* going," Fernando had said.

Dymphna headed up the hill, stopping once to watch Polly skip up the stairs to the Creakside Inn. Dymphna smiled, knowing what put that spring in Polly's step: the prospect of Fat Chance soon being overrun by hungry cowboys.

Pappy was less and less comfortable driving long distances in the Covered Volkswagen. But he'd found a deal on a miniature mule three hours from Fat Chance. The fact that the mule's name was Patsy seemed preordained. Who but Patsy could hold her own with Jerry Lee and Elvis?

He knew he was getting close to the Mighty Mule Ranch as he drove along a pasture full of the tiny animals, grazing on the sweet spring grass. He pulled onto the dusty road leading to the ranch, the potholes rattling what was left of the VW's suspension.

The rancher came out of the farmhouse and shook Pappy's hand. Colby Calhoun was a weathered wrangler in jeans and a faded Cabela's plaid shirt.

"So you're from Fat Chance," Colby said by way of greeting. "I hear you guys are having a grand opening of a barbecue joint any day now."

"Yep," Pappy said, surprised that the news had traveled this far from town. "Tomorrow afternoon. Yes, sir. It's going to be something special." While Pappy was not a native Texan, he had, over the years, grown fond of Southern colloquialisms. "I'll tell you what," he added.

"I guess you want to meet Patsy," Colby said, leading Pappy around the back of the barn. "There she is."

Pappy stared at the tiny animal, who looked up as the men arrived. "That's a mule?" he said. "She's not a llama?"

"Of course she's not a llama," Colby said, staring quizzically first at Patsy, then at Pappy. "Llamas have long necks and shaggy coats."

"I was kidding. It's just . . . I've never seen a white mule before."

"She's got some gray in there," Colby said defensively.

"I was just making an observation," Pappy said, wishing he hadn't. "She's a beauty. What's her temperament?"

"Mulish."

Pappy quickly concluded his deal with Colby and loaded Patsy into the back of the Covered Volkswagen.

"See you at the grand opening," Colby said, shaking Pappy's hand.

"You will," Pappy said.

Colby stuck his head in the back of the van. "You be good now, ya hear?" he said to Patsy. Then to Pappy, with a slight catch in his throat, he added, "She's a good girl. You're gonna love her."

Pappy nodded. He didn't really feel like explaining that Patsy wasn't for him, but for a woman who wouldn't give him the time of day unless it was to discuss mules.

As he headed back to Fat Chance, Pappy came across the cutoff that led to Meriwether's farm. He'd gone by that cutoff at least a hundred times over the years, without giving her a thought. He felt bad about that now. He had been a different man back then, when he'd first laid eyes on the Hill Country with Cutthroat Clarence almost thirty years ago. He made light of it with the men of Fat Chance, but he felt guilty when he thought of how he had virtually disappeared on Meriwether one day. He felt they were getting too close and he couldn't do that. Not then—and maybe not ever. He shook his head; the plans he and Cutthroat had had! Cutthroat, who had an excellent track record and the Midas touch, was sure there was an underground hot spring in the area around Fat Chance. His idea was to open a spa, the first in a line of first-class spas. But the earth had not cooperated. The hot springs were all nestled around Dripping Springs—so near, yet so far. Cutthroat was accustomed to bending men to his will, but he hadn't counted on Mother Nature. He'd washed his hands of the area, but something about the place had worked its way into Pappy's soul.

Pappy was brought back to the present by Patsy's nickering in the back. If he hadn't had the mule in the back of the VW, he might have turned down that road to Meriwether's. As he drove toward home, it occurred to him that in the past he'd ignored Meriwether and now he lavished attention on Old Bertha. He didn't seem to know the right way to go about either situation. He'd learned a lot of lessons over the years. But he still didn't know anything about women.

"Knock it off, Elvis," Powderkeg said, pushing the little mule away from his hat, which the mule seemed to think was a midmorning snack.

Powderkeg was putting the finishing touches on a tiny barn beside the Creakside Inn. The barn was big enough for Elvis and his soon-to-be-delivered companion. Old Bertha came out to inspect his handiwork, the back door of the inn creaking in protest as she pushed through.

"Looks good," she said.

"Yeah," Powderkeg said, lifting his hat and wiping the sweat away with his arm. "I tried to make it lean to the left like the rest of the town, but our gravity-defying architecture is beyond me."

"Well, give it time," Old Bertha said.

"I made an overhang for shade." Powderkeg pointed to a porch-like structure attached to the barn. "You want me to get some of Pappy's grapes and plant them so they trail over? That'd be mighty pretty."

"Aren't you just the poetic soul. Must be love talking."

"Might be," Powderkeg said, then, changing the subject quickly, "You want grapes or not?"

"No, I don't want grapes. That's all I need, two mules getting stung by bees night and day."

"They won't get stung. Pappy says the bees get drunk and just hang out. They don't bother anybody."

"Since when do we listen to Pappy?"

"Since always," Powderkeg said. "I know he seems a little nuts, but I can't imagine what life would have been like if he hadn't been here. He really showed us the ropes. I just don't understand what you have against the man, Bertha."

"He's just so full of himself," she said heatedly. "Buys me a mule, so I have no choice but to buy another one. I had to spend days with him trying to figure everything out. The old fool."

"Sounds like that must be love talking," Powderkeg teased.

"Sounds like you need to get back to work." Old Bertha turned on her heels, starting heavily up the stairs. "Sounds like it might be love talking," she muttered, shaking her head. But then she thought:

It just might be.

PART THREE

CHAPTER 25

The doors were set to open in twenty minutes. As Fernando predicted, there was already a line of cowboys, ranch hands, and folks he recognized from Spoonerville and Dripping Springs. There were also people he'd never seen before, coming down the trail and up from the creek. It was a miracle how many people had found their way to Fat Chance. He saw Dodge Durham from Spoonerville, scowling. Glenannie, the Dripping Springs patron of the arts, stepped daintily down the road. He hoped he got a chance to talk to her about how Titan's crafts were doing in Sedona, but he knew the answer already. Even if she'd lost money, she'd say they had broken even at three thousand dollars. That Glenannie was a good woman.

Polly burst through the door of the café, carrying something red and ruffled. She closed the door behind her. "Have you seen the line outside?"

"I have," Fernando said. "I've already picked out my cowboy."

Polly peeked out window. "Which one?"

"I don't have time for this right now," Fernando said as he set dual lemonade-limeade jars with spigots on a shelf built by Powderkeg. "But he's the one in the really big black hat."

Polly looked out the window. Half the men were wearing really big black hats. "Very funny."

"I just realized something." Fernando stopped in his tracks.

"What?"

"My boots don't hurt anymore," he said, holding up one boot and then the other as if surprised to find them on his feet.

"Welcome to Fat Chance, Texas. You've broken in your first pair of boots. You're a real cowboy now."

"I really need to focus here, Polly."

"You nervous?"

"I know I have enough food for at least fifty people. I'm just not sure I can handle all this by myself."

"I was thinking that myself. I can help! I even made an apron." Polly unfurled her ruffled red apron.

"Tips only?"

"Tips only!"

"And you'll help clean up?"

"I'll help clean up," Polly said. "And I'll ask my new boyfriend to help too."

"Deal," Fernando said.

Polly and Fernando continued to get the Cowboy Food café ready for business as the smell of barbecue smoke traveled on the breeze.

Pappy was proud of himself for finding Jerry Lee's fedora. Last year, Polly had made hats for the mule and Thud for the first (and so far last) Fandango-Up in Fat Chance festival. When the whole thing went sour, with Dodge almost taking over Fat Chance, Thud getting bitten by the rattler, and everyone's high spirits crashing into the earth, Pappy's first inclination was to throw the hat in the trash. Jerry Lee didn't have much use for a fedora and Pappy wasn't one to keep mementos of the past. But these newcomers to Fat Chance had opened his eyes—to possibilities, to life. He saw how sweet Dymphna Pearl got a little farm to call her own; how Polly smashed down the emotional walls she'd been building and hiding behind since she was a child; how Powderkeg, who never took *anything* seriously, renewed his passion for his craft—and for his ex-wife; how Cleo found a surprising part of herself here, but ran from it; Professor Johnson, who took *everything* seriously, found love, even if he had to put that love on hold; Titan, whom Pappy had learned to love like a son, had come to town and given dignity to an old buzzard and sanctuary to a runaway bull, at possible—almost definite—peril to his own well-being. Pappy wanted to remember them.

And of course, there was Old Bertha. He wasn't sure what it was about the woman that tugged at his heart. She was about the most hostile person he'd ever met. Of course, people said that about him too. But she was a survivor and he admired that about her. She was driving him crazy with her mule questions, but he chalked that up to "be careful what you wish for."

Pappy decided that even if he added flowers to the hatband, the fedora would be too masculine for the dainty Patsy. Pappy was much more sentimental than he let on. He had kept not only Jerry Lee's hat but also a few others Polly had made. Polly, along with the other townsfolk, had been so dispirited after their festival failure that the girl just threw them all away. Pappy couldn't stand to see all her hard work go to waste. So he kept them. Besides, you never knew when a costume party might spring up in a ghost town.

He checked to see what else he might have. There was a miniature straw boater that one of the rented mules had sported at the Fandango. Pappy carried the boater to the creek that ran behind the buildings. Spring wildflowers graced the banks of the stream. He thought he'd stick a few in the hatband before he attempted to convince Patsy to wear it. He wondered if this was a good day to present Patsy to Old Bertha. The looming grand opening of Cowboy Food had everyone busy and buzzing. But he'd been hiding the mule for an entire day, and keeping a secret in Fat Chance was almost impossible. He grabbed a fistful of flowers and shoved them in the headband of the tiny hat.

"Check this out, little girl," Pappy said as he showed the hat to Patsy, who peered over the fence at him.

The mule let out a sound that was not a donkey's bray or a horse's nicker. It sounded more like a deep belly laugh. After somehow avoiding detection on his six-hour round trip to buy the mule and getting her down the trail unseen, were all his plans about to unravel? He looked around. His secret appeared safe.

Patsy reached for the hat with her lips, ready to eat the flowers if not the whole hat. Pappy pulled the hat away from her and scratched her ears.

"Not right now," he said. "If you're a good mule and stay quiet for just a little while longer, you can eat the flowers." He looked around again, this time to make sure no one could hear him talking gibberish to a mule. Titan or Dymphna conversing with their animals was one thing. Pappy another.

Pappy wondered if he should take Patsy inside, to keep her hidden— she was small enough—but thought the racket of her tiny hooves on the wood floors would be more of a giveaway than trying to keep her quiet in the privacy of his backyard.

He headed back inside, stopping to look at the grapevines that climbed the arbor. The leaves were bright and abundant. Small clusters of green berries were starting to appear—the arbor would be full of grapes when the hot weather arrived. Pappy always enjoyed sitting in the shade of the arbor, breathing in the wine-scented breeze. With Fernando in town making brandy, maybe Pappy would finally make a bottle of wine or two.

From her porch swing at the Creakside Inn, Old Bertha could see all of Main Street. She marveled at the number of people coming to town. She glimpsed friends like Mikie and enemies like Dodge Durham. She looked around for Titan, but saw that the forge's front door was shuttered.

I guess poor Titan saw Dodge Durham too.

Old Bertha saw Tino weaving his way through the crowd, toward the trail that led to Dymphna's farm.

Where has he been lately? I haven't seen him in town.

She waved as Tino doffed his baseball cap. She noticed he didn't put his hat back on, but ran his fingers through his hair as he climbed the hill.

He wants to make a good impression.

Old Bertha went back to people watching, the porch swing creaking lazily beneath her weight. Suddenly, she stopped swinging. She hoisted herself to her feet and looked into the crowd. She thought she saw . . .

She squinted, trying to follow the slight figure who maddeningly appeared and disappeared into the crowd. Could it be? It was.

Meriwether McMurphy was in Fat Chance.

From her farm Dymphna could see and hear Main Street filling up. She and Thud were ready to head down into the crowd, but her animals seemed skittish as loud bursts of laughter floated up from town. The chickens had all retreated to their coop. The goats bleated nervously and hopped in and out of the barn. Dymphna thought she should hang around a while to calm them. Thud stared longingly down the hill.

If ever a dog lived up to the term 'party animal,' it's Thud.

The only animal who seemed unaffected by all the commotion was Crash, who, in the last two days, had started flying—although "flying" might be an overstatement. He would flap his wings with wild abandon, race around the yard, fly a few feet and then, true to his name, crash back to earth. His frenzied leaps into the air looked somehow familiar. Dymphna worried that the duckling thought he was a chicken.

Thud, who had fallen asleep, suddenly clambered to his feet, tail wagging fast as a whip, sniffing the air but remaining quiet. Dymphna looked up—and into Tino's emerald-green eyes.

Some watchdog. I could have used some warning!

"Looks like I picked quite the day to make my grand entrance," Tino said, entering the barnyard and petting Thud, who had leapt up to place his front paws onto the veterinarian's shoulders. He turned his attention to the dog. "Hi, boy! You miss me?"

Dymphna was happy for the chance to gather her thoughts. "You're just in time for the barbecue," she said.

She wished she could think of something else to say. But everything that sprang to mind—Where have you been? What brought you back? How long are you staying? and What's going on with us?—seemed vaguely inappropriate, since she really didn't know this man well enough to demand answers. It was so frustrating. She didn't know Professor Johnson well enough to demand answers either. Of course, he wasn't showing up for another week, so maybe she'd have time to straighten out what was going on with Tino—if only in her own mind—before the professor arrived.

Tino put Thud's paws back on the ground. The sound of loud applause drifted up the hill. Tino and Dymphna turned and could just make out the sight of Fernando opening one of the smokers he'd placed on the dirt road, far enough from the dry-as-parchment boardwalk to keep the town safe.

"Looks like the barbecue thing is going to be a hit," Tino said.

"I guess." Dymphna hated every minute of this small talk, but wasn't sure what to do about it.

Suddenly Crash took flight, and this time the flight took.

Tino and Dymphna watched as Crash rose into the air and soared gracefully overhead. He disappeared over the hill in a flash. Dymphna waited, knowing she had to let the duckling be free if that's what he wanted, but hoping against hope that he'd return.

"Look at that," Tino said, smiling. "You saved him, Dymphna. He's flown away. Good for you!"

Dymphna felt like she was going to cry. She looked at Tino, who smiled up at the sky, searching for the duckling. She knew that he hadn't been around to bond with Crash as she had. But still she was amazed that he didn't appear to be struggling with his professional detachment in the least.

"I guess he got a better offer," Dymphna said, turning away from Tino so he wouldn't see the tears in her eyes. "He was such a sweet little . . ."

More noise from town cut their conversation short.

"Why are you still up here?" Tino said.

"The animals are nervous. I just thought I'd stay with them."

Tino put his arm around her and kissed the top of her head. "They'll be fine. And you feel down about Crash," he said gently. "Look, I know we've got a lot to talk about, but it looks like the party's getting started. Let's go down and have a good time."

As Professor Johnson navigated the highway the last few miles to Fat Chance, it occurred to him that he might not actually recognize the turnout if the Covered Volkswagen wasn't there. When he started noticing landmarks, he also saw that the two-lane highway was lined with trucks. He slammed on the brakes when he saw the Covered Volkswagen in the turnout, sandwiched between a Chevy Tahoe and a Dodge Ram.

"What in God's name is going on?" Cleo said as the two of them got out of the Outback. "Do you think it's a welcome-home party?"

"It might be." Professor Johnson gestured to all the vehicles. "Except we don't know this many people."

Professor Johnson worried that the U-Haul was sticking out into the road, but as he looked down the highway, he saw cars and trucks parked in a zigzag pattern all the way around the bend.

Cleo beamed, taking a huge breath. "It smells like someone is having a barbecue!"

"Oh! That's right," Professor Johnson said. "Remember? Dymphna's friend Fernando was planning on turning the café into a barbecue joint."

Cleo's smile faded. "Oh yes," she said, slinging her purse onto her shoulder and heading down the trail. "Well, we'll just see about that."

As they turned the curve that offered the first glimpse of town, Professor Johnson and Cleo stopped mid-step. They stared at each other. Their sleepy little ghost town was buzzing with a carnival atmosphere. It even sounded like a carnival, as the tinkling from the player piano floated up to them. They could see the smokers set up in the street by the shuttered forge.

"Have you heard anything about Titan leaving town?" Professor Johnson asked. "The forge looks all boarded up."

"No. Maybe the shop is just closed for the day. Titan must still be around. I think there's a giant cow or a bull or something behind it."

"It's a longhorn," Professor Johnson said. "It's the mascot of the University of Texas."

"Look who knows his football," Cleo said, surprised.

"I don't. I know my universities."

"Everything looks very . . ." Cleo hesitated, looking down the hill again.

"Different," Professor Johnson added dismally.

He realized how little he actually knew now about the everyday comings and goings of Fat Chance. Places changed. People changed. He felt much less confident than when he'd slammed the car door just a few minutes ago. A dust storm suddenly blew up in front of them. Cleo gasped as Professor Johnson was knocked to the ground. Even before the dust cleared, Cleo could see that Thud had managed to sniff out his owner, even above the scent of that ridiculous barbecue.

CHAPTER 26

Powderkeg and Mikie were making out in the carpentry shop.

Mikie giggled. "You're going to ruin my reputation," she teased.

"You have a reputation?" Powderkeg replied.

"Yes, as a no-nonsense woman who loves barbecue so much that nothing and nobody will stand in her way."

"Then you're right," Powderkeg said between kisses. "I'm shooting your reputation all to hell."

"I thought you were one of the town ambassadors." Mikie pushed him gently away. "Won't you be missed?"

Powderkeg looked out the large plate glass window that fronted Main Street. He looked at the crowd, eating, drinking, laughing. "Everyone seems to be getting along just fine without me."

He reached for her and she took a step back. He looked at her in confusion as she walked over to a sawhorse, dusted it off, and sat down.

"Look, I know we've just been goofing around here," she said, blushing.

It was clear she had rehearsed this line to say to him—and even clearer that she was no actress. Her delivery was stilted and self-conscious. This was not territory she was used to treading.

Powderkeg frowned. He had no idea where this was going. "I'm not sure what you're getting at." He leaned against a tool cabinet.

"I just . . ." Mikie averted her eyes. "Look, Powderkeg, you know I kid around with the guys on the ranch. I've figured out how to be one of the boys."

"Not with me."

"Exactly. I've let my guard down with you. And . . . well . . . I know this is all fun and games, but . . ."

"Hold on. I'm a little confused. Are you saying this is all fun and games for you or are you asking me if this is all fun and games for me?"

"It's very hard to be a woman pilot on a ranch," Mikie said, switching gears. "Even in the twenty-first century, I can't be whoring around."

Powderkeg felt as if someone had thrown cold water on him. "Is that what you're doing?"

"You tell me."

He looked at her. She hadn't moved an inch since she sat on the sawhorse. She stared back at him with pleading eyes. He realized she was looking at him with apprehension—and with love.

He looked right back at her.

He was in love with her too.

She stood up and walked over to him. She stroked his face. "From the look on your face, I guess I'm not just whoring around."

They kissed.

"I'll take you out for some barbecue now, if you want," Powderkeg said, nuzzling her neck.

"In a few minutes," Mikie whispered. "I kind of like the smokin' atmosphere in here."

Pappy's enormous plate threatened to topple as he looked for a place to sit. Heaping portions of hot links, baked beans, and macaroni and cheese vied for space with stewed tomatoes that Fernando had made from Dymphna's stocked bounty. Seeing no tables available, Pappy sat on the edge of the boardwalk in front of the Boozehound Saloon. A shadow passed over him. He looked up to see Polly smiling down on him, a pitcher of lemonade in one hand, a glass in the other.

"Want some lemonade, Pappy?" Polly beamed.

Without waiting for an answer, she poured a glass. She sat on the edge of the boardwalk as she handed it to him. They surveyed the crowd together.

"This is awesome, isn't it?" Polly said. "Fernando is amazing."

Pappy nodded, his mouth too full to answer.

Two cowboys walked by on Main Street, tipping their cowboy hats to Polly. She smiled at them as they passed.

"Seriously, Pappy, I haven't seen this many men since I used to go to the firemen's parade with my dad." She watched men lining up for more brisket at one of the smokers. "Here comes another hottie."

Pappy looked up and almost choked as he saw the young man walking toward them. It was Hank, Meriwether McMurphy's new helper, and he wasn't alone.

"Crap," he said under his breath.

Meriwether had seen him. Pappy put his plate down and wiped off his hands on his Hawaiian shorts.

"Meriwether," he said. "Glad you could join us."

"It wasn't my idea," Meriwether groused. "It was Hank's."

"Now I wouldn't say . . ." Hank started, but Meriwether silenced him with a look.

Polly stared at the older woman and wondered, was it possible that Old Bertha was right? Was Meriwether playing hard to get?

"Hi," Polly said, more to Hank than to Meriwether. "I'm Polly. Welcome to Fat Chance."

Fernando's voice cut into the conversation. "Polly, I need you to turn the links," he called.

Polly turned to see Fernando going into the Cowboy Food café. He pointed at the smoker that held the links. The top was down.

"There's no way I can get that lid open by myself, Fernando," she called.

"Then get somebody to help you," he yelled back.

Polly caught Fernando's eye—he winked at her.

Fernando is the best!

"I'd be happy to help you, ma'am," Hank said shyly. Turning to Meriwether, he added, "If that's all right with you, Ms. McMurphy."

"Help me up onto the boardwalk," Meriwether said, "and then you can go ahead."

Hank lifted a surprised Meriwether up by her underarms and set her on the boardwalk, sitting, like a doll, next to Pappy. Hank looked at Polly. She jerked her head, indicating he should follow her. Pappy and Meriwether watched them disappear into the crowd.

Titan wasn't sure how to comfort Fancy, who was clearly upset by all the noise outside the forge. She stalked the floor, climbed up and down her tree, and hid in the recesses of the smithy. Titan wished he could calm her, but even if he could make her understand that all of the people outside would eventually be going away, he'd have to let her know that *he'd* be going away too. The thought of living on the Rolling Fork Ranch was tough enough without thinking about losing Fancy too. But he knew he couldn't safely take the buzzard out of Fat Chance. A working ranch was no place for a wounded animal. He looked out back and saw Rocket. The longhorn was more used to people than Fancy was and just slurped contentedly from the trough.

"I'm sorry I failed you," Titan said, although the bull didn't look up. "I'm going to have to give you back to Dodge. But I promise I'll visit you every day."

He gazed at Fancy, who limped into a darkened corner as a loud laugh from outside their sanctuary startled her. He wished he could make her the same promise. But he knew he wouldn't be able to get back to Fat Chance every day. Pappy would take good care of Fancy, but it wouldn't be the same.

Old Bertha watched as Pappy took Meriwether's hand and helped her hop down from the boardwalk onto Main Street. They were laughing as Pappy steadied her. He left his plate on the side of the board-walk.

Litterer!

Old Bertha kept her distance. While she couldn't actually hear what they were saying, she'd observed their conversation turn from awkward to friendly in a matter of minutes. How could thirty years of bad feelings disappear in the blink of an eye?

Don't these people know how to hold a grudge?

"Hey, Bertha," Polly said, suddenly at her side. "I want you to meet Hank."

Old Bertha lost sight of Pappy and Meriwether as she was introduced to the young man.

"You work for Meriwether McMurphy, is that right?" Old Bertha said.

"Yes, ma'am." Hank cocked his head to one side as he looked at her. "How did you know that?"

"Oh, you know these small towns," Old Bertha said. "Word gets around."

Polly smirked at Old Bertha. The old woman could tell that Polly wasn't buying a word of it. Polly must have seen her spying on Pappy from the beginning. She gave Polly a withering stare, but Polly was enjoying herself too much to be intimidated.

"I better get back to work," Polly said.

"Anything else I can help with?" Hank asked Polly.

"I bet I can find something for you to do. Maybe help me with the dishes?"

Old Bertha could swear the girl was batting her eyelashes. She thought about the glowering Goth Polly had been when she first got to town. When had everybody turned so *happy*?

Hank smiled as if he'd been granted an audience with a super-model instead of an invitation to do manual labor, and followed Polly into the café.

Old Bertha scanned the crowd.

Pappy and Meriwether were gone.

Fernando sent Hank down to the creek to pick up more lemonade, which he'd had the foresight to store in the icy water. Fernando and Polly stood in the doorway, watching him.

Hank waded into the creek, lightly stepping over rocks to keep his jeans and boots dry.

"Good balance," Polly said.

Hank bent over and plunked his hands into the water.

"More importantly," Fernando said, "nice ass."

Hank retrieved a large sealed jar of lemonade from the creek. He stood up and waved it over his head in triumph. Polly and Fernando waved back at him, Polly adding a thumbs-up.

"He's cute as a bug," Fernando said as they watched Hank amble back up to Cowboy Food.

"I know! Is it too soon to tell if he's 'the one'?"

"Oh, honey, who cares?" Fernando said. "Just settle for 'he's one of the ones.'"

"I like your thinking." Polly kissed Fernando on the cheek.

"We've been here twenty minutes and haven't seen anyone we know," Cleo said to Professor Johnson as they wandered through the crowd. "How is that even possible?"

Professor Johnson shook his head. He was about to answer, but realized his aunt was asking a rhetorical question. He'd fallen for that more than once in his life. Suddenly, Dodge Durham was standing in front of them, eating a chicken leg.

"Look who's back," Dodge said, a speck of barbecue sauce on his cheek, muting his naturally threatening presence. Thud growled low in his chest. Professor Johnson put his hand on the dog, although he didn't actually mind the bloodhound snarling at this man.

"If you've come to talk about Rocket," said Dodge, "you can save your breath. Every single one of you has stuck your nose where it don't belong, and I'm sick of all of you."

"I'm sure the feeling is mutual," Cleo said with a sweet smile.

Dodge looked at her, not sure he'd heard correctly.

"In any case, it's nice to see you supporting an event in Fat Chance, Dodge," Cleo said, sounding for all the world like a Beverly Hills matron.

"Yeah, right." Dodge licked his fingers. "I got business here, but no use letting good barbecue go to waste."

Dodge walked on, Professor Johnson and Cleo looking after him.

"What business could he have in Fat Chance?" Cleo said.

"I don't know." Professor Johnson fingered Thud's snakeskin collar. "And who is Rocket?"

Professor Johnson patted Thud, who continued to knock into him, constantly looking up to make sure Professor Johnson was still there.

At least somebody was glad to see him.

Dymphna felt guilty sitting in Professor Johnson's domain with another man, even if they were only eating rice and beans. She looked at the museum display cases shoved out of the way, cases Professor Johnson had tried so hard to fill with historic memorabilia.

It's not too late. When he gets here next week, he'll be able to start again.

Will we *be able to start again?*

"Where's Thud?" Dymphna asked Tino.

"He's around," Tino said. "I saw him a few minutes ago."

Dymphna wasn't really worried about the bloodhound. Thud was a responsible dog. He'd go visit the other shopkeepers or splash in the creek for an hour or so, but always returned to her.

Unlike Crash.

Dymphna thought about the duckling and her throat tightened.

Tino put his hand over hers. "I know you're thinking about Crash," he said. "It's only natural to be sad, but it's just in some creatures' nature to go, and some to stay."

"I know," Dymphna said. "I *do* know. It doesn't make it easier, that's all. Crash was a really great duck."

"He still is a really great duck. Just . . . you know . . ."

"Not here," Dymphna said. "Let's change the subject."

"Great idea." Tino put down his fork and leaned closer to her. "I have something I need to talk to you about."

"OK."

"Not here. Can we go back to the farm?"

"I don't know if we should. That doesn't sound very supportive, to just leave in the middle of Fernando's grand opening."

"Look around. There's a line waiting for our table. And we can always come back. It's just so noisy in here, I can't think straight."

He traced his finger over her forearm, sending shivers up her body.

Speaking of not thinking straight . . .

As they headed up the hill, Dymphna cast a sweeping glance around the town for Thud. She thought she saw a quick flick of his tail, but wasn't sure.

CHAPTER 27

Old Bertha had looked up and down Main Street for the last half hour with no sign of Pappy or Meriwether. She turned to make another loop, when she ran right into Hank.

"Whoa, sorry, ma'am," he said, steadying her. "You all right?"

"Of course I'm all right," Old Bertha snapped. "I was just looking for . . . your boss, that's all."

"I just saw her." Hank smiled.

"Oh? Where was that?" Old Bertha asked casually. She had to admit, those dimples were damned cute.

"I was down by the creek, picking up some lemonade for Polly," he said.

"That's so interesting." Old Bertha tried to control her temper—and her sarcasm. "I mean, where did you see them . . . her?"

"Oh!" Hank said. "They were behind the buildings . . . on some sort of patio."

Old Bertha knew immediately that they were behind Pappy's place. Maybe she'd head over there and surprise them. She could catch them red-handed. But what excuse could she use for going? Her thoughts were interrupted by Hank.

"Excuse me, ma'am. I was wondering . . ."

Old Bertha waited. Hank didn't say anything.

"Speak up," she said.

"I was wondering . . . Do you think Polly might go out with me if I asked? I mean, I'm sure every guy for miles around asks you this, but . . . well, I sure do like her."

Old Bertha stared at the boy. Had he just arrived from Mayberry? Who talked like that?

"I'll tell you what I'll do," she said, forgetting about her own quest for a moment. "I'll put in a good word for you. That might shoot you to the top of her list."

"I bet it would. Polly thinks you're the greatest! Well, I better get back to Cowboy Food. Polly and Fernando are letting me help clean up."

"Lucky boy."

"I'm going to see if Marshall . . . Powderkeg . . . is in the shop," Cleo said to Professor Johnson as they climbed the stairs to the boardwalk. Powderkeg's carpentry and leatherwork shop was the first building on the boardwalk.

"OK," he said, "I'll just follow Thud around. I'm sure he'll lead me to Dymphna." He stared down at the dog, who was drooling on his shoes and looking at him adoringly. "Eventually," he added.

Cleo grabbed Professor Johnson's arm suddenly. He looked at her. She put her other hand to her heart.

"I'm suddenly very nervous," she said. "I mean, I did sort of desert him . . . again."

Professor Johnson touched the hand that was clutching his sleeve. This was alien territory for the Johnsons. They were not a touchy-feely family.

"You just have to put yourself out there," he said. "Whatever happens, it is what it is."

"No need to sink to platitudes." Cleo removed his hand, then softened. "Thank you, Elwood. I'll do what I can. What will be, will be."

Now who's sinking to platitudes? he thought.

Cleo watched her nephew drift down the boardwalk, looking for a familiar face. When she lost sight of him, she reached into her bag and felt for the ring box. She wrapped her hand around it to give her the courage to walk in the door. She hesitated, got out the ring box, and put the tiny engagement ring on her finger. Taking a deep breath, she grabbed the doorknob and pulled.

There was so much noise on the boardwalk and Main Street that no one heard Mikie's shriek when she saw a middle-aged woman enter the store and catch her with her blouse open and her legs around Powderkeg, who sat on a tall toolbox. As soon as Cleo's eyes adjusted to the light, she added her own scream. Luckily, in the few seconds it took for her eyes to adapt to the murky interior of the shop, Mikie had buttoned her shirt and leapt to the floor. Powderkeg also managed to stand, but Cleo caught him mid-buckle.

"The shop is closed," Mikie said, scooping her bra off the floor and stuffing it in her back pocket. "Didn't you see the sign?"

"Who in God's name are you?" Cleo said.

"Who in God's name is asking?" Mikie said, swiveling her head as if she had ball bearings in her neck, all fluster banished.

"Ladies, ladies," Powderkeg said, stepping between them. "Let me introduce you. Lacey Carmichael, this is Cleo . . ."

"Your ex?" Mikie said, eyes widening.

"Yes," Powderkeg said. "You'll have to forgive me, Cleo. I didn't know you were coming back to town."

"There's nothing to forgive, Marshall," she said, looking Mikie up and down dismissively. She wore her best "this too shall pass" expression.

"Marshall?" Mikie asked, turning to Powderkeg.

Apparently he hasn't told her everything.

"Cleo, this is Lacey Carmichael," he said. "My . . ."

The two women turned to look at him. A lot was riding on his introduction.

"Your what?" Cleo demanded.

"My . . ." Powderkeg looked miserable. "My friend."

Cleo turned to watch Lacey Carmichael's big eyes fill with tears before she turned and stormed out the door. Powderkeg followed after her.

"Mikie! Mikie!" he said to the back of the door as it slammed in his face.

He turned to Cleo, shaking his head.

"*Mikie?*" she asked, raising an eyebrow. "Really?"

He glared at her. He was clearly not in the mood for arched eyebrows and sarcasm. "What the hell are you doing here?" he asked heatedly.

"I thought I'd surprise you," she said softly.

"Congratulations," he said, running his fingers through his hair. "You're a howling success."

"Is she . . ." Cleo steeled herself to continue. "Is she really just a friend?"

The noise from outside the walls faded away. There was nothing but silence between them.

"No," Powderkeg said finally. "I . . . it's all new. I don't know how she feels and I didn't want to scare her off."

She stood in front of Powderkeg, who was looking out the window. She tried to remain calm. He said this thing was new. She could fight this. She could win him back. She touched his cheek and drew his face down to look at her. The storm she saw in his eyes took her breath away.

She was too late.

"You better go after her," she said, trying to hide her emotions.

"I might have blown it already," he said miserably.

"Go on, Marshall," she said. "She'll be fine. Just chalk it up to your first fight."

"Are you going to be okay? What are you doing here? Why didn't you say you were coming?"

"I just decided to come with Elwood—to keep him company," she said airily. She saw Mikie storming toward the trailhead. "You better go. You don't want to ruin this."

"Cleo . . ."

"Go!" she said, forcing a smile.

Cleo could see the relief flood over him.

He bolted from the store. Cleo watched as he chased the long-legged woman to the edge of town. He spun her around. Cleo couldn't hear what they were saying, but within minutes, the woman was in Powderkeg's arms.

Cleo touched the window, the star sapphire of her engagement ring twinkling sadly in farewell.

Old Bertha rounded the corner to Pappy's back patio. No one was there. Laughter came from the little barn where Jerry lived. Old Bertha stepped as lightly as she could toward the voices.

When she reached the door, she stared at the sight in front of her. It was like a geriatric version of the Mad Hatter's tea party—Pappy and Meriwether, wearing hats from last year's Fandango-Up in Fat Chance. Jerry Lee wore his fedora from the Fandango as well. Pappy was pouring some of Fernando's peach brandy into two mason jars. He looked up and his smile faded.

"Bertha!" he said.

"Oh!" Meriwether said. "So this is Bertha!"

"Damn, it, Bertha," Pappy said, sounding annoyed. "What are you doing here?"

Old Bertha felt like a schoolgirl. A goofy schoolgirl running into the cool kids in a deserted hallway—albeit cool kids in stupid hats. Maybe it was more like running into the drama kids. She tried to steady her nerves.

What am *I doing here?* she wondered.

"I just . . ." Old Bertha could come up with no explanation that would leave her with any dignity, so she stopped explaining.

"I guess our secret is out," Meriwether said.

"Secret?" She didn't want to know their secret.

"I guess so," Pappy said. "You know that Meriwether and I had some bad blood between us. Well, we've talked it out and that's over."

"Having young Hank around has taught me to live a little," Meriwether said, patting Pappy's arm. "I've just decided I'm too old to keep embracing all that negative energy."

Negative energy? Where does she think she is? Taos?

"I asked Meriwether to come back here to help me with something," Pappy said.

Meriwether fell for that old line? At her age?

Pappy walked to the barn, leaving Meriwether and Old Bertha staring at each other. He returned with a delicate little white mule in a straw hat.

"Meriwether was helping me get everything just right," Pappy said. "Bertha, meet Patsy. Now I know you said you wanted to pay for her, but . . ." He looked right at Bertha, daring her to challenge him. "You would make me a very happy man to accept her . . ."

He faltered. Meriwether moved to his side. She seemed a little unsteady on her feet, possibly from the peach brandy. She rose up on her toes and whispered in Pappy's ear, "As a token of my esteem."

"As a token of my esteem," Pappy said formally.

Old Bertha could feel her eyes welling up. She pulled an old but ironed handkerchief from her sleeve and dabbed her eyes. She turned to Meriwether, who was smiling kindly at her. It occurred to Old Bertha that she might have a new friend as well as a new mule and— she snuck a quick peek at Pappy—a suitor too.

"Grab a hat," Pappy said. "I'll pour you some peach brandy."

* * *

Cleo felt as if she were wrapped in cotton. What was she going to do now? She looked for Professor Johnson but saw that he and Thud were heading up the hill to Dymphna's farm. She couldn't very well run after him. She glanced over at the shuttered forge. She'd assumed that Titan wasn't in Fat Chance. If he was, why wouldn't he be out in the streets with everyone else? But she thought she saw a slight movement from between the gaps in the walls. Avoiding the peril of spilled barbecue at every step, she made her way to the smithy and knocked. There was no answer. But this time she was sure she saw movement within. She knocked again.

"Titan," Cleo called. "Titan, it's Cleo! May I come in?"

The door opened. Cleo was shocked by Titan's appearance. He'd always seemed massive to Cleo, but now he looked diminished. She could see by the muscular chest and massive forearms that he hadn't actually changed size. It was his spirit that appeared to have shrunk. She threw her arms around him, not sure if she was comforting him or asking for comfort.

"What's going on, Titan?" she asked, forgetting her own disappointment for a moment.

Titan dusted off an old stool and offered it to her. She shivered to see Fancy a few feet from her on the wrought-iron perch, staring at Cleo with her one red eye. Cleo listened as Titan filled her in on the dismal deal he'd made with Dodge and how the day of reckoning was here.

"I think Rocket knows something's up," Titan said. "He hasn't been himself."

The back door of the forge was open. The enormous longhorn stood in the doorway. Cleo stared at him. Rocket was certainly not as ugly as Fancy, but Cleo couldn't imagine risking her entire life for the ungainly beast peering in at her.

"You must have known you'd never be able to raise that much money, honey," Cleo said.

"I just thought . . ." Titan turned to look at Rocket. "I don't know what I thought. I just hoped it would all work out."

He walked over to the bull and put his face against the bull's head. The bull closed his eyes. "Things work out here in Fat Chance, you know."

Not everything, thought Cleo.

Titan came back and sat down next to Cleo.

"What about everybody else?" Cleo said. "Couldn't they help?"

"They tried," Titan said, "but it would take everything everyone had. I can't accept that."

"I could . . . ," she began, knowing that she'd promised Elwood that she would not throw her money around.

"No, Cleo. I appreciate it, but that wouldn't be right. You can't go around fixing everyone's problems."

"Why not?"

"I believe in what your father sent us to do. He gave us an opportunity to see what we could make of ourselves. Not the opportunity to see how much we could mess up and have his money bail us out."

"Oh, Titan," Cleo said. "I wish everyone in this town wasn't so stubborn."

"Is that code for you wish everyone would do what you want them to do?" he said, a small smile creasing his face.

Cleo laughed. "I guess it does."

"Are you back for good?" He sounded relieved to be changing the subject.

"No," she said, her smile fading. "Just a visit. I'm actually leaving tonight."

"I guess you met Mikie."

"I guess I did."

"Would you stay with me until Dodge arrives?" Titan said. "He'll be here any minute."

Cleo looked back at Rocket, who stood so forlornly at the back door that it made her want to cry. There must be a way to keep these soulful creatures together. An idea struck her. She grabbed her purse and started rummaging.

"Titan, I need you to do something for me," she said as she pulled the ring box out of her bag. "I can leave here happy if you'll swear you'll do me this one favor."

"Anything," Titan said. "I swear."

She opened the ring box and held it up for Titan to see. The four perfect carats sent sparks around the forge.

"I need you to take this ring"—she took the ring and forced it into Titan's immense hand—"and give it to Dodge."

"I can't marry Dodge," Titan gasped, pushing it back at her. "I don't love him! I don't even think he's gay!"

"Not like that," she said, returning the ring like a hot potato. "For

Rocket. It's worth in the six figures. That has to be more than enough to settle your debt."

"It is. More than enough, but . . ."

"Tell Dodge he can keep the change."

"Cleo, I can't take this," Titan said, although he couldn't resist slipping it onto the first knuckle of his pinkie finger. "My gosh, it's beautiful."

"Isn't it?" Cleo said softly. "But it never did me or Marshall or anyone else a bit of good. So if you don't take it, I'm going to go throw it in the creek."

Titan held his hand to his chest, covering the ring protectively. "You wouldn't," he squeaked.

"You know how rich I am," Cleo said, playing the stereotype of the fabulously wealthy woman for all it was worth. "What's it to me?"

"I can't let you do that!" Titan said hesitantly.

"Take the ring." Cleo reached out and squeezed Titan's forearm, which was like squeezing granite. "Let the damn thing bring *some-body* happiness. Please, Titan."

"All right." He stared at the ring in disbelief. "If you're sure."

"I am sure," Cleo said, standing up.

They turned as they heard the front door. They could make out Dodge's silhouette backlighted against the sky.

"I'm going to go." Cleo kissed Titan on the cheek.

They stood and embraced.

"Will I see you again?" Titan asked.

"Of course."

Although she wasn't sure of that.

Cleo patted Titan on the cheek. She could see how nervous he was. She wondered if she should stay, but realized that Titan would want to handle this himself. She shot a quick look at Dodge, and then whispered in Titan's ear.

"You can do this," she said. "Just make him an offer he can't refuse."

CHAPTER 28

Professor Johnson searched all of Fat Chance for Dymphna. Exasperated, he looked down at Thud. "Where is she, boy?"

The dog wagged his tail and headed up toward the farm. Professor Johnson followed. He wondered why Dymphna would be at the farm when there was so much going on in town. For an instant, he even doubted that Thud had understood the question. But of course, that was just foolishness.

Professor Johnson could feel himself relaxing with every step he took closer to the farm. He could hear the soft cluck of the chickens, and every once in a while a goat peered over the barnyard fence. If he was not mistaken, he thought Dymphna had said a couple babies were born earlier in the spring, but he couldn't be sure. The phone connection was always so bad.

He could only hope the connection would be better now that he was here.

Professor Johnson climbed up on the porch as Thud pushed his way into the house. The door was ajar. Professor Johnson was just about to pull it wide enough to enter, when he heard Dymphna's voice.

"Hey, Thud," she said.

Professor Johnson couldn't see her, but he could hear her thumping the dog's broad side in greeting. A smile stretched across his face. He hadn't actually planned to surprise her, but this might be fun. The smile froze on his face when he heard a man speak.

"We were starting to wonder about you," the voice said. "Where have you been, buddy?"

Buddy? This man knows my dog well enough to call him "buddy"?

Professor Johnson backed away from the door. Dymphna obviously knew this man. She sounded comfortable and at ease. More at ease than she ever sounded with him, he feared. He flattened himself against the house. He wasn't sure what he should do or where he should go. He couldn't see them and he strained to hear their voices, to see if this chum of Thud's was anyone he'd met during his six months in Fat Chance.

"Do you want any more cobbler, Tino?" Dymphna asked.

Tino? Have I ever met a Tino? I don't think so.

Thud came out of the house and looked up at Professor Johnson, wagging his tail furiously. Thud started to whine softly. Professor Johnson put his fingers to his lips to silence the dog. The last thing he needed was for Dymphna and this Tino person to find him skulking on the porch.

"Thud," Dymphna called. "Stay on the porch, please."

Thud looked back into the farmhouse, and then lay down in the doorway, closing his eyes.

Professor Johnson looked for an escape route, but he didn't see one. Even if he could get off the porch without being noticed, if he attempted to leave, Thud would cause a ruckus.

Wouldn't he?

Professor Johnson tried to inch his way down the wall toward the stairs. Thud raised his head with every creak of the floorboards. The professor didn't want to be eavesdropping—or at least he didn't want to be discovered eavesdropping. On the other hand, he wasn't quite ready to announce his arrival. He took a deep breath and waited for the right moment.

Waiting for the right moment—story of my life.

He heard Dymphna cough.

"So . . ." Dymphna's voice didn't carry to the porch like Tino's did, but Professor Johnson could still hear her. "You had something you wanted to say?"

"I'm sorry I've been so mysterious about all this," Tino said. "But I wanted to make sure my plans were going to pan out before I said anything."

"Your plans?" Dymphna asked.

"Right after I treated Thud's snakebite wound, I went to South America for a while. I was in Chile at the International Livestock Research Institute."

"Is that where you've been these last few weeks, too?"

"Yes," Tino said. "That's what I want to talk to you about."

Professor Johnson found himself leaning closer to the wall in order to hear every word. He tried to fit the pieces together. He remembered trying to locate the veterinarian who had saved Thud in order to thank him. But that veterinarian had left Texas by the time Professor Johnson knew about him. What was his name?

Dr. Valentine. Dr. Constantino Valentine.

Tino!

Professor Johnson had missed some of the conversation. He tuned back in.

"It's a fascinating study, and they've asked me to be part of it," Tino said.

"So you're leaving again?" Dymphna said.

Yes!

"I am," Tino said. "And I want you to go with me."

No!

"I can't go with you," Dymphna said. "I can't leave Fat Chance just like that."

Professor Johnson tried not to analyze that response but failed. Did it mean she didn't want to leave? That she could leave eventually?

"Sure you can," Tino said. "You know Pappy would take care of the farm."

"And what about Thud?" Dymphna asked.

Did Professor Johnson imagine that her voice cracked?

At the mention of his name, Thud looked up. He stared at Professor Johnson, who held his breath. Was he about to be exposed by his own dog?

Thud went back to sleep.

"Give him back to his real owner?" Tino asked.

"Professor Johnson and I don't like to think that animals have owners," Dymphna said.

"In any case," Tino said, "I'm sure your boyfriend would be happy to take him back."

Professor Johnson stood up so fast, his glasses slipped down his nose. He smiled stupidly at the sliver of sky he could see through the hole in the porch roof.

Boyfriend? She's called me her boyfriend?

"I can't give you an answer right now," Dymphna said.

"Of course. It's a lot to take in. But just think, Dymphna, we'd be doing cutting edge research."

"You'd be doing cutting edge research."

"I've seen you working with animals. I suspect we'd be doing it together."

Cutting edge research? I'm in trouble now. Who could resist that?

"That sounds very interesting," Dymphna said.

"I guess I should let you sleep on it," Tino said.

"Thanks."

Were they going to sleep on it together? Were they going to walk onto the porch? Professor Johnson's heart started to pound. He could hear chairs scrape against the floor. They were getting up!

"I know you have a lot to think about," Tino said. "Just let me ask you one thing."

"Okay."

"How much is this Professor Johnson my competition?"

Professor Johnson knew it wouldn't be fair to eavesdrop on the answer—or perhaps he didn't want to hear the answer. He turned and walked through the doorway.

He forgot that Dymphna didn't know he was back. All she saw was a man coming through her doorway. She screamed. Reaching out to her was the last thing he remembered.

He woke slowly to Thud licking his face. He could hazily make out voices above him.

"So you know this guy?" Tino said.

"Yes," Dymphna said. "He's . . ."

"Your competition," Professor Johnson said through a swollen lip.

He opened his eyes. Dymphna was kneeling beside him.

She touched his cheek. "I'm so sorry. You scared me. What are you doing here? You're not supposed to be here until next week."

"Miscommunication," Professor Johnson said as he sat up. He always said that Fat Chance had to get better cell service or somebody could get hurt. He had just expected that it would be someone else.

"Sorry, dude," Tino said, giving the professor a hand up. "Dymphna screamed and I decked you."

"I assumed that was the scenario," Professor Johnson said. "Have you seen my glasses?"

Dymphna stood up and handed them to him. He put them on, testing to see if he had a broken nose. It appeared that the only damage was to his lip.

"Tino," Dymphna said by way of introduction, "this is Professor Johnson. He has a PhD in natural sciences. Professor Johnson, this is Dr. Constantino Valentine. He's the vet who treated Thud after the Fandango."

The men nodded to each other. Professor Johnson was acutely aware that in the introduction department, Tino won.

"Tino was just—" Dymphna started.

"I know," Professor Johnson said, holding up a hand. "I heard."

Dymphna flushed.

"How much did you hear?" Tino asked, eyes narrowing.

"You asked Dymphna to go to Chile with you. I believe you were offering her a life of research."

"That's about right," Tino said. "You got something better?"

"Cutting edge research in Latin America?" Professor Johnson said miserably. "Or staying here in Fat Chance while I pan for any relic that might be of interest for a two-bit museum? No, I don't have something better."

Professor Johnson felt guilty calling his museum two-bit. But he had to admit, it paled in comparison to the International Livestock Research Institute.

Dymphna bristled. "Excuse me. I'm standing right here. Do I have a say in this?"

"Of course," Professor Johnson said.

"Where would *you* rather do research?" Tino asked.

Dymphna threw her arms up in the air and walked out the door. The two men stared at each other. Thud barked and broke the impasse. The men followed Dymphna into the yard.

When they caught up with her, Dymphna was looking down at Fat Chance. The din from town had been reduced to a murmur and the smell of barbecue had faded from the breeze. From their vantage point, Dymphna, Professor Johnson, and Tino saw Fernando, Polly, and a young man they didn't know, all cleaning the smokers.

"It was a good day," Dymphna said to Professor Johnson. "A really good day for Fat Chance."

He smiled at her. He knew exactly what she meant. Even given the fact that he had been gone, his heart had been with this town, with her, all these months. It wasn't research in Chile, but it was something. He only hoped it was enough.

"Professor," Tino broke in, "Dymphna has a lot to think about. Why don't you and I call it a day?"

Thud leapt into the air and started barking. The trio turned to him in surprise.

"Thud?" Dymphna said. "What is it, boy?"

Thud stopped barking as suddenly as he'd begun. Professor Johnson covered his head as something whizzed by his shoulder. Whatever it was landed with a clatter, rolling through the yard, scattering chickens. When Professor Johnson looked up, there was a duck sitting in the middle of the yard.

"Crash!" Dymphna called.

She dropped to her knees and the little duck waddled over. Dymphna wrapped her arms around the duckling and kissed its feathered head. For a few moments, nobody spoke. The two men exchanged an anxious glance. Neither knew exactly what was happening, but it seemed like something big. Finally, Dymphna rose to her feet, still cradling the duck.

"He came back," Tino said.

While Professor Johnson had immensely enjoyed his own moment with Dymphna, he realized these two had their own shared history.

"I guess we should go," Professor Johnson said.

The men turned to go.

"You don't have to go," Dymphna said quietly. "I've made up my mind."

Tino and Professor Johnson froze. The professor thought it was interesting that both men had something huge at stake. In a moment, one of them would win and one would lose. This should have made them enemies. But since they were in exactly the same boat, they were also comrades.

Why am I thinking about this?

"Professor Johnson," Dymphna said, "this is Crash." She added, "He's a duck."

Professor Johnson nodded. "I see that."

"Tino brought this duck to me when he was a ball of fluff too small to fend for himself. I raised him, knowing he might leave. I hoped he'd stay. I loved him. But when he flew away, I knew I had to be brave, because he had to follow his heart. We all have to follow our hearts."

Dymphna stopped talking. It was clear she felt she had explained herself, but Professor Johnson was lost. He snuck a peek at Tino, hoping to gauge by Tino's reaction if he should be ecstatic or heartbroken. Tino looked just as confused.

Dymphna walked to Tino and stood in front of him. Professor Johnson looked at his shoes, but he stole a glance and saw that Crash was staring at him from Dymphna's arms.

He was going to lose.

"Tino," Dymphna said, "Crash came back! Don't you see what that means?"

"That I can sure pick my ducks?"

"No. I hoped Crash would never leave, but I was ready to accept the fact that he might. I never considered he might leave and then come back."

"Uh-huh," Tino said. "Could you give me . . . just a little more?"

"He came back because he loves me," Dymphna said. "He came back."

Professor Johnson's head snapped up. "I came back!" he said. "I came back because I love you! I'm your duck!"

"You're my duck," Dymphna said.

She turned and graced him with her beatific smile. He ran and scooped her up, swinging her around. Crash squawked.

"Sorry, Crash," he said as he lowered Dymphna to her feet.

Dymphna laughed and put Crash on the ground. The duck waddled over to the chickens, as if to see what had transpired in his absence. Dymphna and Professor Johnson suddenly remembered Tino.

"Tino," Dymphna said, but Tino put his hand up to stop her.

"No no," he said. "I can see the better man won."

Professor Johnson put out his hand. Tino shook it.

"Seriously," Tino said. "You two are perfect for each other."

CHAPTER 29

Tino climbed the trail toward his truck. It was one of the few remaining vehicles at the turnout. As he got closer, she saw a woman
sitting on his fender. As he got closer still, he could see she was crying.

"Excuse me," he said gently, so as not to scare her.

The woman jumped. He was making all the wrong moves today.

"I'm sorry," the woman said, dabbing at her eyes. "Is this your
truck?"

"Yes, but take as much time as you need. I'm not in any hurry."

"Thank you." The woman blew her nose. "I apologize for the display . . . but . . ." She cried harder.

Tino sat on the bumper and patted her back. "But what?" he asked
gently.

"I just got dumped," she cried.

"Me too."

The woman stopped crying and looked at him. "You did?"

"I did."

The woman started to laugh. "I'm sorry," she said. "I shouldn't be
laughing."

"You shouldn't be," Tino said, starting to laugh himself.

"I'm Cleo."

"Tino. What are you doing up here?"

"Besides crying? I'm hoping to hitch a ride to Spoonerville. I
need to call a cab. This was the only truck left up here, so I thought
I'd take my chances."

He couldn't imagine this sophisticated woman having business in
Spoonerville.

"What's in Spoonerville?" he asked.

"A phone that works," she said bitterly. "I need to call a cab."

"You don't need to call a cab. I'll take you wherever you need to go."

"I'm going to Los Angeles." She sniffled.

"You were going to take a cab to Los Angeles?"

"Oh no, just to Austin to catch my . . . catch a plane."

"I'll take you to Los Angeles."

They stared at each other.

"Can that truck of yours pull a U-Haul?" she asked.

CHAPTER 30

Professor Johnson didn't need to bunk at the Boozehound Saloon. In the cool morning air, Dymphna and Professor Johnson walked hand in hand to the Cowboy Food café. Thud was having so much fun chasing and being chased by Crash that he almost stayed at the farm, but ultimately opted for the tantalizing aroma of breakfast coming from town.

As they stepped onto Main Street, Professor Johnson's back pocket started to vibrate. He pulled out his phone and stared at it.

"It's Auntie," he said.

"Isn't she here?" Dymphna asked.

Professor Johnson shrugged as he answered the phone.

Dymphna nodded. She watched as Professor Johnson paced Main Street, trying to keep a signal going. When he finally got off the phone, the two of them continued their walk to the café.

"She left?"

"She left," he said. "She's on her way back to Los Angeles."

Because Fat Chance was such a small community, everyone was pretty much in the loop by the time Dymphna and Professor Johnson walked through the door. Professor Johnson looked at Powderkeg, who was sitting with his arm around Mikie.

Powderkeg stood up. "Elwood—"

"I just spoke with her," Professor Johnson said. "She'll be all right."

Professor Johnson could see the relief in Powderkeg's eyes.

The seating had been rearranged. Old Bertha was now sitting next to Pappy. Mikie seemed to have her own permanent spot next to Powderkeg. Titan stood up, vacating his spot so Professor Johnson could sit next to Dymphna. He pulled up a chair for himself nearer the kitchen. Dymphna looked at him questioningly.

He beamed. "I still have Rocket. I made Dodge an offer he couldn't refuse."

Dymphna was about to ask more questions, when Polly came out of the kitchen with a pot of coffee. She was wearing her ruffled apron.

"You working here now?" Old Bertha asked.

"Yep," Polly said. "After yesterday, Fernando says it's going to be all hands on deck."

As Polly poured coffee, Fernando came out of the kitchen with heaping baskets of bread. The group applauded him, both for break- fast and for breathing new life into Fat Chance, Texas.

The wonderful smell of the freshly baked bread filled the room. *The sweet scent of promise,* thought Professor Johnson.

The door to the café burst open and an out-of-breath Hank stum- bled in.

"Whoa, whoa, whoa," Pappy said, and the group stood up, offer- ing chairs and water to the gasping young man. "Where's the fire?"

"I brought the mail," Hank said, coughing on a sip of water prof- fered by Polly.

"Who are you, the Pony Express?" Old Bertha asked. "Why the rush?"

"We'll get our mail later this week," said Fernando.

"I was at the store in Spoonerville this morning," Hank said. "Dodge was sorting the mail. He picked up a letter and started laugh- ing. It was that mean laugh, you know the one?"

Everyone nodded.

"Anyway," Hank said, "I asked him what was so funny and he said he had a letter for Fat Chance from the health department."

"The health department?" Fernando exclaimed, and then stag- gered. Titan helped him into a chair.

"I knew Dodge would find a way to cause trouble," Pappy said. "He's going to try to close us down."

"What is wrong with that man?" Mikie asked.

"I told him I was headed over this way," Hank said, casting a glance at Polly. "And said I'd deliver it."

"Isn't that against the law?" Dymphna asked. "A postmaster letting a regular citizen deliver mail?"

"Have you met Dodge?" Pappy growled.

Fernando put out his hand for the letter. Hank looked blankly at him.

"The letter isn't for you," he said, looking down at the envelope. "It's for a Professor Elwood Johnson."

Fernando froze, hand still outstretched. The room was silent. All eyes were on Professor Johnson as he took the letter.

"Lucy, you got some 'splainin' to do," Fernando said in a Cuban accent.

"Yes, well," Professor Johnson began, "it's a little complicated."

"Just start at the beginning," Dymphna said kindly, although her voice telegraphed the confusion that she could see in everyone's eyes.

"I know all of us beneficiaries are in the same situation," he said. "We have our inheritance and we want to make the most of it. When I confirmed that we had Thomas Volney Munson's grapes growing in Fat Chance, I—"

"We have Thomas Volney Munson's grapes growing in Fat Chance?" Fernando said, dropping the basket of bread. His background in Napa Valley gave him an edge over the other people at the table.

Titan caught the basket in one swoop, but a roll fell to the ground. Thud was on it before anyone knew it was missing. Bloodhounds are quick when they want to be.

"Who is Thomas Volney Munson?" Old Bertha asked.

"There are no vineyards in Fat Chance," Mikie said. "I've flown over this place hundreds of times."

"What has that got to do with the health department?"

"Calm down, everybody," Powderkeg said, slamming the table to silence the chatter. "Go on, Professor. Who exactly is this Munson guy?"

"Was," Professor Johnson corrected. "Who *was* Thomas Volney Munson. He died in 1913."

"May he rest in peace," Old Bertha said. "Pertinent information only, Professor, please."

"OK," Professor Johnson said. "Munson was a horticulturalist who tried to develop new varieties of pest-resistant grapes by cross pollination and hybridization."

He looked up and saw the eyes in the café begin to glaze over, so much like the eyes in his classrooms.

"Let me try again," he said. "In a nutshell, Munson failed at his experiments until he moved to Denison, Texas, where the weather and soil were perfect for his work."

"So, basically, he grew grapes?" Powderkeg asked.

"Not just any grapes," Fernando said. "The man is a legend in the wine community. In the late nineteenth century, when the French grape growers had an epidemic of some kind—"

"Aphid phylloxera," Professor Johnson added.

"Yes, that," Fernando said.

"He sent aphid-resistant stock to France," Professor Johnson said. "The French winemakers grafted their vines onto Munson's rootstock."

"The dude saved the French wine industry," Fernando said. "Not that the French are exactly bragging about it."

"Having a PhD in—" began Professor Johnson.

"Natural sciences," all the original Fat Chancers recited.

"Exactly," Professor Johnson said. "Well, my focus is environmental science and that made me curious about what exactly was growing here. I thought a section on horticulture would be interesting for my museum, of course."

"Of course," Dymphna said.

"I took samples of leaves and dirt back to Los Angeles and analyzed everything," he said. "You could have knocked me over with a feather when I found out we had Munson's mustang grapes growing right here in Fat Chance."

"The only grapes growing around here are hanging over my patio," Pappy said. "You don't mean . . ."

"Those are Munson mustang grapes," Professor Johnson said gleefully.

Fernando glowered. "What has that got to do with closing down my café?"

"I'm not closing down the café," Professor Johnson said, tearing open the letter. "I'm getting us a food license—and I'm getting the Boozehound a liquor license!"

Everyone stared at him while he read. He smiled. "God bless Texas," he said, looking around the room. "If this were California, I wouldn't be able to afford this. As it is, I spent almost everything I had."

"I must be getting old," Old Bertha said, "but I'm not connecting the dots."

"We have Munson mustang grapes," Professor Johnson said. "If I've jumped the gun, I'm sorry. But with a food and liquor license, Fat Chance can go into the wine business. We can have a wine-tasting room with an attached café."

"A gold mine!" Powderkeg said.

"Well, no," Professor Johnson said. "I checked that out, and there isn't any gold around here. It's a common mistake—thinking there's gold everywhere in Texas."

Powderkeg opened his mouth, but Mikie put her hand on his arm and patted it.

"Is this possible?" Titan asked.

"Sure," Professor Johnson said. "We can start our own vineyard."

"There's only one problem," Polly said, looking at Thud. "If we get an OK from the health department, old Thud here won't be able to hang out in here."

"I'm going to get him a therapy dog license," Professor Johnson said. "I mean, he's earned it."

Fernando had gone around the room pouring the last of his peach brandy into juice glasses. "A toast," he said.

Everyone stood, glasses in hand.

"Wait," Polly said, getting her cell phone from her back pocket.

Everyone crowded into the frame.

Polly beamed. "OK, Fernando," she said. "Go!"

"One for all," Fernando said, "and all for one fat chance!"

"A fresh, heartwarming voice."
—Jodi Thomas, *New York Times* bestselling author

Home is where your heart is....

Welcome
To
FAT CHANCE,
TEXAS

CELIA
BONADUCE

Be sure not to miss Celia Bonaduce's

WELCOME TO FAT CHANCE, TEXAS

For champion professional knitter Dymphna Pearl, inheriting part of a sun-blasted ghost town in the Texas Hill Country isn't just unexpected, it's a little daunting. To earn a cash bequest that could change her life, she'll have to leave California to live in tiny, run-down Fat Chance for six months—with seven strangers. Impossible! Or is it?

Trading her sandals for cowboy boots, Dymphna dives into her new life with equal parts anxiety and excitement. After all, she's never felt quite at home in Santa Monica anyway. Maybe Fat Chance will be her second chance. But making it habitable is going take more than a lasso and Wild West spirit. With an opinionated buzzard overlooking the proceedings and mismatched strangers learning to become friends, Dymphna wonders if unlocking the secrets of her own heart is the way to strike real gold . . .

A Lyrical e-book on sale now!

the Merchant of venice beach

Take the first step
on the way to
happiness...

CELIA
BONADUCE

The Rollicking Bun—Home of the Epic Scone—is the center of Suzanna Wolf's life. Part tea shop, part bookstore, part home, it's everything she's ever wanted right on the Venice Beach boardwalk, including partnership with her two best friends from high school, Eric and Fernando. But with thirty-three just around the corner, suddenly Suzanna wants something more—something strictly her own. Salsa lessons, especially with a gorgeous instructor, seem like a good start—a harmless secret, and just maybe the start of a fling. But before she knows it, Suzanna is learning steps she never imagined—and dancing her way into confusion.

"*The Merchant of Venice Beach* has a fresh, heartwarming voice that will keep readers smiling as they dance through this charming story by Celia Bonaduce."
—Jodi Thomas, *New York Times* bestselling author

Your best shot at love...

A *Comedy* OF *Erinn*

CELIA
BONADUCE

Erinn Wolf needs to reinvent herself. A once celebrated playwright turned photographer, she's almost broke, a little lonely, and tired of her sister's constant worry. When a job on a reality TV show falls into her lap, she's thrilled to be making a paycheck—and when a hot Italian actor named Massimo rents her guesthouse, she's certain her life is getting a romantic subplot. But with the director, brash, gorgeous young Jude, dogging her every step, she can't help but look at herself through his lens—and wonder if she's been reading the wrong script all along . . .

A VENICE BEACH ROMANCE

MUCH *Ado* ABOUT *Mother*

*When it comes to life's
big questions, who knows best?*

CELIA
BONADUCE

Look out, Venice Beach—the Wolf women are all together again. But when 70-year-old Virginia arrives with her teacup Chihuahua and unshakeable confidence, she senses trouble. Erinn is keeping secrets—like being broke and out of work—and Suzanna is paying too much attention to the wrong man—a Latino dance instructor who nearly broke her heart once before. Virginia's ready for the third act of her life, and she intends to make it rousing and romantic. Now she just has to convince her daughters to throw out their old scripts. If life has taught Virginia anything, it's this: There's more than one way to a "happily ever after."

© William Christoff Photography

Celia Bonaduce is the author of five novels and is currently a Field Producer on HGTV's *House Hunters*. She has covered a lot of ground in TV programming, including field-producing ABC's *Extreme Makeover: Home Edition* and writing for many of Nickelodeon's animated series, including *Hey Arnold!* and *ChalkZone*. Her successful Tea-Shoppe Stops, lectures and readings of the Venice Beach Romance series: *Merchant of Venice Beach*, *A Comedy of Erinn*, and *Much Ado About Mother*, will continue across the country with the Fat Chance, Texas series, although a better venue might be local rodeos. Celia lives in Santa Monica, California, with palm trees, the Pacific Ocean, and her husband, Bill.

Website: http://www.celiabonaduce.com/
Facebook: https://www.facebook.com/pages/Celia-Bonaduce/352890508156101
Twitter: @celiabonaduce
Instagram: Yocelia
Media: http://www.celiab.name/